Flora Lively and the Sign of Seven

by
Joanne Phillips

This novel is entirely a work of fiction. The names, characters, localities and incidents portrayed in it are the product of the author's imagination. Any resemblance to actual persons, living or dead, or events or localities is entirely coincidental.

Mirrorball Books

Paperback Edition 2020

Copyright © Joanne Phillips 2020

Joanne Phillips asserts the moral right to be identified as the author of this work. All rights reserved in all media. No part of this publication may be reproduced, stored in a retrieval system, or transmitted, in any form, or by any means, electronic, mechanical, photocopying, recording or otherwise, without the prior written permission of the author and/or publisher.

Typeset in Sabon, printed and bound by Amazon
Cover design by Blondesign

Flora Lively and the Sign of Seven

by
Joanne Phillips

Mirrorball Books

Chapter 1

Flora Lively took a slow steadying breath. In her cupped hands she held a small wooden monkey, the intricate carving unlike anything Flora had seen before. The delicate paws, uncannily human, covered its eyes, and she could just about see the secret little smile on the primate's face. Or was it a grimace?

Jasmin had told her that the monkey hailed from the seventeenth century, and Flora had no reason to doubt her. Mizaru – see no evil. Its brothers, hear and speak no evil, were missing, probably stolen by looters during an archaeological dig. But this artefact on its own was worth over twenty thousand pounds.

Flora wrapped the wooden monkey in acid-free tissue paper, stopping after a few minutes to do another three-sixty of the dimly lit atrium. She was surrounded by long, rectangular packing crates, each in varying stages of completion, while at the edges of the room stood large glass cabinets, a few of which were now empty. A tarnished suit of armour, disconcertingly small, kept guard by the entrance, its face an inscrutable black hole. Flora couldn't help find the atmosphere decidedly spooky.

The Shropshire White and Co. Museum of Antiquities had contracted Shakers Removals a little over a month ago, the brief being to catalogue and pack its entire collection and transport it to a new home in London. Seemed the good people of Shrewsbury weren't showing enough interest in antiquities – or not enough interest in paying to look at them, anyway. Flora had been delighted with the new contract, even if she had found some of the exhibits downright weird. Anything that made a change from their usual, run-of-the-mill trade made her deliriously happy these days.

She blamed the events at Hanley Manor last year for the slump in her enthusiasm. Getting involved in yet another murder mystery had ramped up the excitement, and nothing could quite match the buzz of solving a crime. Marshall, of course, kept accusing her of being 'full of it', especially when the article appeared in the Shropshire Herald:

Local Business-Woman Cracks Contraband Gang

The headline certainly had a nice ring to it.

But, as Flora liked to remind Marshall, that job had taken its toll on her personally as well as professionally. She'd had to expose her best friend Celeste as a trafficker in fake goods, and they'd discovered that her old school friend Jack – trusted police detective – was a fraud, a thief and a murderer.

Not good. But certainly more exciting that moving Ikea wardrobes and dining tables and sofas with ten years' worth of crumbs and debris lurking beneath them.

Detecting was more glamorous than working in removals. But did detecting pay the bills? It did not.

Flora sighed and laid the tissue-wrapped antique monkey into its designated crate. The monkey was now in the company of various other Japanese antiquities and a selection of Viking pendants, including an enormous bronze angel pendant that must have been impossible to actually wear. There seemed to be no particular order to the exhibits, but Flora was logging everything and taking Polaroid photographs in situ. They would need these to set up the collection when it reached its new home.

Flora fixed the crate lid into place with metal clips and began to seal it with tape.

'Hey, how's it going? You got no home to go to?'

Flora looked up and smiled at Nick Guest, the security guard they had taken on for this job.

'Stuff won't pack itself,' she said. 'Done all this today already. Only another five exhibition rooms to go.'

'It's kind of creepy in here, don't you think?' Nick dropped his rucksack by the entrance and crossed to where Flora knelt. He picked up a cracked, brown skull and regarded it suspiciously.

'Be careful with that,' Flora told him. 'It's from the Hugia tribe in Papa New Guinea. It's five hundred years old.'

'Yuck!'

Nick handed the skull to Flora, then took a red and black striped mask from the floor.

'And this?' he asked.

'African fertility death mask,' she said. The mask was three-feet tall and surrounded by spiky hair. It was definitely human hair. Flora regarded Nick seriously. 'History says that if the fertility death mask is ever touched by a man, he will be struck down immediately by a deadly virus.'

Nick dropped the mask and yelped. Flora giggled, then began to laugh when she saw the look of outrage on his face. Nick was in his late twenties, and would probably be described as buff by the kind of girls he attracted. He certainly worked out a lot. Buzz haircut, little bit of stubble, bright blue eyes. Not too tall, but he filled out his dark blue uniform exceptionally well. He wasn't Flora's type – and besides, she had Marshall now – but he was certainly nice to have around.

And here he was, the tough guy, squealing like a school girl. Flora laughed.

'I was kidding! You're perfectly safe. No deadly viruses here.'

Nick gave her a rueful look and picked up the tribal skull again.

'That was not nice, Miss Lively,' he said, holding up the skull and pretending it was speaking. 'Not nice at all.'

'Sorry.' Flora carried on smiling to herself while she tidied up the tissue paper and piles of tape. Marshall had been set against hiring Nick, arguing they could do the job between them. But Flora knew that was impossible. As soon as Shakers began work the collection became their responsibility, and it had to be guarded at all times. If anything should be damaged or lost there was no way Shakers could afford to replace it – their usual insurance wouldn't cut it for priceless antiquities. So the night guard solution was the only one that made sense.

A bit of eye candy and banter didn't hurt either.

They made their way through the museum, closing doors behind them. Their footsteps echoed dully on the wooden floors, and when Flora spoke she found herself almost whispering. The low-level lighting, which was all about protecting the artefacts, certainly aided the mysterious atmosphere. Flora was getting used to it now, but when she had first visited, one or two of the exhibits had seriously freaked her out.

The museum's owner, Jasmin White, had seen the article about Flora in the local newspaper. A well-groomed woman in her sixties with dark skin and long, silky black hair, she had greeted Flora with a firm handshake and a wide smile.

'We need a firm we can trust,' she'd explained over coffee in her large office on the upper floor of the museum, overlooking the River Severn. 'And when I read about you in the paper I just knew that I could trust a person with such good … morals.'

'Thank you.' Flora wasn't sure that the local rag had promoted her morals as such, but she was glad of the compliment. Within an hour the job brief was signed off and a generous fee agreed.

'Everything is going to the British Museum,' Jasmin

had said as they toured the museum's main exhibition rooms. 'Apart from the stuff in here.' She showed Flora a small storage cupboard. 'This is my personal collection. Just some sentimental memorabilia from my travels. I'll be removing these items myself and taking them overseas with me.'

'Overseas?' Flora said, peering over Jasmin's shoulder. 'Whereabouts are you going?'

'America,' Jasmin replied, closing and locking the door to the cupboard.

'Is it a permanent move?'

'Yes.'

Flora had waited for more, but on this subject her new client seemed unwilling to elaborate. Not so on the background of the exhibits. For any that Flora showed a passing interest in, Jasmin had extensive knowledge, and delighted in regaling Flora with gory tales associated with the artefacts in her possession.

'Oh, that!' she exclaimed when Flora pointed to a particularly striking vase. 'Legend has it that this is the very same silver vase that was made in the fifteenth century for a bride on the eve of her wedding in Napoli, Italy. Tragically, she never made it to the altar.'

Jasmin paused, and Flora took the bait.

'Why not? What happened to her?'

'She was brutally murdered that very night with the vase in her hands. It's said that she drew a heart on the vase in her own blood.'

'Oh my!' Flora exclaimed, taking an involuntary step away from the cabinet housing the silver vase. 'That's so sad.'

Jasmin continued, her dark eyes shining. 'The vase was passed down her family line, but anyone who took possession of it is said to have died a similarly horrible death soon after. The family boxed the vase away with a warning, but it resurfaced in the nineteen-seventies with a note that read, *Beware. This vase brings death.* That was when I acquired it.'

'You bought a cursed vase that brings death?' Flora said incredulously.

Jasmin waved her hands vaguely. 'I acquired it, yes. The story is probably just there to make it more valuable.'

'Probably,' Flora repeated, eyeing the vase warily. 'Oh now, what about her?' she exclaimed, pointing to a particularly evil looking doll sitting alone in a lit glass case that hung from the wall. 'Now, she must have some kind of horrible history as well. That is one creepy toy.'

'Now that little darling,' Jasmin said with a cheeky grin, 'belonged to the daughter of a prince. She has a particularly nasty story to tell.'

'I think I'll pass on that one.' Flora walked on, glancing over her shoulder at the doll. One of its eyes was slightly out of alignment, giving the impression of the eye following Flora's progress out of the room while the other eye stared blankly ahead. Its blonde hair, ivory skin and Victorian clothing were so realistic that the effect had been decidedly unsettling.

She and Nick were walking past the same doll now, and Flora shuddered again. She hadn't been able to bring herself to pack it away yet – even taking the positioning photographs had disturbed her. She would let Marshall do this space when he came in tomorrow.

'So, you've got your set of keys, my number, and Marshall's number, right?' Flora said to Nick. 'I've got some paperwork to do so I'll be here for a while anyway.'

'Cool,' Nick said, holding open the office door for her.

Flora flopped into the not-particularly-comfy chair in the corner of Jasmin White's office and grabbed her oversized tote bag. She rummaged inside it and pulled out the folder of photographs, along with an unravelling woollen scarf, which had somehow attached itself to the folder, and her knitting bag, which had become entangled with the scarf. She sighed in annoyance and began to tug at the scarf to free it.

She'd started to wonder lately whether the vintage style she loved so much might in fact be a little shabby. Her slight frame and lack of curves made her feel like a child in grown-ups' clothing whenever she tried to dress more sophisticated, but she knew she could make more of an effort with her appearance. And were Marshall's jokey comments about her 'quirky look' really a veiled criticism? Not that Marshall was often subtle. The co-manager of Shakers with whom her father had left her lumbered, had become indispensable to Flora – in more ways than one – over the years since Peter Lively's death, but he still drove her crazy on a daily basis.

Flora ran a hand through her cropped hair. She was growing out the bright red colour but her own plain mousey brown was not doing anything for her either. Maybe blonde again? Or something more up-to-date, like rose gold? Or one of those blue or green shades the youngsters liked so much?

Youngsters? Jeez. She really was sounding old.

'Hey, Flora?' Nick was waving his hand at her from across the room.

'Huh?'

Nick grinned. 'I'm off to do a circuit. You be okay?'

'Sure. No problem.' Flora smiled and shook her head. 'Watch out for the death masks.'

'Ha. Very funny.'

Flora smirked and shuffled her chair over to Jasmin's sprawling metal desk. She opened up the folder and began to paste photographs into place, with quick notes to help them do an efficient job at the other end. On the wall above her hung a painting of a woman wearing a white veiled hat, her face a study in sadness. The eyes, large and mournful, seemed to pull Flora in. Flora shivered involuntarily. Magical and exciting it might be, but it was still a job, and she'd better get on with it.

***

Flora woke up with a start. She lifted her head from the desk and blinked her eyes. Her neck hurt and her back felt stiff, and she was absolutely freezing cold.

'Hey? What are you doing still here?'

Nick was leaning over her, looking concerned.

'I must have fallen asleep,' she said blearily. 'What time is it?'

'Nearly midnight. I've been in the war room for a while now. There's this geezer outside, he's acting a bit weird.'

'What? The what room?'

Flora got up awkwardly from the chair and stretched through her body, arching her back. Even though Nick wasn't especially tall, Flora still only reached his shoulders at full height. She rubbed her eyes and tried to focus. God, she was tired. How long had she been working on that inventory before she fell asleep?

The woman in the painting looked down at her sadly. Too long, she seemed to be saying.

'The war room,' Nick was telling her. 'I call it that because it's full of all that ancient weaponry stuff. And that skeleton thing. It's seriously creepy in there, Flora. I've got to tell you, this is one of the weirdest jobs I've ever had.'

'Me too.' Flora looked around for her poncho. 'It's so cold in here! Aren't you cold?'

'I don't feel the cold. Too much muscle.'

Flora stared at him. Was he serious? She opened her mouth to question whether that was even a thing, but before she could form the words a piercing scream cut through the ambient sounds of a ticking clock and a low-humming fridge. The scream was so loud, so sudden, it was almost inhuman, and it seemed to come from all around them – from the walls and the floorboards and the very air itself.

Then it stopped as suddenly as it had began, leaving an echoing silence in its wake.

'What the hell was that?' Flora whispered.

Nick had moved to the door with lightning speed. 'Stay here,' he told her authoritatively. He hunkered down, all shoulders and narrowed eyes.

'What?' Flora said. 'No! I'm not staying here on my own.'

Another scream ricocheted through the corridors, and Flora and Nick jumped in unison. And then the lights went out, all at once, and the office and surrounding corridors were plunged into darkness.

There was a moment of pure, complete silence.

'Jesus,' Nick said, clearly rattled.

'Wait.' Flora laid her hand on his arm when he made to move away again. She couldn't see his face clearly but she could feel the tension coming off him in waves. 'What's that?'

They listened, Flora straining in the dark to orientate herself. She could make out a blue blinking light in the corner of the office. The computer hard drive. So not all the electricity had gone off. Just the lights. But how?

'I hear it,' Nick whispered.

Flora nodded. So did she. Footsteps. Solid, echoing footsteps. Slow, a regular but unnatural gait, getting closer, but also not getting closer. The dark made it difficult to gauge. Flora could hear and feel her own heart beating; she could hear the blood pounding in her head. Her teeth began to chatter, not only from the cold. Nick stood tense beside her, his body positioned across hers, as though protecting her from whatever might come through the door. And then the footsteps stopped.

Silence.

'What the hell is happening?' Flora whispered shakily. Her eyes had adjusted to the dark now; there was enough light from the waxing moon to illuminate the museum's office into a blurry greyness.

Nick placed his forefinger to his lips. He pointed to Flora and then pointed to the floor. She shook her head furiously in response. No way was she staying on her own while he went to look around. Nick nodded firmly. She shook her head again. *I'm your boss*, she mouthed, but she didn't think he could lip-read well enough to understand. He began to move towards the door again; Flora became his shadow.

A clock began to strike, loud and ringing. Flora recognised it as the grandfather clock in the entrance lobby on the ground floor.

'Midnight,' Nick said quietly, showing Flora his watch. The watch face had tiny green illuminated dots that cast an eerie light over his strong wrist. Flora nodded. She counted the chimes in her head as she and Nick inched forward. One chime. Two. Then Nick flicked on a torch and cast the beam in a wide circle down the corridor ahead of them.

Three.

'You've just this minute realised you have a torch?' Flora hissed.

Four.

Nick shook his head. 'Didn't want to alert the enemy,' he whispered gravely. Flora rolled her eyes in exasperation. Men! *War room. Alerting the enemy.* He was turning it into something right out of a shoot-em-up video game.

Five. Six.

'Where are we actually going?' she asked.

'The basement. Get the lights back on. Then we – *I* – can investigate properly.'

Seven.

Flora wasn't sure about that. She decided she might forgo the security of Nick's sturdy presence rather than head into the basement of a creepy museum with no lighting.

But then, as they neared the end of the corridor, she stopped. It was silent again. There was only her heart, still pounding too loudly, and Nick's slowly padding footsteps.

He looked back questioningly. 'What's wrong?'

'The chimes,' Flora said.

'What about them?'

'They've stopped.'

'So?'

'There were only seven of them. Seven chimes. It might have been eight ... No, I'm sure it was seven. But it's midnight.'

'What?'

'It's midnight. But the clock downstairs only chimed seven times.'

'Are you sure?'

Flora nodded. She felt a creeping sensation across her back, like her skin was moving.

'Maybe it's broken,' Nick said quietly.

'No, it isn't. I heard it earlier. It was chiming when I called Marshall, and I was downstairs cos the signal is best there, and it was really loud so I waited until it stopped. It chimed five times and it was five o'clock.' Flora got all this out in a whisper, then drew in a ragged breath.

Nick shrugged and adjusted the beam on his torch. He swung it around the room they were about to enter. Flora glimpsed a painting of a weeping child, a stuffed bear with a terrifying expression of intent, and the doll with the wonky eye. She shivered. The old building with its antique polished floorboards and flaking plaster walls suddenly seemed more forbidding than quirky; the exhibits more menacing than creepy. She was aware of a scent now, sweet but also oddly bitter. She was sure she hadn't smelt it before.

Suddenly she really wanted Marshall to be here.

'Well, as soon as we get the lights on–'

But whatever Nick was about to say was drowned out by a high-pitched wail and a number of loud, echoing bangs that came in quick succession.

'What the ...?' Flora stared at Nick. 'What the hell is going on here tonight?'

'I don't know,' he said. 'But I'm going to find out. That's definitely a woman screaming. This way.'

He took off at a jog, doubling back and heading towards the atrium. Flora hesitated for a second, then followed. She pulled out her phone as she ran and dialled Marshall's number. He wouldn't mind being woken up. Not for this.

She left a message, keeping the details brief. Marshall was the one who had wanted them to complete this job with just the two of them. If she'd gone along with that, either she or Marshall would be here alone right now. Even as she finished speaking she was thinking how vindicated she felt. Any museum was a potential target for thieves, and possibly vandals or kids messing around. And it was their responsibility now to keep it safe and secure.

Flora caught up with Nick just as he reached the central atrium; she crashed into his solid form when he stopped dead at the entrance.

'Flora! Don't look.' Nick reached back to prevent Flora's progress into the room, but it was too late. In the circle of light from Nick's torch, Flora could see the group of crates that she had packed earlier. One of the crates was open now, its wooden lid thrown off at an awkward angle. And lying inside the box, slumped on top of tissue-wrapped antiques and artefacts, was the lifeless body of a woman.

Chapter 2

'Who is she?'

Flora couldn't raise her voice above a whisper. It was hard to process what was going on, everything was happening so fast. First Nick had whipped out his phone and called the police, then Marshall had arrived, his face grave with concern. Flora had fallen into his arms, sobbing. Not again, was all she could think. Not this again.

It was all well and good to think about detecting and mysteries when you were bored out of your mind packing up people's mis-matched china. It was another thing entirely to be faced with a dead body in the middle of the night, in the dark, in a crate that you yourself had sealed shut only hours before.

'Who *was* she, you mean,' Marshall said grimly.

'I can't believe this is happening again,' Flora whispered for the tenth time. 'I mean, are we cursed or something? Everywhere I go, someone dies.'

'Come on, it's not everywhere you go. We've done loads of jobs this year and no one's died.'

'You know what I mean.' Flora shuddered. Men were so literal. Surely anyone could understand that it didn't feel normal to come across three dead bodies during your working day in little over three years?

'I see Mr Muscle over there is strutting his stuff again,' Marshall said, his voice taking a distinctly snarky turn.

Flora shook her head. 'What do you have against him, Marshall? He was lovely to me tonight. I'd have been terrified if he wasn't here.' She sighed shakily. 'I was terrified anyway.'

Marshall grunted and pulled Flora closer to his chest. He smelled of his usual musky scent, and Flora breathed it in gratefully.

'Anyway,' she said, feeling her heartbeat finally settle somewhat, 'Mr Muscle is a cleaning product. That's not really the insult you were looking for, is it?'

Flora liked to tease Marshall about his American-English, and never failed to point out when he used a particular phrase in a way that a native Brit wouldn't. But Marshall merely cuddled her harder. Flora laid her head against him and closed her eyes.

It made her even more anxious that he wasn't rising to the bait.

'Miss Lively?'

She looked up to see a police officer glowering down at her. Late fifties, white stubble on his jaw line, and at least six feet tall, the man was solidly built in a way that said danger rather than safety. Flora swallowed and moved imperceptibly closer to Marshall.

'She's given her statement.'

Marshall replied for her, his West-Coast twang more incongruous than ever amongst this odd tableau. They were cordoned off now by the entrance to the atrium, where a team of police investigators had taken over, efficiently turning it into a flood-lit crime scene. Forensic personnel wearing white paper overalls, masks and shoe covers surrounded the crate; every surface was being inspected and tested; a woman with the word 'Coroner' on her jacket stood by looking bored, tapping at her phone. Flora shook her head. She couldn't take it in. Only a few hours ago it had been just her and the Mizaru monkey. See no evil. Someone had seen evil here tonight. There was no way a woman had gotten inside that crate and died without help from someone else.

'I've still got some questions, if you don't mind.' The officer's voice was gruff, and his tone implied that he didn't care too much even if they did mind. He told them his name was Curtis, Detective Inspector Curtis, and that Flora should take him through the events of the night again. In as much detail as possible. She sighed. It wasn't like she hadn't been through this kind of thing before. But it always amazed her how much time the police seemed to waste getting the same story from the same people. That's not how *she* would go about figuring this out.

Flora complied, keeping her voice moderated and sticking to the facts.

'You heard a woman screaming at what time?' the Inspector asked.

'Just before midnight. I'm certain of the time because the clock in the lobby began to chime when we heard the footsteps–'

'Footsteps?'

'Yes,' Flora nodded. 'We heard footsteps coming from somewhere, and then the chiming of the clock. Except ... well, there were only seven chimes, not twelve. But it was twelve o'clock. Definitely.'

'Seven chimes.' D.I. Curtis's face bore no expression whatsoever.

'Uh huh.' Flora bit her lip and thought some more. 'Then there was another cry, and then some banging, and then we – well, that was when we found the body. In the atrium.'

'In the box that you think you packed and sealed earlier?'

'In the crate that I *did* seal earlier,' Flora corrected hotly. For goodness sake, it was ridiculous how many times she'd had to stress this already. She wouldn't mind betting that if it was Marshall who had been here – if it had been he who had packed that crate – they wouldn't be questioning him about it so doubtfully. 'It was in that exact position. Right next to the African mask there. There's no doubt it's the same crate.'

'Anything else you can remember?' the detective asked, scribbling in a tiny black notebook. Or maybe it only looked tiny because his hands were so huge.

'Well, there was a strange smell at one point,' Flora said.

'A smell?'

This time it was Marshall sounding incredulous.

'Yes,' Flora said, exasperated. 'Like … Oh, I don't know. Something sweet. Not perfume exactly, but like that. When we were walking through one of the rooms. The room with the creepy doll.'

'Creepy doll?'

'Can you stop repeating everything I say,' Flora snapped. 'It's very irritating.'

Marshall held up his hands in a gesture of surrender.

'So what you're saying is,' D.I. Curtis summarized, 'you heard the woman scream, then you heard her attacker running away, making some kind of banging noise, and that the attacker was wearing perfume. And something about a broken clock.'

Flora just stared at him, speechless. Marshall made a coughing sound; she could tell he was trying not to laugh.

As if any of this was funny.

Kicking Marshall sharply in the shins with the heel of her boot, Flora replied, 'I'm sorry, I think you're confused. The footsteps were strange and weren't necessarily coming from the atrium. Neither was the banging. And the clock isn't broken. You can go and have a look at it yourself if you like.' She sniffed, aware that her voice had veered into overly formal and British. 'I've heard it chime the correct hour a number of times throughout the morning while we've been waiting around for you to be finished with us.'

Flora stopped talking. She would keep her opinions to herself. Nick could confirm everything she'd said, if he hadn't already. Experience had shown Flora that the police were rarely interested in or impressed by so-called 'outside help', even when it might be key to providing a solution.

Which was why she was completely left-fielded when D.I. Curtis put away his notebook and said, 'So, Miss Lively, do *you* have any ideas about how this suspicious death might have occurred?'

Flora stared at him for a moment, then opened her mouth to answer.

'She has no clue, and why would she?' Marshall cut in, throwing her a warning glance.

'Actually,' Flora responded, smiling at the detective, 'I do have a few thoughts. I–'

'No, no. She doesn't,' Marshall said decisively. 'She was just here in a professional capacity – representing Shakers Removals, that is. Nothing else to say. Nothing at all.'

'Marshall!' Flora glared at him. What was he doing? The first time she was actually being asked outright for her opinion and he was ruining it. She knew he could get jealous, but this was unfair.

She turned back to the Inspector. 'What do we know about the dead woman?' she asked, lowering her voice. 'Who is – I mean, who was she?'

It worked both ways. If he wanted to pick her brains, he could share some information too.

D.I. Curtis nodded once then began to move his grizzled head very slowly from side to side. 'Yes, I know who you are, Miss Flora Lively of Shakers Removals. We've all read about you, down at the station, sticking your nose in, playing detective. And I'm telling you now, you'll stay out of this. Do you understand? You'll stay right out of it or I'll have you barred from this building entirely.'

'What?' Flora's mouth gaped open. She looked from the policeman to Marshall, then back again. 'But you just this minute asked me what I ...?'

Marshall wore an expression that looked more resigned than annoyed. 'Yeah we get the message. Come on, Flora. Time to go.'

'But I ...' Flora was still processing it, and she didn't like this feeling one bit. 'Oh,' she said. 'Oh, I get it. You were making fun of me. Ha. Very funny. Very professional to have a joke at my expense when there's a dead woman not six metres away from where we're standing.'

'Very professional to interfere with a police investigation not once but twice already,' the detective countered, looking entirely nonplussed by Flora's criticism. 'You just make sure you don't make it three times.'

'Well!' Flora's face began to burn. Anger rose up from her belly, and when Marshall took hold of her arm she shook him off violently.

'I'm going,' she snapped. But as she wheeled around, her long skirt flaring, she collided with two uniformed paramedics pushing an empty gurney. The gurney fell clattering to the floor, and Flora let out a anguished cry, much to the astonishment of every person in the atrium.

***

Downstairs, she found the museum's owner Jasmin White talking quietly to a female police officer. Flora caught her client's eye, then took a seat by the ticket office, which was really no more than a low bookcase with some leaflets on it and a cash box on a table behind. She still felt shaky after her encounter with that horrible police detective, although the hot chocolate Nick had made her was helping a lot.

Now why hadn't Marshall thought of making her a hot chocolate?

This was not the time to be making comparisons. If she was having doubts about her relationship with her handsome co-manager they were certainly nothing to do with Nick, nor with the making of hot chocolate in extreme circumstances. Besides, they weren't doubts as such. More mild misgivings. Like, were they truly compatible, for example? Their differences gave their love its fire, its spark, but also could be frustrating. And, more often than Flora cared to admit lately, just plain exhausting.

'Hello, Flora my dear.' Jasmin wafted into the chair next to Flora's, all white linen and clean perfume. She was as unlikely an owner of crusty old antiquities as you could hope to find, yet somehow the role fitted her. Jasmin exuded class and wealth and knowledge. It was immediately obvious that the lady was well-travelled, and there was something exotic about her, something almost regal.

'How are you holding up?' Flora asked, watching the policewoman head towards the staircase that led to the second floor.

'Ah,' Jasmin sighed. 'It's a sad thing to have a death. But the watchers will see her over to the other side.'

'The watchers?' Flora looked puzzled. 'Who are they?'

'What, not who. It is difficult to explain.'

Jasmin leaned back and closed her eyes. Flora waited. After a few minutes, when it seemed clear that her client wasn't going to elaborate, she said,

'Jasmin?'

The older woman opened her dark, brown eyes. 'Yes?'

'The watchers. What do you mean?'

'Hmmm.' Jasmin sighed again. 'It is a difficult thing to find words for. So, there have been many lives lived over and over, and the watchers are the eyes of souls that live on in the material – in the elements of the objects that I collect.'

'You mean like ghosts?'

'Ugh, no. Your ghosts are stupid clumsy inventions for Halloween and mystery books. I'm talking about souls, souls that become watchers. A very different thing.'

'And these souls live on inside the exhibits?' Flora said dubiously. 'Is that what you're saying.

'It's difficult,' Jasmin repeated, waving her hand vaguely.

'Yes,' Flora murmured. 'It sounds it. Jasmin, do you know anything about the woman they found? Did they tell you anything yet?'

'No,' Jasmin said sadly. 'That police lady would tell me nothing. But I have to go and look at the atrium shortly. We both do. We need to tell them if anything is missing. I'm afraid we'll have to open and check the crates you've already packed, my dear. It's extra work for you.'

Flora nodded. That made sense. Maybe the dead woman was trying to steal an artefact. Perhaps she had an accomplice and he killed her and kept the haul for himself. Oh, watch out for your assumptions, she told herself sternly. The killer could have been a woman. It paid to keep an open mind.

'Do you know of anyone who might want to steal from you?' Flora asked.

A smile spread across the woman's beautiful lips, but then disappeared as her eyes grew serious. 'Why, Flora, of course. I had forgotten how you are also a detective in your own right. You will find out what happened here, will you?'

'Erm, no. I don't think that's going to happen.' Flora pulled a face. 'The police have already made it clear they don't want me interfering.'

Jasmin smiled again, and poked Flora in the ribs with a manicured finger. 'Ah, but you interfere anyway, no? Because that is what you do.'

Before Flora could think of a response, Jasmin said a

swift goodbye. Yes, Flora thought, I suppose that is what I do. And there didn't seem any good reason to stop now.

***

As far as Flora could tell there was nothing missing, but until the police had finished with the actual crime scene it would be impossible to know for sure. And there was obviously one box they couldn't search through yet; the crate where Flora had packed away the Mizaru monkey only hours earlier was covered by a white tent and would remain off-limits long after the body had been moved. That a woman had died inside a crate that Flora herself had packed and sealed shut only hours earlier seemed incredible.

'You know we can't carry on with this job until they give us the all clear,' Marshall told Flora when they had finally been allowed to leave the museum. They were walking along the riverbank, hand in hand, heading for a favourite coffee house that was open early for breakfast. The sun was just beginning to give a little warmth to the day, and the sky was clear now, a washed-out pinky-blue.

'You're right,' Flora agreed. 'Ugh, what a thing to happen!'

'Should we get out there and find something else, do you think?' Marshall said, guiding her to the side of the path to avoid a particularly deep puddle. It had been raining all night, and the air was fresh now, properly autumnal. Sharp, but with an edge.

'Like what?' Flora said. 'I mean, work is picking up at last, but it's still slow. We can't ditch this museum job, Marshall. We'll have to see it through. We can't afford to start letting big clients down.'

'I guess.'

Now he was in one of his gloomy moods. Look how

his shoulders hunched, how his head sat just a little more forward than usual. God, she knew him so well. Every tiny detail of his body, his mannerisms, his voice, his moods, was so familiar. Was that a good thing, she wondered?

'Cheer up,' she said. 'It'll only be a day, most likely. Then we can get back to it. We might even be back in there tonight.'

'Yeah. I guess.'

Flora watched the swans on the river, enjoying how they glided so gracefully across the water. They had it all going on underneath the surface, didn't they? Maybe Marshall was like that. Cool, calm exterior. Cool, *grumpy* exterior. But full of unspoken thoughts and passions and ideas and motivations underneath.

Maybe. Or maybe he was just plain grumpy.

'Has anyone ever told you that you're a very grumpy guy,' Flora said, slipping her hand out of his.

'Yeah,' Marshall replied. 'You have. Many times.'

She glanced at him, looking for the twinkle in his eyes that would tell her the game was on – that their banter was back in play. But the twinkle wasn't there.

'Marshall,' she began, 'do you think–'

'No,' he said, 'I try not to think.'

'Very funny. But seriously, sweetheart, do you think that–'

Her phone began to ring. She pulled it from her pocket and looked at the screen.

'It's Jasmin,' she said, swiping to answer.

'Flora! Oh, Flora, you have to come back.'

Jasmin's voice was high-pitched and frantic. Flora held the phone away from her ear, and gestured to Marshall to listen in.

'What's wrong? Are you okay?'

'It's the seventh … No, I can't say it, Flora. Not over the phone. You have to come back, right now. Please. Please can you come back to the museum? I really need your help.'

'Okay. Yes, of course.' Flora looked at Marshall and widened her eyes. He shrugged and nodded. 'We're on our way. We'll be about ten minutes.'

'Meet me in the basement,' Jasmin said. 'And Flora, don't tell anyone. I mean it. It's a matter of life and death.'

Chapter 3

'It's known as the Seventh Tablet of Lamassu.'

Jasmin moved around the basement, lighting candles with a safety lighter, speaking softly as she walked.

'What I have to tell you, Flora, must not leave this room. I cannot express how important it is to me that I have your solemn promise about that.'

Flora watched the older woman warily. Jasmin had not wanted Marshall to hear what she had to say, even though Flora had insisted that she would be sharing whatever Jasmin told her with him later. Marshall, taciturn as ever, seemed content to wait upstairs. Flora thought it just as well. He'd no doubt find the atmosphere down here, with the candles circling the room and the space freshly cleared for two old armchairs, positioned facing each other across a low round table, decidedly kooky.

'You have my promise that I won't tell anyone other than Marshall,' Flora repeated. 'Unless it's something that I have to tell the police, Jasmin. None of us are above the law.'

Jasmin lit the final candle and weaved her way back across the basement, around the discarded display cabinets and empty crates, to sit opposite Flora.

'Quite,' she said. 'However I think you'll see that this is a matter for us alone. It really doesn't affect anybody else.'

'Well, if that's the case …' Flora trailed off, not sure how to finish. Jasmin had opened a small wooden box of photographs and was now leafing through them. The flickering light reflected off her black hair, which hung smoothly over one shoulder. Flora could hear muffled voices above. The investigation team was still in full force.

'This,' Jasmin said, handing Flora a dog-eared photograph, 'is a Lamassu. This was one of the monuments at the entrance to Nineveh. It was destroyed by Isis in twenty-fifteen.'

Flora took the photograph and held it up to the light. She saw a giant winged creature, half man, half beast, intricately carved from pale grey stone. Its human head was majestic, proud, with a long sculpted beard and turban. 'I've seen this before,' Flora said. 'Where have I seen this before?'

'Such a tragedy,' Jasmin sighed. 'So much pointless destruction. These Lamassu had survived since the eighth century B.C. Can you imagine that? Protecting all who passed by. Only to be disfigured with an electrical power tool, just to draw attention to a militant agenda.'

Flora could only agree; clearly Jasmin knew far more about it than she did. 'I'm sure I've seen something like this before, though,' she said again.

'At the British Museum, perhaps? They have some Lamassu statues from Nimrud on display there. It's quite dramatic.'

'No, I've never been to the British Museum.'

'You've never been to the British Museum?' Jasmin looked confused. 'Oh,' she said, her expression clearing, 'I suppose the Victoria and Albert is more your thing. The history of fashion?' she added when Flora shook her head blankly.

'The thing is, I don't really go to–'

'Oh well, the Natural History Museum then, or whichever is your favourite. My point is, there are Lamassu at the British. Full size. Very impressive.'

'Okay,' Flora said meekly. She didn't think it would be a good idea to push on with the fact that she hadn't set foot in a museum, until this one, since she was a child. She handed the photograph back to Jasmin. 'So how is this Lam ... Lamas ...'

'Lamassu.'

'Right. How is it connected to what you wanted to tell me?'

'Ah yes.' Jasmin seemed to deflate before Flora's eyes. 'Yes, of course. That is why we are here. So, I am going to tell you, and then I am going to ask you for your help. I hope that you will help me, Flora. I hope I can rely on you.'

'I'll do whatever I can,' Flora said quickly, concerned to see tears collecting in the older woman's eyes. She leaned forward to show she was listening. Was this another mystery to be solved? And if it was, what kind of a ride was she in for this time?

* * *

'The Seventh Tablet of Lamassu is absolutely priceless. It has been in my family for hundreds of years, through thick and thin, across continents. People have sacrificed unimaginable things to protect it. Our Lamassu isn't a statue – it is carved in relief, onto a small stone slab. Many years ago it would have been painted in bright colours, like the original statues in Assyria. When my father died he entrusted it to me. He told me never to let it out of my sight.'

Jasmin told her story in a hushed voice that Flora had to strain to hear. It was chilly in the basement, among the remnants of a failing museum, and the environment did little to cheer up the gloomy atmosphere.

'So it's here in the museum?' Flora said. 'That must be why I recognised the photograph. I probably packed it yesterday.'

Jasmin let out a loud sob. 'Oh, Flora! The Seventh Tablet of Lamassu has gone! It's been stolen – taken from my family, ripped away from me like someone has ripped out my heart.'

Flora sat back in surprise. 'But …' she began, 'well … I'm sure the police will get it back.'

'No, it's gone forever,' Jasmin wailed. 'You were here all night, you and your security man. A woman dead, my Lamassu taken – it's all too much for me to bear.'

'Now hang on a minute.' Flora jumped up and stood behind her chair. She gripped the fabric-covered back with shaking fingers. 'I hope you're not suggesting that it was my fault, because–'

'Not fault, Flora, no. But responsibility, yes? It is in our contract, no? That is why you have the security man, why you take over looking after the precious antiquities while they are carefully taken to their new home in London.'

Flora turned away so that Jasmin couldn't see the dismay on her face. Of course she was quite right. There had been a theft as well as a death, and any losses incurred were absolutely on Shaker's watch, and therefore her and Marshall's responsibility.

Marshall. Flora's heart did another unpleasant somersault. He was going to kill her.

The insurance would cover it. Wouldn't it? Although, how could any insurance cover something that was literally priceless?

'Jasmin, listen. You need to tell the police right away. I don't even know why you're telling me first. I mean, I appreciate being given a head's up, obviously, and I'll get on to the insurance company as soon as I get back to the office, but you've got to let the investigators know that there's more to this than a suspicious death.'

Flora couldn't help thinking that Jasmin seemed a lot more upset about the loss of this carving than she was about the death of someone's daughter or sister or even someone's mother. But one thing she'd learned from all her years of moving customers from one home to another was this: people got more attached to stuff than made any logical sense.

'Where exactly was it taken from?' she asked.

'What?'

'Where did you have this tablet thing? Was it on display?'

'Yes, of course.'

'Was it insured?' Flora asked. She stood and began to circle the basement, her mind working hard. 'Was it ... secured in some way?'

'It should have been locked away,' Jasmin said, her distress palpable.

'But it was insured, right?'

Jasmin looked at her hands briefly. 'You can't always insure things, Flora,' she said. 'Not when you need to show provenance. It's … it can be complicated.'

'Hey, are you guys done down there?'

Flora met Jasmin's startled stare. 'It's Marshall. I guess he's tired of waiting for me. We have been up most of the night, you know.'

Jasmin had the grace to look chastened. 'I'm sorry. This is too much for you right now. I panicked when I saw that my precious Lamassu has gone. Let's talk again tomorrow.'

When Flora reached the bottom of the stairs she looked back to check that Jasmin was following. The sooner they got this missing artefact thing handed over to the police the better. But Jasmin was still perched on her chair, her eyes glassy in the flickering light.

'Aren't you coming?'

Jasmin shook her head.

'But we need to–'

'Flora, no. Don't you remember? I said you couldn't share this with anyone. This is for you and you alone.'

'For goodness sake, why? I don't get this, Jasmin. You must know that even if our insurers cover what that carving was worth, if it's as priceless as you say they won't pay out without a crime number. Besides, it's far more likely that your own policy would be a better option.'

'It's not the money, Flora.' Jasmin crossed the room and took Flora's hands in hers. 'No amount of money could replace the Seventh Tablet of Lamassu.'

'Then what do you want?' Flora was perilously close to losing her temper. After only a couple of hours sleep with her head on a desk, then waking up to a screaming banshee, finding a dead body and being grilled by the meanest police detective ever, and now having all this guilt dumped on her – not to mention the threat of financial ruin for Shakers Removals – she wondered how much longer she could hold it together.

'I thought it was obvious. I want you to take the case.'

'The ... you want me to what?'

Marshall's head appeared, peering down from the top of the basement stairwell. 'Is everything alright?'

'I'll be up in a minute,' Flora told him.

'Right. Okay then.' His expression said it was far from okay, but he retreated all the same.

Flora began to climb the ancient wooden treads. Her legs felt as heavy as lumps of granite; she was dizzy from lack of sleep. And food, she realised. It had been almost twenty four hours since she last ate anything substantial. She gripped the handrail grimly and hauled herself up the last few steps.

'I'm serious about hiring you,' Jasmin called just as Flora reached for the door. With a tired sigh, Flora turned and forced a smile.

'I know, Jasmin. You've already hired us. And I promise we'll see the job through to the end. Just as soon as the police let us carry on with our work.'

'Not that job, although yes, please do continue. But I'm going to hire you as my own private detective, and I'll pay you well. I want you, the Flora Lively from the newspaper, to investigate my missing Lamassu. I believe that you are the only person who can find it.'

***

Ever since that night in the yurt at Hanley Manor, Flora and Marshall had been inseparable. It made sense for Marshall to rent out his mid-century townhouse and move in with Flora – his house was on the wrong side of the river, for one thing, and it was a soulless box, in Flora's considered opinion. The rent covered Marshall's mortgage, with enough left over to start a joint savings account. Neither of them were entirely sure what they were saving for, but it seemed like the sensible, 'coupley' thing to do.

Everything else – food, bills, travel, going out – they split fifty-fifty. There was no mortgage to pay on Flora's apartment; she owned it outright. She was lucky, she knew that, but she'd still rather have her parents alive than have the financial security afforded to her by a generous inheritance. Still, it gave her a sense of security to be the sole person on the deeds, and she knew that was something she wouldn't give up lightly.

Her apartment was light and airy, one of two penthouses in a converted former school building. The ceilings were high, the floorboards stripped back and sanded, and the walls were painted white and hung with bright, eclectic, oversized artwork sourced from local thrift shops. Flora loved it. Marshall, she could tell, was ambivalent at best. If he had his way, she suspected, he'd chuck out all her mix-and-match retro furniture, along with the homemade curtains and the knitted throws, and decorate the flat with a careful combo of neutrals, finished off with oak furniture from Oak Furniture Land.

She smiled to herself now, sipping a freshly brewed coffee, happy just sitting on a tall stool with her elbows on the kitchen counter, listening to the rain make patterns on the skylight. Such a soothing sound. And boy, did her nerves need soothing. She'd spent an hour that afternoon working on the patchwork cover she was quilting, enjoying how the sandwiched wadding rose between the lines of stitching, like little mountains and valleys. Sewing and making always relaxed her, and today was no exception.

Marshall's key in the door jolted her out of her reverie. She jumped down from the stool to greet him, happy to see that he was smiling.

'Well?' she asked, grabbing a mug from the shelf to make him coffee.

'We're on.' He planted a kiss on top of her head. 'Save the coffee honey. I'm gonna take a shower.'

Flora watched him cross the apartment and walk through the bedroom, undressing as he walked, dropping first his sweater, then his jeans, onto the floor. It drove her crazy when he did that, but she had to admit it was also very sexy. Should she go join him in the shower? Was the undressing on the go a display for her benefit, or just male laziness? She touched her hair where he'd kissed her chastely, the way you would kiss a friend, or worse, a sister. That wasn't so sexy.

Why were men so damn hard to read?

Flora picked up the mug and stuck it under the filter. But then she changed her mind and dumped the mug in the sink. Being tired and wired wasn't going to help her tonight. Marshall had said they were on – that meant that the police had lifted the embargo on the museum, and there was a whole day's worth of packing to make up. Why, it might even turn into a night shift. Flora smiled again, feeling a familiar bubble of excitement. Plenty of time to look for clues. Plenty of opportunity to have a really good snoop around. And this time she wasn't prying, or sticking her nose in where it wasn't wanted. This time, she was on official business. Her first proper case.

'Flora Lively investigates,' she whispered under her breath, enjoying how important it sounded. Then she pulled a face, annoyed at herself. Murder was a serious business, not a game. A woman was dead; a priceless heirloom missing. And Jasmin was relying on her for help. She wouldn't let her down.

'Whatcha doing?' Marshall drawled, appearing back into the kitchen wearing only a towel, trailing wet footprints across the living room floor. His chest, broad and muscular with just a light scattering of golden hair, glistened attractively, and his eyes sparkled with mischief.

So it had been for her benefit after all.

'Nothing,' Flora said briskly. 'Come on, Mr Goodman. You better get dressed. We've got a job to do.'

Chapter 4

'Is there really any need for us all three of us to be here?'

They'd been back at the museum for a little over four hours, but despite the great progress they were making, Marshall clearly had a problem with Nick. Flora had asked him about it twice already; she'd started to get the crazy idea that Marshall was actually jealous – which would be the first time ever as far as she was aware – but he denied it vehemently.

'Keep your eyes on the bottom line, Flora,' was his response, which she figured was something to do with having to pay Nick's wages, rather than her boyfriend telling her to look at another man's arse.

Flora was glad to have the two guys there with her. The Shropshire White & Co Museum of Antiquities had taken on an even more ominous atmosphere. Approaching the medieval building earlier that evening, the sun dipping low in a red sky, Flora had experienced a genuine feeling of foreboding. What had previously been charming – uneven leaded windows, blackened beams, awkward jutting gables – now appeared to bear down on them like a warning. The windows were hooded eyes; the timber facade a shrunken face.

The inside was a little less intimidating. With Marshall by her side, Flora made light work of the two smaller rooms on the same floor as the atrium; fewer and fewer exhibits on display made for a far better environment in which to work. They took a break just after ten-thirty, taking coffee from the little kitchen into Jasmin's office. Flora perched on a stool with her feet tucked up under her, and Marshall sat back in the adjustable chair, stretching out his long legs under the desk. Nick announced that he was going to do a quick check outside, and Flora thanked him with a broad smile.

'It's so reassuring having our own private security guard,' she said to Marshall once Nick's footsteps had faded. 'We should take him on permanently.'

Sure, she was winding him up. But that was what passed for sport between them. He was just as bad as her, and they both loved it. She braced herself for a clever comeback, and a bit of flirty banter.

'That's just plain stupid, Flora, and you know it,' Marshall responded flatly.

Flora sighed and sipped her coffee. It was horrible, but at least it was hot. Unlike her relationship right now.

They finished their drinks in silence, then Flora said,

'You know, sweetheart, I think I'll go and do a reccy of what else there is to do tonight. Is that okay?'

'Sure. Go for it.' Marshall held her gaze.

'What?' she said.

He smiled slowly and held out his hand. Flora got up and crossed the room, gasping as he took her wrist and swung her onto his lap.

'Oh, wow.' Flora laughed, putting her palm to her throat. 'That was a very nice sup–'

Her words were cut off by Marshall's mouth on hers, the kiss warm and soft, an intimate promise of more to come. She closed her eyes and gave herself up to it. My, he smelled good. She reached for his hair, feeling the curls fold around her fingers. The fluttering in her stomach swelled into heat, travelling all over …

'Hey, guys, get a room why don't you?' The amusement in Nick's voice was clearly audible.

Flora groaned inwardly. For once, she was in complete agreement with Marshall – she definitely wished right now that their security guard was anywhere but here. She kept her eyes fixed on Marshall's as she pulled away and slowly stood, a light smile playing on her lips, waiting for him to wink at her or give some other mischievous indication of camaraderie.

But his expression was stony, which Flora knew now was a mask for furious. She shook her head and threw Nick a cross glance.

'Time for you guys to do some male bonding, or whatever the hell it is you do. Spray your testosterone around, hit each other with sticks, whatever. Just get over it.' She picked up her bag and glared at them each in turn. 'I'm gonna be here for another half an hour then I'm calling a cab and going home. I'll be back in the morning to take over.'

She swung around and stalked out of the office, aware all of a sudden that she really was angry. When she'd started talking she'd been part joking, but now she had a fire in her belly – and not the desiring kind. What was it with men? Women weren't like that around each other. Sure, there might be a bit of bitching, but it was always behind each other's backs. And women always made sure they didn't make other people feel uncomfortable when they hated each other.

Really, women were just so much better at being horrible than men.

Flora smiled at this as she pushed open the doors to the atrium. But the smile fell away as she remembered the scene that had been played out here twenty four hours ago. An involuntary shiver ran across her back. She squared her shoulders, then marched purposefully into the room. She had a job to do. It was time to look for clues.

***

The only problem was, Flora had no idea where to start. Nor did she know what she was actually looking for. It was all very flattering of Jasmin to think that Flora was some kind of amateur investigator, but the truth was, her past triumphs had been mostly down to luck.

At least, that was what Flora began telling herself now, as she tried to piece it all together.

She began in the atrium, walking through her actions in her head. The Mizaru monkey, Nick coming in, sealing up the crate. The police – that hateful Detective Curtis – had grilled her on this detail. They clearly thought she was lying, and just hadn't bothered.

Flora knew different. Jasmin had even specified the kind of tape Shaker's were to use, a special type of tape that created an air-tight bond. And it was damn difficult stuff to cut, too. So if the investigators' theory was that a random woman had wandered into the museum at night, fallen into an open box and then died ... Well, that just couldn't be.

But what then, Flora thought? Obviously she had no idea how the woman might have died, but she did know that the police were treating it as suspicious. No shit, Sherlock. Flora hadn't got a good look at the body – nor had she wanted to – but she was pretty sure that there were no obvious signs of injury. It wasn't the first time she'd seen a dead body – the murders at Hanley Manor last year had been grim enough to give her nightmares for months. She wondered for the hundredth time just how on earth that poor woman had ended up in a museum crate right under their noses?

And how was it linked to the noises she and Nick had heard?

Flora inspected the remaining crates, which had been moved to the perimeter of the room now, but found nothing untoward. Next, she examined the entrance lobby, checking the door to see how easy it might have been for someone to break in. Not that easy, she figured, but then she wasn't a burglar.

She was starting to have serious doubts whether she was up to this task at all.

Flora was on her way upstairs, circumnavigating the atrium along a narrow corridor that ran parallel to the street and was lined with a row of small diamond-leaded windows, when she saw the man. The glass in the windows was single-glazed and draughty; it was shivery cold in here, not helped by the fact that she'd left her sweater in the office with the warring males. Flora glanced down towards the road outside, her eye drawn to a movement in the shadows. Dimly aware that it was midnight, or near to, she wondered idly what it could be. Her attention grabbed, she paused and looked more closely.

A man stood on the cobbled pavement, staring directly up at Flora. He wore a peaked cap that partly shaded his upper face, but the direction – and intensity – of his gaze was unmistakable. Flora took an involuntary step backwards, catching her breath. She peered out again, staying hidden behind the deep black timber frames. He was still there, but was no longer watching the museum. Instinctively, she began to take in details of his appearance. Not particularly tall, but solidly built. Dark clothing – something like a windbreaker over black or navy trousers. Impossible to see much else.

Suddenly, the man tilted back his head and looked up at her again. Surely he couldn't see her? The windows were so tiny and the corridor so badly lit. But now Flora could see his face in the yellow glow of the streetlight, and something about it affected her deeply. She pressed her back flat against the cold wall and closed her eyes.

She knew him. Flora was sure of it. From where she had no idea, but there was something familiar about that face ...

'Flora?'

She blinked and there was Marshall, close enough to kiss, his face concerned. 'Are you alright?' he said.

'There's a man out there,' Flora whispered.

'Outside?'

She nodded. Marshall stepped closer to the window.

'There ain't no one I can see, honey.'

Flora took a tentative look. The street outside was empty.

'He's gone now.'

'I see that.'

'There was someone there!'

'I didn't say there wasn't.'

'Okay then.' Flora paused for a moment, then pressed herself into Marshall's arms. His warmth was comforting, reassuring, and she didn't want to admit how shaken she felt.

And then a thought occurred to her.

'Marshall! There was a man outside!'

'Erm, I know, Flora. You just said that.'

'No, idiot. I mean, there was a man outside the museum last night as well. Nick said he saw someone. Oh, I can't remember what he said now – it was just before all those weird noises started. Maybe he had something to do with them. Maybe he had something to do with the murder.'

'Whoa there lady,' Marshall said, looking alarmed. 'When did it become a murder? I thought it was just a suspicious death.'

'Oh, come on. What else could it be? She didn't break open a crate, climb in and then die.'

'Suicide?' Marshall ventured uncertainly.

Flora gave him a look that said, *Seriously?*

'You're shivering,' Marshall said, rubbing her back. 'Anyway, I thought you were going home?'

'I was investigating,' she said sulkily, as they walked towards the relative warmth of the office.

Marshall snickered. 'Did you solve it yet?'

'Listen, Mr Sarcastic, what you don't know is–'

But her words were cut off by the sound of a woman screaming. Flora stopped dead, her fingers gripping Marshall's upper arm.

'It's the same as last night,' she hissed.

Marshall's usual laconic coolness had temporarily left him. His face was pale in the dim light; Flora tried to slow her breathing.

'This is what you and Nick heard?' Marshall whispered.

'I think so,' Flora said quietly, all but holding her breath. 'And listen ... footsteps.'

Marshall nodded; he heard them too. But they were different to last night, Flora thought. They sounded more regular, and they were getting closer, not moving further away. In fact, they were getting really close. Soft footsteps, padding along on the other side of the door, almost on top of them ...

'Hey, what are you guys doing huddled in here? Did you hear that scream again?'

'Nick!' Flora sighed. 'I thought you were the, you know. The footsteps we heard last night.'

'I heard them just now, outside the office.'

'We didn't hear them. Just yours.'

'Weird,' Nick said. He took up a stance that struck Flora as comical but kind of cute, with his hands on his hips, legs wide, holding his torch to one hip like a weapon. Marshall had yet to acknowledge Nick's presence; Flora guessed the male bonding hadn't gone too well after she'd left them alone.

The lights went out. One minute Flora was looking at Nick, the next he was a grey silhouette against the window.

'Great,' she whispered. 'What time is it?'

'Nearly midnight,' Nick said, using his torch to check his watch.

'Do you think the clock will strike all the way this time?' Flora asked, not expecting an answer.

'Why are we waiting here in the dark?' Marshall said. 'Why don't we go down to the lobby? He pulled out his phone and switched it to torch mode, clearly not wanting to be outdone.

Flora nodded. That was smart. 'Let's do that,' she said, swiping to the torch on her phone too.

'I'll stay here,' Nick told them. 'Keep a look out.'

'I think we should all stay together,' Flora said. 'Just in case.'

'If you like,' Nick agreed. 'I can protect you both if there's another intruder.'

'Like you protected that woman last night,' Marshall said.

'Oh, come on!'

Flora began to march Marshall down the corridor, with Nick close behind. They each jumped when a loud bang sounded somewhere overhead. No, more than one bang – maybe five or six in succession.

'Jesus!' Marshall exclaimed. 'What was that.'

'I told you,' Flora said, feeling oddly vindicated.

'This place is weird,' Nick sighed.

Flora agreed. 'Listen,' she said. 'The clock is striking.'

They all stopped and listened. Marshall counted the chimes under his breath.

At three chimes, Nick whispered, 'I've lost count.'

'Shhh,' Marshall told him. 'Four. Five.'

'Six,' Flora said. 'Seven.'

Then silence. In the cold, eerie light from their torches, the silence seemed louder than the chiming of the clock below had been.

'It's stopped,' Flora said, stating the obvious.

'It must be broken,' Marshall said, shrugging. But even he looked rattled.

'Come on,' Nick said. 'Let's go and see.'

They walked quickly through the atrium. When they reached the entrance to the lobby, the lights flickered back on. They stopped moving, and Flora blinked, shielding her eyes momentarily. How long had the lights been off for, she wondered? And, more importantly, how did they go out and why?

She was speculating whether the noises they had heard could be part of the fabric of the old building – pipe work, heating, plumbing, or some other quirky feature – when she remembered the man she'd seen.

'Nick, last night you said you'd seen a man outside. When you were in the – what was it you called it? The war room?'

'Yup.' He nodded, and held open one half of the double doors that led to the main lobby.

'Can you describe him? And what did you mean when you said he'd been acting weird?'

'He was just hanging around, you know. Like, just standing there. When he saw me watching he ran off.'

'He ran off?' Flora asked, trying to suppress a yawn. She felt like she could sleep for a week.

Nick crossed the room and stood in front of the grandfather clock. 'It seems to be working fine. The second hand is moving. It's ticking.'

'It's so weird,' Flora said, shaking her head. 'There were definitely only seven chimes.'

'We should head home,' Marshall said, laying his arm across Flora's shoulders. 'We're back in here at nine. And you look wiped out.'

'Sure. Just give me a minute, okay?' Flora turned back to Nick. 'Would you say he was young, or older?'

'Who?'

'The man you saw last night.'

The man Flora had seen just now had given her the impression of being late fifties, possibly older. She wasn't sure, though. It was just an impression.

'He was a white male, about five seven, eighty kilos, dark clothing, running shoes, one of those flat caps like they wear on Peaky Blinders.' Nick paused and thought for a moment. 'I'd say he was ex-forces. Possibly fifty-five, sixty, but fit.'

'Thorough,' Marshall commented.

'Did you give that description to the police?' Flora

asked. When Nick nodded, she smiled ruefully. I bet they were impressed with that, she thought. Nick's account of the night's events, with his matter-of-fact tone and his laser-sharp memory, was exactly the kind of thing they liked.

Not so her woolly recounting, that always seemed to come out like some kind of made-up story.

Why oh why had she bothered mentioning that stupid smell?

Chapter 5

In the good old days of Shakers Removals, they would have had at least three jobs on the go at any one time. Even after Peter Lively died, Flora had employed two full-time staff and a few casuals – this was pre-recession, when everyone was moving house, upsizing, climbing the ladder, ringing the changes. Back then, there had been little need to go touting for commercial work like this museum job – or the film crew gig last year, or the sensitive document storage and transport they took on a few times a month. Domestic removals remained the mainstay of the business to date, but only just.

There were still some regulars, though, and Flora loved them like family. Even returning customers rarely moved more than once a year, so it had been great to hear that Bobbi was on the move again after only six months. This time it was out of her rented three storey on one of the newer estates, and into a four-bed, two-bath out by Albrighton. Compared to Bobbi's usual abodes, this was a veritable mansion.

'Wowsers, Bobbi,' Flora exclaimed for the third time. 'This place is like a palace.'

'And ain't I the queen of the castle!' Bobbi, with her bubble-permed hair, Snapchat-filter make-up, spiked heels and spray on jeans, strutted for Flora's benefit across the white tiled kitchen floor. Flora grinned. Bobbi's cheer was infectious.

'You are a tonic,' Flora said. Already her shoulders were relaxing a little, her face losing some of its tightness. The past forty-eight hours had been crazy, and the craziness showed no signs of abating.

Nice to have a bit of light relief by doing some heavy furniture lifting.

They'd drafted in help from Marshall's temp pool to help load the lorry – a sign-written pantechnicon that Flora had only recently mastered driving. She now had her professional license, a source of pride for a diminutive woman who'd always worked in a man's world. How she loved to manoeuvre the pantec into a particularly difficult driveway, then clamber down from the cab and see the surprise on the faces of any men within view.

Right now, all Bobbi's belongings were packed nice and tight in the van, while Tom and Dick – who were actually called Brian and Julian, but Flora always thought of Marshall's temps as Tom and Dick, which came from a joke neither she nor Marshall could remember but which had been hilarious at the time – were having a fag break.

Marshall was at the museum, meeting D.I. Curtis, who had 'pertinent information' apparently. It was a task Flora had been glad to delegate, even if it did mean that she had the job of helping lug Bobbi's super-sized mattress down two flights of stairs, not to mention about a hundred boxes of make-up and shoes and more cushions than a soft furnishings store.

And now she had to help lug all that stuff out of the van and into its new home.

Flora couldn't help thinking that Bobbi's slightly shabby belongings, seen in situ in countless locations over the years, would look completely out of place in these posh surroundings.

'It's not a rental house this time,' Bobbi said, watching Flora's expression closely. 'That's what you're thinking, isn't it? How can Bobbi afford somewhere like this?'

'No! That's not what I was thinking,' Flora said quickly. What she had been thinking was much worse.

She felt her face starting to redden.

'It's okay, love. I know this ain't the same as my usual gaffs. Got myself a man, didn't I?'

'Ah.' Flora smiled. 'And this is his place, is it?'

'Asked me to move in with him. Wasn't gonna say no, was I?'

'I don't suppose you were.'

'He's a dentist,' Bobbi offered. 'Works in Wem.'

'That's ... nice.' Flora didn't know what to say. She regarded Bobbi carefully. Was she happy, she wondered. Would she settle here? How easy would it be to just move yourself in to someone else's home, lock stock and barrel, and make it your own?

But wasn't that exactly what Marshall was trying to do? And how was that working out? Flora didn't think she'd be able to manage it so well if it was the other way around.

'There's always a downside, Flora,' Bobbi said with a wide grin.

'What do you mean?'

Bobbi pulled a plastic kettle from a cardboard carton and filled it at the tap. 'I mean, even when you land on your feet – find a great relationship, a great job ...' she waved her free hand to take in the kitchen, 'or a great house like this, say, or even being left a wonderful family business.'

Flora gave a heavy sigh. 'What exactly are you getting at, Bobbi?'

'Nothing.'

The older woman winked, then rummaged in the carton for cups, producing two matching Cath Kidston mugs in lurid red and green.

'I know I'm lucky, if that's your point. You don't have to tell me. Early thirties, own flat, own business–'

'Good health, slim, cute as a button,' Bobbi finished. 'And there's that handsome boyfriend of yours.'

'Yeah. He's great.' Flora pulled a face. 'But it's not all

fun and games, you know. Marshall is gorgeous, obviously, and sexy as hell, but he can be so damn moody! And the business is hard work, just to keep it afloat. Sometimes I wish ...' Flora shook her head. She didn't want to go there. It felt too disloyal to her dad.

'As I said, honey, there's always a downside.' Bobbi plonked a mug of builder's tea in front of Flora. 'For instance, I've got to share this palace with a dentist who thinks those –' she pointed at the set of venetian blinds that hung above the sink '– are a suitable window dressing in twenty-nineteen. It's a cross I'll have to bear,' she said with a shrug. Then she winked again, and nudged Flora in the ribs. 'For now, at least.'

***

'Boy, am I glad to see you!'

Marshall met Flora in the museum lobby with such evident relief she felt her heart give a little flutter of happiness. See, she thought. They worked so well together that he missed her when she was off on another job. She squeezed his arm and said, 'I missed you too, sweetheart,' and reached up on her tiptoes to give him a loving kiss.

But then he went and ruined it all in typical Marshall Goodman fashion.

'What are you doing, crazy lady? There's no time for shenanigans – we've got serious trouble going on here.'

Flora rolled her eyes. She wished she'd never taught him that expression for fooling around – how he loved to use it against her.

'Can I take my coat off?' she said, shrugging out of it anyway.

Marshall raised his eyebrows. 'You call that a coat? It looks like you mated with a mountain goat on the way here.'

'Cheek!' Flora whacked him lightly on the chest. 'This

is an Appalachian poncho made from alpaca wool.'

'It smells like an alpaca,' Marshall laughed.

Flora laughed too, but inside she was stung. Yet another slight on her personal styling, she thought. It was definitely time to ring the changes.

'So, if it's not shenanigans you're after, why are you so pleased to see me,' she said, packing her poncho away in her big tote bag and hiding her face so Marshall couldn't see the hurt there.

'They've identified the dead woman,' Marshall said quietly.

'Oh my god.' Flora stood up, dropping her bag on the polished floor. 'Was that what the detective inspector wanted to talk to you about?'

Marshall nodded. 'Apparently she's called Lucy Akopian. She hadn't been reported missing or anything, didn't have any ID on her. But that Curtis guy said they'd put her photo on the system and it matched her passport. She'd been staying in London. He asked if we knew her.'

'A photo of her dead face?' Flora said, grimacing.

'I guess.'

Flora looked around for somewhere to sit, but there were only the chairs by the ticket office and they were piled high with leaflets and stationery and other paraphernalia. 'Can we go out and get a coffee?' she said. 'I just need to … I really want to get out of this place.'

'Sorry, sweetheart, no can do. The detective wants to talk to you. They're interviewing Jasmin just now, up in her office, but he told me to keep you down here when you arrived.'

'Fine.' Flora pulled her poncho out of the tote and flopped on the floor in the warmest corner of the lobby.

'How's the packing going?' she asked.

Marshall narrowed his eyes. 'The police are here, Flora. They're interviewing a suspect. You think they're gonna let us carry on packing up the museum around them like nothing's happened?'

'A suspect?' Flora jumped to her feet. 'What do you mean? Who?'

'Jasmin. I just told you that.'

'What? No you didn't. You said they were interviewing her, not that she was a suspect. Why is she a suspect? Did D.I. Curtis tell you that himself or are you just guessing?'

'Flora, hey. Take it easy.' Marshall took hold of her hands. 'They said that she knew the victim. This Lucy person was Jasmin's business partner, apparently. Hey, I'm sure they'll clear it up. Just breathe, okay.'

'Sorry.' She took a few steadying breaths. 'But tell me everything. Remember – Jasmin asked *me* to investigate, so it's really important that I …'

She stopped talking as she noticed Marshall's expression. It took a moment or two for it to sink in.

'She asked you to *investigate*? You?' Marshall's eyes were two black stones. 'To investigate what, Flora? And in what capacity? And why the hell am I only just hearing about this now?'

Shit. Shit on a stick. Flora could kick herself. So much for keeping it secret. But in her defence, she usually told Marshall absolutely everything – every little detail of her life – and had for such a long time now it was completely alien for her to keep a secret from him.

Hence it slipping out at exactly the wrong moment.

Speaking fast, and not meeting his eyes, Flora gave a brief account of what Jasmin had told her the day before. She didn't leave anything out. She was hazy on the details of the winged half-bull half-man creature, but that was only down to her memory. Marshall's face hardened even more when Flora mentioned Jasmin's veiled allusions to the theft being Shaker's responsibility – at least from an insurance perspective.

'Which was partly why I felt that I had to agree to

help her,' Flora said earnestly. It was a little disingenuous of her to use this as an excuse, but only a little. She *had* felt pressured. And also flattered. But mainly pressured.

'I was going to tell you,' she said. This much at least was true. 'I told Jasmin right from the start that I couldn't promise to keep it from you, or from the police. It only happened yesterday, Marshall. I just sort of assumed she was going to talk to the police about the missing artefact, and then we'd meet up again and discuss our next steps.' She waited for him to respond. He was sitting on the floor now, his back up against the wall, just staring ahead. 'Well, say something. Come on, it's not like I've done any actual investigating. I'm not really a private investigator, am I? I wouldn't have a clue where to start.'

'Exactly,' Marshall snapped. 'And that is my point. You're just a woman who co-manages a removals firm, Flora, nothing more. Why do you keep having to try to push yourself forward like this? It's ...'

He stopped and bit his lip.

'It's what,' Flora said, her heart pounding. 'Go on. What were you going to say?'

'It's embarrassing,' Marshall said softly. He laced his fingers together and propped his elbows on his knees. 'I'm sorry, Flora, but there it is.'

'Right. I see.' She picked up her bag and poncho and placed them both carefully over her arm. 'Well, clearly that needed to be said.'

'Listen, I–'

'No.' Flora held up her hand to cut him off. 'I don't want to talk about it anymore. There's just one thing I need to put you right on, Marshall. I don't *co-manage* a removals firm. I'm the sole owner of that removals firm. And you'd do well to remember that.'

***

Jasmin's face was a study in terror when she was led out of the museum and placed in the back of an unmarked police car. Flora had been waiting outside for over an hour, snuggled up in her woolly coat, silently fuming at Marshall but determined not to shirk her responsibilities, both to the police and to Jasmin White.

She'd had only the briefest moment to speak to Jasmin, and that had been over the top of a police constable telling them that they really should not be conversing.

It was far from conversing – more like shrieking.

'I didn't know that it was her, Flora, I swear,' Jasmin had cried as soon as she saw Flora outside. 'They're saying I tried to hide that I knew her, but I did not know it was poor Lucy.'

Flora had raced to her side and kept pace with the little entourage of police and suspect as they negotiated the wide cobbled pavement outside the museum. Thank goodness for Shrewsbury's pedestrianised areas and the need to park the police car across the road; Flora had just enough time for Jasmin to gush out her side of the story.

'It's been over twenty years since I last saw Lucy Akopian,' Jasmin wailed. 'How could I know it was her?'

'Did you see her body?' Flora asked, glaring at the policeman who was trying to jostle her out of the way.

'Not closely. Who wants to look closely at a dead body? I am a squeamish person! I saw a woman, that was all. I didn't know it was Lucy. You must believe me.'

'I do,' said Flora reassuringly. 'But you have to tell me more about this, Jasmin. Do you think it's connected to the … you know what?'

Jasmin shot her a terrified look. 'Yes. Yes, I am sure it is. She must have come here to steal it. Flora, you have to help me. Please find out who did this to Lucy. What if they come for me next?'

'You'll have to stand back now, Miss,' one of the policemen said, firmly positioning himself to block her progress. It was early evening, and even though the shoppers had finally gone home, theatre goers were out in force, gazing with interest at the tableau being played out for free. Flora hung back, watching the other constable dip Jasmin's head as he put her in the back of the car, then round the vehicle to jump into the driver's seat. They drove off quietly, no siren or lights or squealing tires. You'd have no idea there was a potential murder suspect in the back of that shiny grey BMW. Just a middle-aged woman with her anxious face pressed against the window, mouthing words that Flora couldn't hear.

Chapter 6

'Are you okay?'

Flora looked up to see Nick smiling at her, holding out a vending machine hot chocolate. What joy! A proper drink at last.

'I am now,' she said, taking the cardboard mug gratefully. 'You're here early. Did Marshall call you?'

Nick nodded, popping open a can of energy drink. 'He did. Brought me bang up to date. Also, Marshall's added me to his list of approved temps or something, so I can be here alone to keep an eye on the place.'

It was Marshall's way of trying to make it up to her, Flora supposed, and also to make her go home so they could talk. Half of her was desperate to be home – it had been a long day and she was absolutely exhausted. A hot bath, a glass of wine, and a Netflix series on the TV beckoned. But the other half of her just did not want to face Marshall after what he had said.

Embarrassed by her? That was a whole other level of messed up.

'Go home, Flora,' Nick said kindly.

'Can I drink my hot chocolate first?' she answered with a smile.

'Oh, go on then.' The security guard began to get himself kitted out with his regulation torch and utility belt, checking batteries and phone signal. Flora watched with interest. This was a guy who loved his job. It might be a pretty boring job but she absolutely envied him.

When had she started to dislike her job, she wondered?

No, Flora. Now was not the time to be thinking

about that.

'Will you be in tomorrow?' Nick was asking.

'I don't know,' Flora said, wiping froth off her upper lip. 'The museum move is on hold again while we wait to see if Jasmin is charged with anything.'

'Marshall told me about Mrs White. That's just awful. I mean, if she killed that woman, right here under our noses ...'

'Nick!' Flora reprimanded him sharply. 'She is our employer. You shouldn't talk like that. Jasmin says that she didn't even know it was her former business partner who died, and there's no reason for us to doubt her word. And anyway, as far as I know they haven't said it was definitely murder yet.'

Nick nodded his agreement, but he looked doubtful. Flora sighed.

'Look,' she said, 'Tonight it's really important that you listen out for anything unusual. Or, considering the past two nights, anything usual.'

'You mean screaming and banging and all that weird stuff?'

'Exactly.' Flora shook her head and gazed out of the window for a moment. The darkness seemed absolute. 'If those noises are just part of the building, some kind of freaky natural occurrence, then they are going to happen every night, right? So I want you to log everything. No matter how small or insignificant it seems.'

'I would anyway,' Nick countered. 'It is my job.'

'Yes, of course. But tonight, just be especially vigilant.' Flora paused, then got up and headed for the door. She turned and looked at Nick. 'And be careful. We really do not have a clue what's going on here.'

He called her back when she reached the end of the corridor.

'Flora, I forgot to tell you that I saw that man again. He was outside when I came in. He ran off, though, when I approached him. I think he's just the local weirdo.'

Flora nodded, trying to ignore the chill she felt in her stomach.

'Do you want me to walk you out?' Nick said. He was tying up the laces on his black trainers, crouched in the doorway, all broad shoulders and thick thighs. 'I'll only be a minute.'

'No, don't be soft,' Flora said. 'Jeez, Nick. I walk around this town all the time on my own. I'll be fine, thank you very much.'

But when she exited the museum, the night air cold on her cheeks, the sky black and unforgiving above her, she wished she'd taken him up on his offer, no matter how ridiculous it would have made her feel. A pair of teenagers swerved by, clearly drunk, the girl staggering in platform heels, the boy wearing low jeans that most of his underpants. Flora pulled her poncho closer around her body, and set off in the direction of home.

She'd only walked about five steps when she sensed someone behind her. Swirling around on instinct, the scream fell from her lips when she saw it was Marshall.

'What the hell are you doing here?' she gasped.

'Just thought I'd make sure you got home okay,' he said. He had a sulky air about him, and although Flora was touched she was also instantly irritated.

'Well, how did I manage to get about unmolested before I had you in my life,' she snapped.

'Fine,' he said, immediately turning away with an exaggerated shrug. 'Suit yourself. You're the boss, after all. As you just love to keep reminding me.'

Flora gaped at his retreating back. How dare he? Why, she'd only said that because he diminished her in the first place.

She took a step after him, ready to go into battle. But then she saw movement out of the corner of her eye. Adjusted fully to the darkness now, Flora could easily make out the shape of a man in the shadows. A man wearing dark clothing, and a peaked cap.

He walked towards her slowly, his eyes completely shadowed. Flora couldn't move; she stared at him, glued to the spot. There was something about his face, or his gait, or perhaps the set of his shoulders, that drew her to him. He seemed familiar, even though he clearly wasn't. She told herself, *Run now, Flora.* She thought it over and over. But somehow, she did not move a muscle.

He stopped walking about two metres from her. She could hear his breath, low and even. There was an energy about him, as though he could run a marathon straight off the bat, or jump a wall. Or kill someone.

He reached out his hand. Flora stared at his hand, then looked up at his face. She could see the eyes now, and once again she felt that jolt of recognition. Or was it just in her imagination?

'Flora,' he said.

As soon as he spoke the spell was broken. Flora began to move. She swung around and ran in the opposite direction. But then she heard a commotion behind her; she turned her head as she ran unevenly and saw Marshall – Marshall who had come back, who had probably not gone far at all. He had hold of the older man's arm, was twisting it behind his back. Flora stopped running and watched warily, her heart pounding against her ribs. The man in the cap, although at least a foot shorter than Marshall, was clearly strong; he put his body against Marshall's and shoved hard. Marshall staggered backwards.

'Flora, listen' the man said, dismissing Marshall and walking quickly towards her. 'I have to talk to you.'

'What is your problem?' Marshall demanded, rounding on him again.

Flora took a step away, nearly tripped on the curb, then righted herself. 'I don't ...' she began. 'Who are you?'

'This is going to be a shock,' he said, moving closer.

His expression was intense – Flora could take in only the dark eyes, the narrow nose and lips.

Marshall lunged again, this time grabbing both the man's arms behind his back. 'Leave the lady alone.'

But the stranger never took his eyes off Flora, even while Marshall tried to pull him away. He said, 'I'm your father, Flora. Your real father. And I'm so sorry to be telling you like this. I'll be back soon. I promise.' And then he dipped his legs, bent forwards, and flung Marshall over his head and onto the ground.

In a matter of seconds it was over. Marshall staggered to his feet; the man walked quickly away in the direction of the river. Flora held her hand to her mouth, her eyes wide. She felt her legs give way beneath her, and she sat down heavily on the edge of the curb.

'Are you okay?' Marshall asked, his breath ragged. Flora didn't answer.

He had said he was her real father.

Was there even a chance that could be true?

***

Flora's uncle Max lived out in deepest Whixall, a rural village to the north of Shrewsbury and home to a network of unnamed country lanes that swallowed up any visitors who were crazy enough to think they could rely on SatNav to get around.

It also swallowed up those who thought they could rely on maps. The only people who knew their way around Whixall were those who had lived there for years. And even they got lost occasionally.

Sometimes, when Flora visited, she would get lost for fun. She'd go out for a walk, taking off up a single-track lane, a day-sack on her back with water and a waterproof and perhaps a snack or two. Coming to a crossroads or a fork in the lane, she would simply follow her instinct in choosing which way to go. Left or right, east or west, straight on or veering off along the hedge line. Oftentimes she would go with the most sheltered path, but not always.

If she saw a particularly big dog wandering about in the road – which was a more common occurrence than you might imagine – Flora would do an about turn and head a different way. It didn't matter. All the roads were the same, the view was the same, the trees and fields were the same, the air was the same. If she saw people up ahead she'd try to avoid them. People were rarer than dogs. She could walk for hours and see no one, and not once retrace her steps. She loved to have absolutely no idea where she was.

Eventually she'd either see a signpost and figure out her way back to Max's farm, or else she'd walk until she got a signal on her phone – which was also pretty rare out here – and then call her uncle. With the smallest of details, Max would know where she was. She might say, 'I passed a farm about ten minutes ago with a caravan outside, and up ahead there is a field with cows in.' And Max would ask, 'Does the road have a ditch to the left or the right?' Or perhaps, 'How high are the hedges where you're standing?' and he'd know exactly where to drive to. It was uncanny. Only once did Max get a little tetchy with her, and that was when she was absolutely sure she was helping.

'I'm in front of Bank House,' she'd said confidently. Max had snorted his derision.

'There are at least five Bank Houses that I know of,' he'd told her. 'Now tell me something useful like what colour are the markings on the sheep's backs in the field nearest to you?'

This visit, she needed the space more than ever, so she was grateful that the weather was fine for October, and that Max was occupied with his menagerie of animals; he would leave her alone until she was ready to talk. After a six mile hike around the lonely lanes of Whixall,

Flora was ready for a hot shower, a tot of Max's single malt whiskey, and a good chat with her uncle.

'I don't know what to tell you, Flora,' Max said finally, after Flora had elaborated on the incident from the night before. 'I mean, sure – he *could* be your real father. Why would someone lie about something like that? What else did he say?'

'Nothing,' Flora sighed. 'Marshall chased him off.'

Max chuckled. 'Good old Marshall.'

'Not "good old Marshall" at all. Honestly, you won't hear a bad word about him, will you? I know you think of him like a step-son, Uncle Max, but seriously. Can you take my side just once?'

Max was the reason Marshall had come to England in the first place. Quite the heart throb in his youth, Max was on good terms with almost all of his exes, and always kept an eye out for any offspring that he had played part-time step-dad to, no matter for how short a time. He and Marshall had kept in touch, and when Peter Lively needed a helping hand at the family firm, Max persuaded his brother to hire Marshall, the son of an old flame. Much to Flora's annoyance at the time. To say her feelings for Marshall had been a slow burn would be an understatement.

'I'm always on your side, my dear,' Max reassured her now.

'Hmm,' Flora murmured. 'Well, to be clear, I prefer the term birth father to real father. As far as I'm concerned I had a real father. And a real mother. The fact that I was adopted is neither here nor there. They were my parents.'

'That's good to know,' Max said, giving her a big bear hug. He settled back in his favourite armchair, a reeking cigar smouldering away at his side. Flora had long since given up trying to get Max to stop smoking, just like she'd given up trying to get him to stop letting the chickens run around the kitchen, or to tidy his crazily messy yard. This was how he liked to live, and it was his business, not hers.

Besides, she loved him exactly how he was. The chaos was oddly comforting. It was good to know that at least one person in her life lived exactly how they wanted to and the world did not crumble and fall apart.

'Do you remember anything about my birth family, Uncle Max?' Flora asked, her hands clenched on her knees. 'You weren't around when I was adopted, were you?'

Max shook his head. 'I was in America,' he said regretfully. 'But I do know that your dad and Kitty would have been more than happy for you to find your real ... I mean, your birth family, Flora. They would not have minded at all.'

A warm feeling enveloped Flora and she smiled gratefully. Until that moment she hadn't realised that this was among the things that bothered her the most. Of course, she had wondered about her birth family all her life, ever since the first time her mum and dad took her aside and explained how she was special to them, how they had chosen her. But there was always that guilt, the feeling of being disloyal.

'So what will you do now?' Max asked.

'What can I do?' Flora replied.

'I'm not sure. I suppose you could start to look for your birth parents via the usual channels. Then, if this man is your birth father, you'll find him yourself and know for sure.'

It was sound advice, which was no less than Flora had come to expect from her uncle.

Max heaved himself up and threw another log on the open fire; the effect was only to dampen the existing flames, but Max didn't seem remotely concerned.

'Ah, it'll soon pick up again now,' he said, sinking back into his armchair. 'Flames burn brightest when they are just about to go out.'

Flora nodded, only half listening. 'I suppose you need to poke it or something,' she suggested.

'You can poke at things too much, Flora,' Max said sagely. 'Sometimes it's best to just leave well alone.'

'Are we still talking about the fire.' She looked at him quizzically.

He shrugged. 'Fire, life, love. Take your pick.' Then he flashed her a wide smile, teeth surprisingly white against the ruddy cheeks and grey-grizzled chin, a mischievous glint in his faded blue eyes. 'But what do I know, hey? I'm just an old man with chickens as best friends.'

'Marshall and I argued afterward,' Flora said quietly, staring into the smouldering fire.

'About what exactly?'

Flora thought back to that awful walk home, the tension between them, the violent shivers that would not leave her body. Marshall had tried to hold her but his arm around her shoulders had felt like an unbearable weight. And then, when they reached her apartment, she had been infused with hope – a bubbling, overflowing, welling of hope that spewed out of her mouth without thought or reason. What if it was true, she'd gushed. What if he really was her father? It made sense, didn't it? He'd been waiting for an opportunity to speak to her. He was nervous, shy, didn't know how to approach her. He'd tracked her down through her work, perhaps at first had just wanted to see her from afar, to make sure she was okay. To see what she looked like, even! And then he'd plucked up the courage to speak to her, to tell her who he really was …

But Marshall had a different viewpoint. He said the man was undoubtedly a crook, a con-man, the whole thing stank. No genuine person would make an approach that way, at night, outside, in the dark. Why not write her, asking to meet? Why not make a call? It was bullshit.

Of course, Marshall was angry about being bested by a man twice his age – a fact Flora wasted no time in pointing out. Fanning the flames of his anger, just as his dismissal poured water on the flames of her budding hope.

Flames burn brightest when they are just about to go out.

Max wasn't just an old man with chickens as best friends. He was well-travelled and experienced and he knew a thing or two about the vagaries of love.

Was the fire that had been passion for Marshall turning into something else for her? And perhaps, for him too? Was their flame about to go out? Flora swallowed down a rising knot of fear.

With the awful mess that was their current work situation, a possible murder at the museum, a stolen artefact to track down, and a question around her birth father hanging over her head, the last thing she needed was a break-up on her hands as well.

'It never rains but it pours,' Max murmured, as if reading her mind. Flora started to speak, then stopped and shook her head. Tears were misting her eyes; the lump in her throat made talking impossible.

'There, there,' Max said. 'That's okay, my brave girl.'

But Flora felt anything but brave. She felt small and fragile, like a breakable doll. Like one of Jasmin's ancient, worn-out artefacts – but nowhere near as valuable.

She sighed, the thought of going back to the museum later a further burden on her mind.

'Coffee before you go?' Max asked, getting up and patting her on the head like a pet dog. Flora smiled.

'Okay.' She looked at her watch. It was another hour before her train back into town. 'Stick a bit of that whiskey in it, will you? I have a feeling I'm going to need it.'

Chapter 7

The good news was, Nick reported no strange noises at the museum the night before. He'd listened out all night, done several circuits inside and out, and heard and seen nothing untoward. No screaming, no unexplained banging, no footsteps.

At first, Flora was relieved. But that didn't last long. Her rationale had been that if the noises occurred every night there was more likely to be a logical explanation; she was even prepared to consider a ghost! Pipes banging, beams creaking, the wind whistling through holes in the roof – it wasn't so hard to imagine that a medieval building might have an unusual sound-scape, especially at night.

Nick's assertion that he'd heard nothing, however, rendered this explanation unlikely. Flora decided to put it out of her mind for now; there was nothing she could do about it, and there were a few more pressing issues to attend to. For one thing, she was required to go to the police station to give a statement, and apparently this had to be done today. As it was already nearly five o'clock by the time her train got into Shrewsbury, Flora reluctantly agreed to go with Nick to the community police station in Monkmoor.

'It's typical of them,' she complained as soon as she got into Nick's car at back of the museum, 'to just expect people to drop everything with no warning.'

Nick nodded, but didn't answer.

'And that they shut at six-thirty, I mean that's convenient,' she added sarcastically. 'Like they couldn't have given us a teeny bit more notice.'

'Hmm.' Nick stared at her, his hands on the wheel. He'd yet to move and they were double parked.

'Your seatbelt,' he said.

'Huh?'

'You need to put your seatbelt on, Flora.'

'Oh, right.'

Flora buckled up, pulling a face at him when he turned away to filter into traffic. What was it with grumpy men at the moment?

Nick drove a newish small black Fiesta, which was not what Flora had expected. He had one of those vanilla scented trees hanging from the rear view mirror and a cushion in the back. At a glance, Flora pegged it as his parents' car. It made her feel sad for him, but she didn't know why.

'This is usually your time of day to go to the gym, isn't it?' she said, trying to lighten the mood.

'I went earlier,' Nick answered. He sounded a little subdued.

'Well, that was lucky,' said Flora. She fidgeted with her bag, putting it first on the floor, then lifting it to her knees, then shoving it back down into the footwell.

'Look, I'm sorry,' Nick said, not glancing her way but keeping his eyes firmly on the road ahead. 'I feel bad. I did know about this police thing earlier. I mentioned it to your fella. Just assumed he'd told you. It was only when you called from the train, and I said about going … Well, I guess I should have called you directly.'

'Oh.' Flora's face began to burn. This seemed so unprofessional. And for Marshall to fail to pass on a message like this – why, that was just so unlike him.

He must be really pissed off with her. Or just pissed, as he would say.

'Maybe he called and left a message?' Nick offered helpfully.

Flora nodded. It was highly likely, and Uncle Max's house had zero reception. And she hadn't checked her messages on the train, preferring to sit and stare out of the window at the dusky landscape zooming past, losing herself to that feeling she loved so much on trains, the sense of being both somewhere and nowhere at the same time.

'It's my fault,' she said, smiling. She made her voice sound confident and secure. 'Nothing to worry about at all.'

Nick visibly relaxed, and Flora's smile became a little more genuine. She said,

'So have you heard anything from Jasmin? What did the police tell you when they came by this morning?'

'She's still being questioned, apparently. They went into her office and took another bunch of stuff. They're just bagging things up randomly, is what it looks like to me.'

'Won't be much left for us to pack soon,' Flora said, only half joking. 'Did Marshall get much done in the basement?'

Nick shook his head. 'I think he's a bit frustrated, to be honest. It's hard to work around the investigation. That policeman, the big one, he was talking about closing it down again, for the foreseeable future he said.'

That wouldn't be good, Flora thought. Not for them or for Jasmin. If they had to walk away from this job, even temporarily, there was barely anything to fill their time with until next month. Flora couldn't invoice until the work was complete, and the fee from this museum move was covering both of their salaries for the next three months.

Which included Christmas.

Once again Flora had the free-falling sensation that maybe the time had come to close down Shakers Removals and walk away. Just get a job, a regular salary, no stress, no trauma. Maybe it would do her and Marshall good to not work together day in, day out.

Or maybe that was the glue that held them together.

Nick parked carefully on the street outside the police station, and jogged round to open the car door for Flora. They entered the building together, but soon parted company, with Flora being asked to go through first, into a small office-like room with a table and four chairs. The building was squat and unfriendly; in contrast someone had made an effort with the interior. She was offered a drink – tea, coffee or water – and then told she wouldn't be kept waiting long.

'Miss Lively? Thank you for coming in to talk to us.'

Flora looked up, surprised. She had been expecting D.I. Curtis, but instead found herself facing a smiling woman of around her own age, not in uniform but wearing her ID on a lanyard around her neck.

'I'm D.I. Buxton,' the woman said, taking the seat next to Flora. 'Sarah Buxton. Just call me Sarah. None of this detective inspector nonsense. And can I call you Flora, or do you prefer Miss Lively? I don't mind either way.'

Taken aback by her friendly tone, Flora stammered, 'Erm, Flora, yes, that's fine. Thank you.'

'Great!' Sarah Buxton said brightly. 'Right, let's get down to business shall we. I've got your statement here, we had it typed out for you. So all you need to do now is read it through, if that's okay, and let me know if there's anything – anything at all – that should be added to it. Anything you might have remembered since. No matter how small.'

Flora took the stapled sheets of paper and looked at them. 'I thought you got me here to question me again,' she said.

'Oh, god, no!' D.I. Buxton laughed. 'Don't you get tired of going over the same thing again and again and again ... I know, it's just how we have to do things, but we've got it all down here, so take your time.' She nodded at the statement, an indication for Flora to begin reading. 'I'm not in a hurry. You go ahead.'

The detective took out her phone and relaxed back in the upholstered chair, crossing her legs loosely. She wore a plain grey trouser suit with a bright pink sweater, and flat ankle boots. After Flora had read the first page of her statement – surprised by how much it actually sounded like her original description of events – she glanced over at Sarah Buxton's phone. Flora was astonished to see that the woman was playing Candy Crush.

'Just passing the time,' the D.I. said, grinning. 'It's bloody addictive this, isn't it?'

'I've never played it,' Flora said.

'Well, don't. It's a nightmare. Like crack cocaine.'

Flora turned back to her statement, her eyes widening. So much for her stereotyped image of police officers – this woman was completely left-field. She couldn't help liking her, there was something infectious about her smile, and the lack of pretension was completely disarming.

The description of the night Lucy Akopian died made no mention of the unexplained scent Flora had detected, but other than that it was perfectly accurate. Flora debated whether to furnish Sarah Buxton with this additional bit of information. After a couple of minutes, she decided not to.

'All done?' the D.I. said, shutting off her phone.

'Absolutely.' Flora took the proffered pen and signed the final page in a space marked with a cross. Today's date was already typed neatly above, along with her name and a string of alpha-numeric figures.

'And,' Sarah Buxton said, standing, 'now you can tell me the rest of it.'

'Excuse me?' Flora looked up, surprised.

The detective held the door open, gesturing for Flora to walk ahead. In the corridor, she said, 'Whatever it is that Jasmin White told you, now is the time to share it with me.'

'There's nothing else,' Flora said. 'I don't know what you mean.'

'The thing is, my colleague – I think you met him, Detective Inspector Curtis?' She paused and smiled at Flora's grimace. 'Yeah, he's a bit intense, right? So anyway, he told me about your clandestine meeting with Jasmin, down there in the basement. It'll be better all round if you tell me what was said.'

'Nothing was said,' Flora responded automatically.

'Ah, I don't think that's true, is it?'

Flora stopped and turned around, but D.I. Buxton was smiling that same disarming smile.

'Don't worry,' she said, moving around Flora to press in the code for reception. 'You're not in trouble.'

'Trouble?'

'Not yet, anyway.'

Back in the reception area, Sarah Buxton turned her back on Flora and began flicking through the statement. Flora waited, biting her bottom lip. The room, which was lined with blue plastic benches and Perspex leaflet racks, had only three other occupants: a young couple, huddled in the far corner, the woman crying softly, and an old man, a pensioner, with a ruddy face and the unmistakable stink of alcohol. Staff sat protected behind a glass screen; it was against this screen that the detective leaned, assiduously ignoring Flora.

What should she do? She looked around for Nick. Had he given his statement already? He would wait for her, surely, to give her a lift back into town. But that meant hanging around here, when all she wanted to do was get the hell out of this place and think. Was she free to go? Flora could kick herself for coming down here in the first place without talking to Marshall first. He'd know what to say, how to play it. She always felt safe with him, Flora realised. Marshall always had her back.

'So?' the detective said without looking up.

'What?' Flora answered, playing for time.

D.I. Buxton leaned back on the counter, elbows tucked in, ankles crossed.

'I'm on your side, you know,' she said, smiling. 'And see, whatever you tell me now doesn't even have to go in your statement. So if you're worried about anything, there's no need to be.'

'Why would I be worried?' Flora said, shrugging. She hoped her tone came across as nonchalant, but her stomach was churning.

'You're right,' Sarah Buxton said, standing suddenly. 'I shouldn't be trying to help you out. I'm going to get into a shit load of trouble for it. Sorry, Flora. It was unprofessional of me.' She looked at her phone and grimaced. 'Okay, so if you just wait here D.I. Curtis is on his way in and he'll have a chat with you.'

'What! Why?'

The detective's expression became serious for the first time. 'I probably shouldn't tell you this, but it's a murder investigation now. We haven't released that information yet, but the coroner's report has come back. It was death by unnatural causes. Probably strangulation.'

Flora wasn't shocked. 'It seemed kind of obvious, really. She couldn't have gotten in there otherwise.'

'Lucy Akopian wasn't killed there, Flora. She was placed there some time after her death.'

'What?'

Flora's mind was beginning to race. Someone had carried a dead body into the museum, opened up the crate she'd sealed only hours earlier, then deposited the body in it? Why?

'There's more,' Sarah Buxton said quietly.

'What?'

'Something Mrs White said in her statement that you haven't told us. The view is, it looks a bit suspicious that you're wilfully keeping it from the police.'

'Said about me?' Flora asked, confused.

'I can't tell you any more than that. Look, if you

don't want to talk about it, that's fine. I mean, I'd prefer to share it with someone a bit more friendly than Inspector Curtis, especially now it's a murder investigation, but that's just me.'

Flora tried to think. Her mind was buzzing. Jasmin had been questioned at least twice now since she and Flora had spoken; it was highly likely that Jasmin had told them about the missing artefact. Therefore, if Flora didn't mention it, it would look like she was hiding something from the police. From which, she reasoned quickly, they might infer that Shakers Removals had something to hide. As in, either she or Marshall or Nick had something to do with the theft of the artefact. And by association, with Lucy Akopian's death.

With her murder.

Suddenly, the threat of losing business over a potential scandal seemed like a minor concern. Being implicated in a murder and stolen antiquities case would be catastrophic. And not just professionally.

But Jasmin had pleaded with Flora not to tell the police about the missing Lamassu tablet. Yet what possible reason could the museum owner have for not reporting it to the police in the first place?

'Okay,' Flora said finally.

Sarah Buxton visibly relaxed. 'Do you want to talk about it here, or grab a coffee?'

Flora sighed. 'Coffee,' she said. 'Definitely coffee.'

***

Sarah Buxton took a pool car and drove them to a tiny coffee house close to Abbey Foregate. Flora had a view of the Abbey itself from her window seat, the warm red sandstone walls beautifully lit against the darkening sky.

'The Cadfael mysteries were set there, did you know that?' Sarah said, setting down a tray with two steaming coffees and a bag of mini chocolate muffins.

'I did know that,' Flora said with a smile. She wondered whether the detective also knew about Flora's amateur detecting past; there was no way she could know that Brother Cadfael was one of her favourite fictional characters.

She sipped her cappuccino and ate a muffin, while D.I. Buxton listed other famous landmarks. Flora couldn't help liking the detective; there was something almost innocent about her enthusiasm.

'I did grow up here, you know,' Flora said, laughing, when the conversation seemed likely to turn into a travel guide to her own home town.

'Sorry,' Sarah said, pretending to zip up her mouth and throw the key on the floor. 'Over to you, Flora. What did you want to tell me.'

Flora paused, wondering how best to start. But like most tricky conversations, once she had begun, the rest was easy. She kept it brief: the meeting in the basement, the Lamassu artefact, Jasmin's insistence that it should be kept private. Flora thought private sounded better than secret. She told the D.I. that the museum owner had asked her to look into the matter, managing to imply that this was simply as part of their existing contract. The disclosure took no more than five minutes; when she'd finished, Flora picked up her coffee again. It was still hot.

'Okay,' Sarah Buxton said slowly. 'Well, that's really interesting, Flora, and I'm so glad you decided to share it with us.' She nodded, smiling, and Flora relaxed a little.

'You can see why I didn't mention it, though?' Flora said, reaching for another muffin. 'I mean, it was more to do with the museum move than the dead woman.'

'Oh, of course. Yes, I do see that. It's just … Ugh, this is difficult, isn't it.' The detective made a face like she was in pain. Flora raised her shoulders and let them drop.

'What?' she said.

The policewoman leaned forward conspiratorially. 'Flora, there's something you don't know. Your boss, Mrs White, told us that she didn't know the woman who had been killed. Well, she was lying.'

'I know about that,' Flora said, her mouth full of cake. 'She didn't get a good look at her. She only knew when you lot told her the woman's name.' Her words came out muffled but the detective nodded.

'Ah, she did know. For sure. One of our officers showed her a clear photograph of the dead woman's face. She knew exactly who she was, and she lied to protect herself.'

Flora swallowed hard. 'No, that's not right.'

'It is right. Jasmin White recognised Lucy Akopian immediately, which isn't surprising considering they were in business together for years.'

'But ... but why would Jasmin lie? Surely she'd know you'd find out soon enough.'

'You'd think.' Sarah gave a rueful smile. 'Criminals aren't always the brightest buttons in the box, Flora.'

'Criminals? Jasmin isn't a–'

'Apparently, Miss Akopian bore our museum owner a long-time grudge for losing a significant amount of money when they were partners,' the detective continued, cutting Flora off. 'Losing probably being a euphemism for stealing. Jasmin claims that's why she lied, because she panicked, thinking it would look bad for her. Which it does. And then, of course, she tries to get the upstanding Flora Lively onside by flattering her and telling her some crackpot story about stolen antiquities.'

Flora let this sink in. 'Has Jasmin admitted this?'

'She has. On record.'

'And that she told me a "crackpot story"?'

'No. Not that. She's mentioned nothing about this missing tablet business. Which says it all, don't you think?'

'But what if ...'

Trailing off, Flora looked out of the window. It was almost dark now, and the Abbey loomed over them, its west tower like a castle turret against the sky.

'Are we done?' Flora said, finishing her coffee with one gulp and scooping up her bag from the floor. She would need to text Nick and let him know to go home. And also Marshall, who was no doubt wondering what the hell she was up to.

The detective was regarding Flora with mild amusement. 'Sure. You in a hurry to get somewhere? Do you need a lift?'

But Flora just shook her head. She'd said enough, and was far from certain whether she could trust this policewoman, no matter how friendly and affable she seemed.

'She's playing you,' Sarah called as Flora opened the door. A gust of cold air hit Flora in the face but she didn't stop; whatever D.I. Buxton said next was lost to the night. Flora swung her tote over her shoulder determinedly and set off towards English bridge.

Chapter 8

Are you okay? Shall I come down there? Xx

Two kisses in a text from Marshall was practically a proposal of marriage. Flora smiled to herself. She texted back:

All fine here, see you soon xxx

His reply came within seconds:

Miss you xxxx

Flora stared at her phone, considering. Did four kisses mean extra love and happy feelings, or was it Marshall's way of playing a game of text one-upmanship. He did two kisses, she did three, so he does four. She was tempted to text back and add five kisses, just to see what he did next, but then realised that would be ridiculous. Not to mention childish.

Really, she was no better than him.

Which was probably why they were so perfect for each other.

Despite the revelations from D.I. Buxton, Flora remained steadfast in her opinion of Jasmin White. It didn't make sense that Jasmin would have lied about all that Tablet of Lamassu stuff, and there was no way she could be capable of such a horrible murder, especially right under Flora's nose.

Now all Flora had to do was prove it.

She set to work, first by going through the inventory they'd made when they originally costed the job. Flora sipped water, and munched on the sandwich she'd grabbed on her way across town, but didn't move from the office desk until she'd finished her task.

There was no record of the Seventh Tablet of

Lamassu.

Flora sat back, tapping a pen against her teeth. Now, why would that be? Jasmin should have provided a list of everything, except for the items she planned to take with her to America. But she'd said herself that the Lamassu had been in Flora's remit.

Although, Flora mused, why would Jasmin gift to the British Museum an item that was so precious to her family? For safe-keeping, she supposed. You couldn't just carry around with you a priceless artefact – you couldn't pop it on your mantelpiece or keep it in the attic. No home insurer would cover that.

The clock in the lobby below struck eleven. Such a long day, Flora thought, and yet she wasn't tired at all. If anything, she was a little hyper. Probably all the coffee, and surviving on snacks and chocolate muffins. Reassured after Nick's report of an uneventful night, Flora was happy to be in the museum alone, even after dark. Over half of the exhibits had been packed away now, making the space more forlorn than spooky. It was becoming familiar, losing the strange mystique of those first exciting hours. Flora even found herself humming as she crossed the upper landing to use the toilets.

She washed her hands, inspecting her face in the bevel-edged mirror. Not good, she thought. The lack of sleep was starting to show. Her pixie features looked blurred; her eyelids were pinker than usual. In the sickly yellow light she appeared older, late rather than early thirties, and the hue did nothing for her skin tone.

Her phone buzzed in her jeans pocket. Flora smiled at another text from Marshall: *You OK? x*

She typed back: *Won't be long x*

Back in Jasmin's office, an idea hit her. Flora felt a flutter of excitement. She searched through the desk drawers systematically until she found what she was looking for: a set of keys for the filing cabinet that lurked in the far corner by the window. The cabinet was ancient – an artefact in its own right – but the keys turned easily enough in the silver-coloured locks, and the drawers slid out smoothly on their metal runners. Flora started at the top, standing on the stool so she could see inside. She used the torch on her phone for extra light; it would also be handy to take photos of anything interesting she might find.

She heard a noise outside, and stopped to listen. Just people out on the street, probably going home from one of the pubs in town. Inside the museum it was deathly quiet. Flora leafed through the manila files a second time. They appeared to be fairly mundane: a receipt for some stonemasonry work, invoices for cleaning and office supplies, leaflets from local businesses and some health and safety documents. Nothing useful there.

In the next drawer down, Flora found personnel folders, which she flicked through quickly. This made her feel a little uncomfortable, so she took care not to read details about any individual person. Really, she thought, stepping down off the wooden stool, it would have been wiser to clear this with Jasmin first. 'Well, you did ask me to find the missing artefact,' Flora said out loud, imagining she was talking to her employer. 'And I couldn't achieve that without doing a bit of digging.'

Satisfied that she had her snooping-permissions covered, Flora allowed herself a peek at a summary report. It was clear that in the past, the Shropshire White and Co. Museum of Antiquities had been a successful enterprise, employing quite a few people. Sad to think that the town was losing one of its cultural attractions to the big smoke, although Flora herself had never heard of the museum until the day Jasmin contacted her for a quote; neither had any of her friends. It was a specialist interest, she supposed, and these quirky little museums, displaying private collections, were becoming more and more of a rarity.

The next drawer down was empty. Flora noted fresh-looking finger marks on the dusty rails. Had Jasmin cleared this herself or had the police taken its contents? With a sigh, Flora slipped the final key into the bottom drawer. She had no intention of prying into Jasmin's personal life, but finding some information about this Seventh Tablet of Lamassu seemed pretty key. If someone *had* taken any important files, however, it was unlikely Flora would find anything of use.

The key wouldn't turn. Flora tried again, taking it out and putting it in again, then turning it gently, then more firmly. She shook the drawer, hoping to dislodge the mechanism. Was it stuck? Frustrated, Flora went through all the keys again. None of them worked. Sitting back on her heels, and glaring up at the filing cabinet, which towered over her like the hull of a ship, she hissed, 'Damn it!' and dropped the keys on the floor. Lock-picking should definitely be in her skill set by now.

Flora grabbed her bag and pulled out her phone. You could Google practically anything these days – why not how to pick the lock of a rusty old filing cabinet? She'd typed in the first two words of her search when the office was plunged into sudden darkness. Eyes wide, Flora stared into the thick blackness that surrounded her, her heart thudding in her chest.

What now? A power cut? She glanced at her phone; the screen's glow cast an eerie blue light onto her face. Two minutes to midnight. She swallowed, hard, and folded her arms around her body. When the clock began to strike the hour, Flora began to count.

***

Even though she was half expecting it, when the scream came it was startling none the less. This time the womanish wail seemed to come from further away – still inside the museum, as far as she could tell, but not as close as before. Thank goodness. With goose bumps on her arms, and slightly shaking hands, Flora began to type a text to Marshall.

She was fine on her own. She'd just rather not be on her own for this.

The text wouldn't send. She checked the bars on her phone. No signal. Oh, just great. Perfect timing for the mobile reception to go nuts. She ran her hand over the back of her neck. The feeling that there was someone standing behind her, the urge to turn around, was so strong. But of course there was no one there. Jasmin's office was large, with high ceilings and three wide windows, but there was only one door, and Flora was facing it. The only person watching her was the woman with the sad eyes and the white veiled hat, frozen in time by some unknown artist.

Flora sat with her back pressed against the filing cabinet, her phone torch trained on the door. The clock had stopped striking at seven chimes. Just like the first night. And the second night. Yet last night Nick had heard nothing, no screams, no footsteps, no seven chimes, nothing at all. Was it just for her benefit, she wondered? Which was ridiculous, of course.

But not for the first time, Flora considered who might be playing a nasty trick on her. Someone with a grudge, perhaps. An ex employee? Was it revenge for one of the so-called cases she'd helped solve? Thanks to her, three people had gone to prison. There would be relatives, friends, those who did not feel grateful at all for Flora's mystery-solving abilities.

Don't let your imagination run away with you, she told herself. Keep calm. These noises, whatever they are, can't hurt you. If they were going to, they would have already.

That made sense, right?

Sure, until whoever or whatever is doing this comes through that door and gets you good, her mind answered back.

'Hmm, that's the way to stay calm, Flora,' she whispered. Her voice broke the silence, and she relaxed a little. 'Talking to yourself now,' she carried on. 'The sign of a completely sane person, obviously.'

Just to be on the safe side, Flora searched Jasmin's desk for something she could use as a weapon. The heaviest, deadliest thing she could find was an antique glass paperweight. She cupped it in her hand speculatively. It would have to do. By the light from her phone, she also grabbed her poncho and a bottle of water from her bag.

Back at her vantage point, Flora made a kind of nest facing the door. She tested the signal again, but still no luck. Stupid building, not having wifi. No point trying to use the office phone; Jasmin had stopped the contract for comms a week ago.

Into the silence, a new noise intruded. Flora held her breath, ears straining. Footsteps. Unmistakable. Distant, but ... yes, getting closer.

'No,' she whispered. It was more of a whimper, in fact. Barely breathing, Flora stared at the glass door, willing it to not open. Her eyes seemed to play tricks on her, seemed to show the door opening in tiny increments, but when she blinked it was still shut just as tightly as before.

'I'm losing it,' she said to herself. More than anything right now she wished Marshall was here.

Keeping one eye on the door, Flora lifted her phone up to her face and tried again to send a text. To her dismay, she saw that the battery was almost out of charge. Five percent remained. Five percent, and then her torch would go out and she'd be here, in the dark, alone. No phone, no way to call for help, no protection. And on the other side of that door ... what?

Suddenly, the lights in the office clicked back on. Flora winced: it felt as blinding as the sun after sitting in darkness.

She stayed where she was for fifteen minutes, maybe twenty. When her feet had well and truly gone to sleep, and her back had begun to stiffen painfully, Flora stood unevenly and lifted her bag to her shoulder. She wrapped her favourite poncho around her shivering body and checked her phone: four percent remaining. Enough to book a taxi and get herself home, if she could get mobile reception downstairs.

Getting herself out of the office, through the empty museum spaces, and into the lobby, took an effort of will Flora had not imagined she was capable of. She called a cab, glad of the brusque, matter-of-fact shortness of the cab controller. Finally, she stepped outside and locked the main entrance door, then let out a huge sigh of relief.

In the taxi, she deleted the text to Marshall. She was fine, she reasoned. No need to worry him. Besides …

No. There was the most awful, niggling thought in her head, but she had to put it out of her mind. It could not be that. Best not to think about it at all. Because that was a road to all sorts of troubles.

'You work there?' the taxi driver said, glancing over his shoulder. 'At the White museum?' He was a big man with a bald shiny head. The cab smelt of cigarettes and pine air freshener.

'Kind of,' Flora said, sighing. Then, registering his question fully, she asked, 'Do you know the museum? Have you been there?'

'Of course,' he answered, as though surprised to be asked.

'Oh, well … that's great,' said Flora. 'It's just, I suppose I haven't met many people who've visited. Before it closed down, I mean.'

'Loved it, we did. Me and my boy. Used to go all the time a couple of years ago.'

'Ah, that's really nice to hear.'

Flora's eyes began to close. It had been one hell of a day. The man's words washed over her like a waterfall of sound, his voice deep and soothing. He was listing their favourite exhibits: an Egyptian mummified cat, a display of Roman coins, something that sounded like a Sutton Hoo helmet. A pair of jade lions, or foo dogs as they were apparently called to those in the know; various gruesome instruments of weaponry; some original pieces of the Parthenon. He laughed as he said this, and Flora laughed too, but she wasn't entirely sure why they were laughing. In fact, she wasn't really listening – it was about as much as she could manage to simply stay awake.

'Of course it all started to go wrong about the time of the garden shed fakers, didn't it?' the driver said, pulling up outside Flora's apartment block. He turned and rested his beefy arm on the back of the seat. 'Folk lost confidence in antiquities, they started clamping down on the whole export import thing.' He laughed again, shaking his big head joyfully. 'British Museum nearly bought those Assyrian relics, didn't they? I think one of the big museums actually did buy that Amarna Princess. Paid a fortune for it! Made themselves look right idiots – the guy knocked it up with some tools he bought at B&Q.'

Flora smiled and handed over a ten pound note. 'You know loads about this stuff,' she said, yawning.

'My lad got into computer games,' the taxi driver told Flora. 'Didn't want to go anymore. Shame, really.'

He counted out her change, but she gestured for him to keep it. 'Cheers, love,' he said. 'You take care now.'

'You too,' she replied. And then, as she hauled her tired self up the carpeted stairs, she thought how kind he'd sounded. *You take care now.* As though he really meant it.

'What a nice man,' she said to herself, slipping quietly into her apartment so as not to wake Marshall.

But there he was, sprawled on the sofa, a coffee in one hand and his phone in the other.

'I've been worried about you, Miss Lively.'

'My phone ran out of charge.'

'I was just about to come and look for you.'

'That would have been stupid. I was in a taxi on my way home.'

'I see that.'

Flora yawned again.

'You look dead on your feet,' Marshall said, and then he crossed the room and picked her up. He carried her to the bedroom and laid her gently on the bed.

'When you walked in just now,' he whispered, his face close to hers, 'you said something about me being a nice man?'

Flora kissed him once, then turned over and closed her eyes. 'Not you. You're horrible.' And with a smile on her face, she fell into a deep, dreamless sleep.

Chapter 9

The next morning, Flora awoke to two types of singing: birds outside her bedroom window making a big deal about the dawn chorus, and Marshall making coffee while humming along to the radio.

'You sound happy,' she said, coming into the kitchen to give him a kiss on the cheek. He deftly avoided the cheek-peck and planted one on her lips instead. Smugly, he turned back to their expensive coffee machine and started to froth the milk.

'Feeling better?'

'Much, thanks,' Flora replied, jumping up onto a bar stool. 'Oh my god, I don't think I've ever been so tired.'

'I know.' Marshall winked. 'You were snoring.'

'I was not!'

'Sure were.'

'You'll have to produce evidence of that to make me believe you.'

'I'll record you next time,' Marshall said, ruffling her hair. Flora batted his hands away.

'Hey! I look enough of a mess as it is.'

'You said it, not me.'

The buzzer to their apartment sounded. 'Who could that be?' Flora wondered.

'I know a great way to find out,' Marshall joked, strolling over to the intercom. He spoke into it, then pressed the button to open the main door. When he turned to look at Flora, his eyebrows were raised.

'Well? Who is it?'

'It's Jasmin,' Marshall said resignedly, 'and she's on her way up to talk to you.'

'To talk to us,' Flora corrected.

'No, Miss Lively. To talk to you. Seems I'm becoming more and more surplus to requirements these days.'

***

They decided to walk and talk, with Flora wanting to get out from under Marshall's judging gaze and also desperately needing some fresh air and sunlight. Too many hours spent in the darkened rooms of the museum were not having a great effect on her mood, or her skin.

She was surprised to see Jasmin – pleased, but surprised. As tactfully as she could, Flora raised the issue of the police's suspicions regarding the death of Lucy Akopian.

'Ah, it was certainly murder, Flora. Didn't you know?' was Jasmin's response. Flora nodded, momentarily thrown.

'Yes. Yes, I did know. I meant – it was more that I got the impression that the police … that they …'

'Think I did it?' Jasmin White provided.

'Well, yes. I suppose so. Yesterday, when I met with that female D.I., I kind of got that impression.'

'They know different now, Flora.' Jasmin paused for a moment, clearly wanting to give her next sentence maximum impact. 'I have an alibi for the night of the murder. A cast-iron alibi.'

They had reached the riverside path now; recent heavy rain had raised the water level quite a lot, but the Severn hadn't broken its banks. Yet. Swans glided towards the opposite bank; dog walkers were out in force. Just a typical late autumn morning.

Except this wasn't a typical conversation.

'An … alibi?' Flora repeated.

Jasmin nodded, her long shiny hair swinging gracefully in the weak sunlight. 'So you see. They had to release me and, what did they call it? Eliminate me.'

'From their enquiries?'

'Precisely.'

Flora thought about this. They followed the path as it curved towards the Quarry. A suspension footbridge rose up behind the trees in the distance. Flora had dressed warmly in her old faded jeans, hiking boots, and one of Marshall's old sweaters. She'd wrapped one of her own hand-knitted scarves around her neck; it felt snug and comforting. Jasmin, on the other hand, wasn't really dressed for walking. Long thin cardigan over a neat tube skirt, leather ankle boots, cashmere polo neck, all in shades of her trademark white.

She looked elegant though, Flora had to give her that. There was nothing ramshackle and hobo-like about Mrs Jasmin White.

'If you must know,' Jasmin said, sighing, 'I was on a date.'

'Oh.' Flora felt her cheeks redden. 'I wasn't going to ask – it's really none of my business.'

'Well, I think it probably is, Flora. I think I'm making it your business, aren't I?'

Flora had to admit this was true. And yet, if she was completely honest, she didn't want it to be her business. In fact, she'd quite like to finish packing up the museum, drive the stuff down to London, get it installed in the British Museum, and then never think about artefacts and antiquities again as long as she lived.

In the past, she'd been eager to get involved in mysterious happenings. At the Maples retirement home, the deaths had directly affected someone she cared about deeply. Flora still visited Joy, although the old lady's memory wasn't so great now and sometimes she didn't know who Flora was. Which was sad – painful, actually – but it didn't stop Flora going every month. At Hanley Manor, working for the film crew, the death of the director had initially been pinned on Marshall – plus Flora's best friend had also been involved in the drama.

Too involved, as it turned out.

But this time? This time it was too close for comfort, yet not close enough for her to care so deeply. Maybe I really am just a nosey parker, Flora mused. Not any kind of detective at all.

'It was a Tinder date,' Jasmin said quietly.

'Excuse me?'

'Tinder. It's a dating app. You swipe right or left, depending on whether you fancy the man or not.'

Flora laughed, astonished.

'Yes, I know what Tinder is, Jasmin. I just didn't ... I mean I–'

'You just didn't think that old people like me used it?'

'Oh my god, no! That's not what I meant.'

But Flora was lying – that was exactly what she'd thought, and both of them knew it. Jasmin smiled, her dark brown eyes lighting up briefly. She said, 'I met a nice man, Flora. We had a date, and I ... I spent the night with him. Am I embarrassed about it? Well, yes I am. Did I want to keep it from the police? Yes I did. But that was only making things more complicated. So I owned up. What can I say? I'm a woman – a not-unattractive woman, so I'm told – and older people have needs too.'

Flora stared fixedly ahead, wanting the ground to open up and swallow her. Perhaps she could pretend to fall into the river. Fake an important phone call and run back to her apartment?

This was very possibly one of the most awkward conversations she'd ever had.

But Jasmin wasn't done yet.

'That detective, the big one with the shaved head, he wanted all the details. Clearly he thought it was hysterically funny.' For the first time, Flora thought she saw a chink in the older woman's composure. But then Jasmin smiled serenely and threw her shoulders back. 'I gave him more than he bargained for,' she said, marching on. They had rounded the sharp curve of the river now and were heading back towards town. Flora jogged a little to catch up.

'What do you mean?' she said.

'Told him all the gory details,' Jasmin replied. 'And it was more than he could handle, if you know what I mean.'

'We really don't need to talk about this,' Flora said, wincing inwardly.

'Oh, any embarrassment I felt was cured by having to sit in a police cell and recount every last detail of my Tinder date and subsequent sexual encounter.'

'They had you in a cell?' Flora asked, shocked.

'Cell, interview room, what's the difference.' Jasmin slowed a little, linked arms with Flora, then continued briskly. 'Do you want to know the best thing about a Tinder date, Flora?'

'Not really.'

'It's that you never have to see them again if you don't want to,' she said with a wink.

Flora chuckled, despite her embarrassment. 'And did you want to see this one again?'

Jasmin shook her shiny hair. 'I did not. However, I had to give his name and address to the police so they will check my alibi.'

'Awkward?'

'Very.'

They walked on, turning to climb the path that led away from the river. Flora was feeling comfortably warm now, snug in her woollen scarf. She snuck a sideways glance at Jasmin White. The woman had so much composure. She'd been detained by the police; a former business partner found dead in her museum. But to look at her, you'd think she'd merely been through something mildly taxing.

At the museum, Jasmin asked Flora to come inside for a coffee. Flora demurred. It wasn't only that the instant coffee drink was disgusting. Flora hated to admit it, but she could hardly bear to face going inside the gloomy building again.

Get over it, Lively, she told herself. You've got to see this through.

'You're doing a great job here,' Jasmin said as they crossed the atrium. 'Looks like you're nearly finished. When do you expect to make the journey to London? Flora, are you okay?' Jasmin asked. 'You look very pale.'

'The thing is ...' Flora stopped. How to say it without sounding ridiculous? She swallowed and tried again. 'The thing is, I'm kind of freaked out. Being here. To be completely honest, Jasmin, I'll be glad to see that back of this place. No offense.'

'None taken,' Jasmin replied quietly. She held her office door open for Flora to pass through. 'I have been feeling the same way myself.'

Her voice was so soft Flora barely made out the words, but she was pretty sure she understood the sentiment. Yet now there was something else to worry about: across the room, next to the towering filing cabinet, was the evidence of Flora's vigil the night before. And, worst of all, the evidence of her snooping was all too clear. One of the drawers still stood open; the set of keys lay on the floor; the hair clip Flora had used to try and pick the lock of the bottom drawer stuck out of the lock like an accusation. Flora closed her eyes briefly and sighed. Yes, she thought. Definitely losing her touch.

Maybe Jasmin wouldn't notice. Maybe she'd go straight to the kitchen area and Flora could put it all back to normal and ...

'Flora?' Jasmin said, staring hard at the filing cabinet.

No such luck.

'Yeah, I'm sorry about that,' Flora said tiredly, dropping into the corner chair with another heavy sigh. 'In my defence, I was investigating for *you*, like you asked me to. But I'm going to have to say that I can't do it, Jasmin. I'm sorry. You need someone proper to look into this stolen tablet for you, not an amateur like me. I don't have a clue where to start, and I'm totally freaked out by these noises here at night. You haven't heard them, have you? If you had, I think you'd understand. It's like, I keep wondering if it's someone playing tricks on me, or whether it's just some kind of weird coincidence …' Flora stopped talking, noticing the expression on Jasmin's face.

'What noises, Flora?' Jasmin said, crossing the room and taking hold of Flora's hands. 'You must tell me at once.'

'Well, you know. The noises we heard that first night. The night Lucy Akopian died.'

'But that was …' Jasmin White drifted into thought for a moment. 'I thought you and your security guard heard the killer.'

'We've heard it again, though,' Flora replied earnestly. 'And I'm telling you, it was really scary.'

'Describe it.' Jasmin's voice had taken on a different tone; her usually tuneful accent now completely flat. 'Describe everything you heard, and anything you saw. Leave nothing out.'

Flora described it just as it had happened, detailing what she and Nick and Marshall had heard, collectively and individually, and trying to be as accurate as possible. The timeline, when she got it straight in her head, was pretty clear.

'I guess last night was the most upsetting,' Flora finished, 'because I was here on my own. I gotta tell you, Jasmin, I was fairly shaken when I left.'

But not as shaken as the museum's owner looked right now. Flora pulled out the desk chair and guided the older woman into it, concerned.

'Jasmin, what's wrong?'

'It's the Sign of Seven.'

'What?'

Jasmin's face looked ashen. 'The Sign of Seven,' she said, her voice breaking. 'No. Oh, no. I cannot believe it is true.' She stood and pushed past Flora, rushing towards the bathroom across the landing. Flora followed, but stopped outside the door. She listened to the sounds of vomiting; should she go inside and offer assistance, or leave well alone? After a while the retching stopped and all was quiet. When Jasmin emerged, she looked terrible. The groomed hair was dishevelled, her perfect make-up streaked from tears, her brown eyes bloodshot and watery. She shook her head when Flora began to speak, and gestured that she needed to sit.

'Jasmin, what on earth is wrong?' Flora perched on the stool while Jasmin slumped over the desk looking exhausted. She got a cup of water from the sink and waited while Jasmin drank from it weakly.

'I haven't been completely honest with you, Flora,' Jasmin said finally.

Here we go, Flora said to herself silently.

Why couldn't this job have just gone smoothly?

Flora went to the kitchenette again and ran the cold tap. She splashed water on her face, then dried her face and hands with a paper towel. She boiled the kettle, put instant coffee, dried milk and sugar into two mugs, then took the drinks back into the chilly office. Jasmin had recovered slightly, and regarded Flora with luminous eyes.

She said, 'It's time for me to tell you about the Sign of Seven and what it means. It's not good, Flora. It's not good at all.'

Chapter 10

'I first met Lucy Akopian in Turkey,' Jasmin began. Her voice was soft, her gaze far away. Flora shivered a little and hugged a blanket around her shoulders. 'This was back in the late seventies, before the UNESCO convention had really taken hold. I travelled the world then, went wherever the digs were, and everywhere they had already been. It was my life. I never stopped to think about cultural property or so-called illicit trade. Back then, it was all about the acquisition. It was about collecting and preserving. We – myself and my peers – we were fascinated by histories – by our own ancient legacies and by those of other civilizations. I suppose, with hindsight, it might look as though we crossed many a line that should not have been crossed. But that was how things were done then. In truth, things are still done this way in much of the world.' Jasmin glanced at Flora, then looked away with a barely perceptible shoulder shrug. 'I live within the law, of course. I have no choice.'

While the older woman paused to take a drink, Flora sifted through the myriad of questions in her mind. She didn't know enough about the world of antiquities to fully understand all that Jasmin was saying, and she made a mental note to look into it further as soon as possible. There was something very off here.

Jasmin put down her mug and continued. 'Lucy was a dealer. She had many contacts, important contacts, and she knew how to charm. She charmed me! We became best of friends, first of all, and then we went into business together. Our project was linked with certain Greek artefacts ...' She waved her hand dismissively.

'The details are not important now. Our connection lasted for a little over six years. It was lucrative for both of us. We had fun along the way.' A wistful smile flitted across her mouth momentarily. Then, with a small shake of her head, Jasmin clenched her fists on the desk and straightened her back.

'You're probably wondering why Lucy and I fell out. Well, I can tell you now, it wasn't over money. We were good business partners, and I've never met anyone like her, before or since.'

Flora nodded. 'I was wondering that, yes. And also, what she was doing here, less than a week ago. You said you hadn't seen her for years?'

'Over twenty years. Possibly more. I've no idea why she came here, Flora. And I wish she hadn't. Why? Because if she hadn't she might still be alive and then we could talk and drink cocktails and reminisce about old times. Although, I expect she'd want to punch me in the eye first.'

'There was some kind of feud?'

'Lucy,' Jasmin said, 'was married to a very handsome man. As I said, she was a charmer, and quite attractive in her own way, I suppose.'

Flora suppressed a smile at this. The rivalry between the two women lived on, and it was an easy step to imagine Jasmin White, thirty years younger, with her exotic looks and polished beauty, enjoying the limelight everywhere she went.

'Fed, Lucy's husband, began to work with us. He travelled with us and we became ... close. We were all close. It's like that when you travel together.'

'You had an affair with him?' Flora ventured.

Jasmin inclined her head gracefully. 'He fell in love with me. There was nothing I could have done to stop him. By the time I was aware of the depth of his feelings, he'd already announced to Lucy that he was leaving her. For me. She was devastated. Bitter. She destroyed the business when she left. Fed and I practically had to start again with nothing.'

The clock in the lobby chimed midday. Flora felt her stomach rumble. She was hungry, but didn't think she could actually face eating. She wondered where else this story was going.

'You said something about a sign of seven?' she prompted.

'I'm getting to that.' Jasmin stretched out her neck, then stood and began to circle the room. She stopped by the door and leaned against the part-glass wall. 'Lucy, I happen to know, bore me a fatal grudge. Whenever we ran into a mutual acquaintance, they would tell us stories of how she railed against me, the awful things she said. Never Fed, oh no. It was not his fault, apparently. It was all my fault. What, did I bewitch him?'

The hands held aloft, the innocent wide eyes, the sceptical tone – Flora wondered how many times Jasmin had told this story in this exact same way. Probably enough times to convince herself that she had done nothing wrong. But Flora didn't find it hard to imagine a woman like Jasmin bewitching a gullible man today, right here and now, never mind when she was much younger and even more beautiful. Some women were just like that – they have to have the admiration of every man they meet. And some men were suckers for it. It was just the way of the world.

Feeling even more sad for the unfortunate Lucy Akopian, Flora prompted Jasmin again. 'You said earlier that you hadn't been entirely honest with me. What did you mean?'

Jasmin's sudden loss of composure exposed a rawness Flora hadn't seen before. She looked her age for a moment, but that wasn't all.

She also looked guilty.

'I told you that the Seventh Tablet of Lamassu had been in my family for generations.'

Flora nodded, yes.

'Well,' Jasmin continued, 'that wasn't accurate. In fact, it didn't belong to my family at all.'

'You lied?'

'I suppose so. I was … ashamed. You see, the Tablet of Lamassu was one of the artefacts that Lucy and I acquired together. We went through a lot to get it. And I wasn't exaggerating when I said that it is priceless. But technically, I'm not … How can I say it?'

'You're not supposed to have it?' Flora provided.

Jasmin sighed. 'Yes. You see now?'

'See what?'

'Why I can't tell the police about it. Or get it insured.'

'Because you stole it.'

'Because I acquired it in a way that isn't acceptable to your country's government anymore,' Jasmin said coldly.

'You mean, illegally,' Flora countered.

'It's illegal now. It wasn't always so.'

Flora drained the last of her disgusting coffee. 'What I'm hearing is this – there's an artefact that you shouldn't have had, that has now gone missing. You can't claim for it on your insurance, nor can you report it to the police. And you tried to guilt me into looking into its disappearance, but actually you know that it isn't our fault either. So I kind of feel off the hook, if I'm completely honest.'

Jasmin nodded. 'I am sorry. That was unfair of me.'

'It really was,' Flora said, pursing her lips. 'But what about London? Was the museum okay with taking the tablet as part of your collection? Surely if it was acquired illegally, they wouldn't want to know.'

'Museums have a way to … how shall we say? … absorb such issues in the cause of a greater good.'

'I don't understand,' Flora said.

'Lord Elgin?' Jasmin said, raising an eyebrow. 'The marbles of the Parthenon?' Seeing Flora's blank expression, Jasmin shrugged. 'It's not important right now. Do you know nothing about history or culture, Flora? Nothing at all?'

'I hardly think that's the issue here, do you?' Flora retorted. Jasmin shook her head, chastened. 'Look, I want to help you find the missing tablet,' Flora continued. 'And I really want to find out what happened to Lucy. I'd probably have tried anyway,' she added ruefully. 'Seems I just can't keep my nose out of stuff like this.'

'I know,' Jasmin admitted. 'Which was why I took you on for the job in the first place.'

Flora sighed. 'So what now?'

'I need you to know that I had nothing to do with Lucy's death,' Jasmin said earnestly. 'But we must find the Lamassu. And we have to find it as soon as possible.'

The woman's eyes seemed to be filled with genuine terror. Flora paused, an uneasy feeling deep in her stomach.

'Why?' she said, not sure she wanted to hear the answer.

'Because the tablet is cursed, Flora. And now the curse has been released. Once the Seventh Tablet of Lamassu has been disturbed, the curse will return at midnight for seven nights. And on the seventh night, someone else will die.' Jasmin swallowed hard, her eyes dark and unreadable. 'It happened before, when we first acquired the tablet. That's how I know the legend is true.'

***

A morning mist was still hanging low on the river when Flora finally escaped the museum. She wrapped her poncho close around her body and blinked into the hazy light, enjoying the feather-light rain that fell onto her face. She decided to walk the long way home. There was just too much to think about, too much to process. A walk, then coffee. Then Marshall.

'Flora.'

Her name, spoken softly by a voice she didn't recognise, came out of the grey shadows by Saint Chad's Church.

It was him.

Flora stopped by a towering set of iron railings and waited for the man to cross the empty street. She should have felt scared, but she didn't. If anything, she felt preternaturally calm. Jasmin's story, the museum, the Lamassu tale – it was all so surreal. A man claiming to be her natural father was just another part of the whole crazy mix. She wondered if anything could happen right now that would surprise her. A dinosaur could emerge from the River Severn, right there in the mist, and she'd probably pull out her phone and calmly take a photo.

'Hey,' she said. 'How's it going?'

The man smiled. It was the first time Flora had seen him clearly, and she took a moment to observe. Mid to late fifties. Shaved hair under the cap. His eyes were twinkly, possibly blue, lined at the corners and heavily bagged. He was clean shaven.

He held out his hand. Flora noticed that it was shaking slightly. Nerves, she wondered, or something else?

'John Hopper,' the man said. 'Pleased to meet you.'

Flora nodded slowly. She felt a strange calmness settle over her; felt her shoulders drop and her face relax. She took his hand and shook it formally.

'Flora Lively,' she responded. 'Pleased to meet you too.'

***

Two hours later Flora put her key in the door of her apartment and turned it. Then, she took it out again without opening the door. She had called Marshall on her way home, and to say the conversation had gone badly would be an understatement. She stood in the cold quiet hallway and stared at the door. Her door. Oversized and panelled, painted a beautiful shade of peacock blue. The lengths she had gone to to find that exact shade of blue.

Suddenly the door swung open and there was Marshall, tall and glowering and undeniably gorgeous.

'What the hell are you doing? Standing there like a bozo. Get the hell in here already!'

Flora smiled, suppressing the urge to laugh. 'Bozo?' she repeated. 'What, is that the insult of the day?'

'Idiot, then,' Marshall said, kissing her on the head as she walked past him into the living area. 'Chump, dumb broad, schlepper, boob, turkey.'

'Enough!' Flora pleaded. 'Let's stick with idiot, please.'

'Fine by me. My idiot girlfriend, standing in the hall like she's had her brain sucked out by zombies.'

'Maybe I have,' Flora ventured, throwing her bag onto the sofa and kicking off her boots. 'Honestly, Marshall, these past few days have been insane. I mean, truly insane.'

'I know, honey.'

And then he was holding her, murmuring into her hair, kissing her neck and her forehead and her mouth, and she wondered how she could ever doubt their relationship at all.

Not that the doubts went away completely. But she was happy to leave them at the bedroom door for a while.

They had cold chicken salad for lunch, then headed to the museum, wrapped up against the cold and ready for the long shift to come.

'I have to say, I'm sick to death of this job,' Marshall told her as they marched, arm in arm, over Welsh Bridge.

'You know I am too, right?' Flora agreed.

'No more jobs like this, Flora. We need to move in a different direction. If we're not doing proper removals anymore then what are we?'

'I agree,' she said. 'And I've been thinking about that. We'll talk, okay? But not now.'

'Okay.'

Marshall was quiet for a moment, then he said, 'Listen, Flora, about this man who says he's your–'

'No.' Flora cut him off, stepping away and holding up her palm. 'No, Marshall. We leave it there. We agreed earlier that we wouldn't discuss it any further.'

Although it hadn't been much of a discussion. When Flora had phoned Marshall, flushed with excitement and eager to share all that John Hopper had told her, Marshall had responded with such cold, hard disbelief it had been like a slap in the face. He had called her a gullible fool; she'd told him he was cruel beyond reason.

Marshall: 'You're so desperate for a family you'd believe anything.'

Flora: 'You're so controlling you're terrified I might have someone else in my life other than you.'

'You're pathetically needy and he's obviously playing on that.'

'You're insecure and mean and suspicious and never give anyone a chance.'

And on and on it went.

Now, Flora walked a few steps ahead, trying to focus. No point dragging it all up again. Before the row, she'd managed to tell Marshall how John Hopper had explained all about his background. Breathlessly, almost running back along the river path, she'd gushed about how he'd been in the forces, travelling for years, but had always thought of her and had been trying to find her for a decade. How he'd been keeping up with her life now for a couple of years but was worried about approaching her.

There were a couple of things she hadn't told Marshall, and now never would. Like, the way she had felt when she looked into the older man's eyes standing there by the river, certain of an undeniable connection. And how touched she'd felt when he insisted on paying for breakfast, even though it was pretty clear that he wasn't well off at all. In fact, Flora felt anxious that he might be living in a hostel, or even rough on the streets. He hadn't said so explicitly, but was so cagey about his home address she thought this might be the case.

The story he'd told of how he'd had a letter from his childhood sweetheart that she'd had their baby and then given her up for adoption was delivered with such genuine regret it was hard to doubt the truth of it. She could see in his grizzled face the shadow of a younger man, serving his country far from home, burying his sadness in camaraderie and learning how to hide his emotions even as he learned how to strip down and reassemble a gun. And it answered so many questions for Flora; questions she'd long ago learned not to ask.

'So you're just going to accept everything he says at face value and that's it?'

Marshall's voice cut into her reverie. His tone was moderated, softer but still with that annoying edge of judgment.

'What would you have me do, Marshall?' Flora snapped, whirling around so fast she nearly knocked over an old man with a walking frame who was edging along behind her. 'Oh, I'm so sorry,' she said, tears prickling her eyes.

'That's okay,' Marshall responded, his lips twisting into a sarcastic smile.

'Not you,' she hissed.

They reached the museum's entrance, and Flora paused, trying to compose herself, resting her hand on the large brass handle.

'Maybe you should hire a private investigator to look

into his background,' Marshall suggested. 'I hear there's a pretty good one lives near here.'

Flora glared at him. 'Go to hell,' she said, letting the heavy door fall shut behind her.

Chapter 11

When the lights went out at midnight, Flora was ready with her torch. She barely flinched at the footsteps, merely registering them solemnly in her head. And the screaming was just as creepy as before, seeming to come from everywhere and nowhere, all at once.

It was four nights since Lucy Akopian's death. Including that night – if her death was the start of the curse – made five. According to Jasmin there were only two more nights until another death. But if the noises were part of the curse, then why didn't they happen every night? When Nick was here alone, no spooky noises.

Flora still couldn't be sure that the events occurring here weren't just a weird coincidence, or a combination of other odd factors. It was the number seven that seemed to hold the key – specifically the clock only striking to seven instead of twelve. It was just too much of a coincidence to let go.

The Seventh Tablet of Lamassu. She wished she'd stayed last night and asked Jasmin more about this supposed curse. Would that have shone any light on what was going on here?

Flora shook her head in the semi-dark, and let a small sigh. This was not the time to start believing in silly curses and the like. It was time to get serious and start some proper investigating.

She stood at the entrance to the main atrium. In her pocket, some pepper spray. Just in case. She had a proper torch in one hand, and her phone in the other. She was videoing everything tonight. Just let the police tell her she was crazy or imagining everything once she showed them this.

Bracing herself, Flora waited to see if she'd hear banging. When it came, it was even more horrible than she remembered. Strange and ricocheting, both far away and close by, the rattling bangs reminded her of that first night, cowering in the office with Nick. She shivered, shaken despite her intent to stay composed.

Come on, Flora, she thought. You have a job to do. Do it.

Of course, the real job was almost finished now. The collection was completely packed up and ready to be moved. Tomorrow they would transfer all the boxes to Shakers' warehouse; they needed extra hands on deck to do this in a day, so tonight was the final night here in the museum building. Her last chance to figure out what the hell was going on.

Monday she and Marshall would drive the collection to London and begin to install it in its new home. It would probably take two days. A month ago, the idea of an overnight stay in the capital – hotel bed, room service, the city at night – had seemed romantic. They'd both been excited. Now Flora wouldn't exactly say she was dreading it but ...

The banging stopped suddenly and silence filled its place. Flora swung her torch around. Empty cabinets, dusty floor, patches on the walls where exhibits had been. Crates piled up against the far side of the room. All as it should be.

And then she froze. Footsteps, closing behind her. But hadn't she already heard the footsteps? These were the same irregular footsteps she'd heard before, only this time they were closer than ever. She closed her eyes, feeling her heart thump in her chest. There was something about that sound. That gait. It seemed ... inhuman.

A cold kind of terror crept over Flora's body. She

wanted to turn around and shine the torch directly in the direction of the footsteps, but she couldn't move. She wanted to call Nick – Nick who was downstairs watching out with his own torch and phone and pepper spray, waiting for her to text him as per their plan. But she couldn't speak. Her very breath seemed to have stopped in her throat. The footsteps moved closer, and closer.

Then something touched her hair.

The softest sensation, like a spider settling from the end of a web, moved over the crown of her head, so quickly and gently it wouldn't have registered if every fibre of her being hadn't been tense and alert. She shuddered violently, dropping her torch. She fell into a crouched position, scrambling to pick it up again. Finally, Flora found her voice and shouted for Nick, then she twisted around, still in her crouched position, and flared the beam of light up to where the footsteps and the strange spidery touch had come from.

There was nothing there.

'Nick!' Flora screamed. 'Nick, where the hell are you?'

With shaking hands, Flora adjusted the beam to a wider setting and, scrambling backwards towards the side of the atrium, she tried to illuminate as much of the room as she could. Empty. She shone it over towards the crates. Nothing there either. Back to where she'd been standing moments earlier. Nothing. Had she imagined that touch? She didn't think so. But she really did not want to sit here and wait to find out.

The lights flickered on again. Flora let out a long, shaky breath. The room was empty except for the crates. No sign of anyone or anything unusual at all.

Flora backed out of the atrium until she reached the main stairwell, then she bolted down the stairs, shouting Nick's name all the way. A sickness was welling up inside her. What if something had happened to him?

Maybe this was the seventh night – maybe the curse had started before Lucy died. No, that was ridiculous. And there was no curse. Get a grip, Flora. But there was a killer, and Nick wasn't answering her. And she was here, alone. Again.

Damn Marshall and his refusal to do another night shift with them. Damn his stupid pride and his irritating logic. You'll be fine, he said. There's no need for three of us to be here. Someone has to be well-rested for tomorrow, he said. Remembering how he and Nick had kicked off at each other the last time, Flora had readily agreed. She'd been happy to stay, she reminded herself now as she burst through the set of double doors into the entrance lobby. She'd wanted to do some investigating.

Right now all she wanted was to be at home snuggled up with a box set and a cup of hot chocolate.

'Nick?' she called, her voice sounding hollow and too loud. 'Where the hell are you?'

And then she saw him. He was sitting on one of the benches over by the desk, a gas heater glowing at his feet. Flora called his name again but he didn't respond. He seemed to be slumped forwards awkwardly, his hands in his lap as though holding something. He wasn't moving.

'Nick!' she cried, running now. The clock was chiming, but Flora wasn't counting. She reached out to touch the guard's shoulder, crying and calling his name.

* * *

Nick looked up at her and smiled. He pulled a pair of small black earphones out of his ears and then pressed something on his phone. 'Hey, Flora,' he said. 'What's up?'

'*What's up?*' Flora stared at Nick, her mouth dropping open. 'Are you serious? I've been shouting for you. I've been shouting for ages. I thought you were dead!'

'Why?' He looked so bemused Flora wanted to hit him. She shook her head angrily and grabbed his phone out of his lap.

'Candy Crush, Nick? Really? Well, that's a great use of your time, isn't it? So we're paying you to sit here and listen to music and play on your phone? Just wonderful.'

'Hey, Flora, hang on.'

Nick jumped up and ran after her as she stormed away. 'Wait,' he said. 'Look, I'm really sorry. It was only for a minute. What's the big deal?'

'The big deal,' Flora said, punctuating each word with an angry glare, 'is that I needed you. And you were supposed to be on duty.'

'I'm sorry. You're right. I just thought ... Well, you know.'

'What?' Flora said. 'Really, what?'

Nick shrugged, looking embarrassed. 'You know. It's kind of boring, being a security guard. And there's nothing really to do here anymore, is there?'

For a moment, Flora couldn't speak. Not struck dumb from fear, as she had been a short time ago, but by sheer outrage.

'Okay, look,' Nick began, backtracking quickly. 'I can see that you're angry. But I promise I won't do it again. Don't sack me, please. My dad will kill me. I'm paying off a loan with this money, and I promised him I wouldn't get fired again, and seriously if I lose this job my life is just over.'

'Oh, don't be so ridiculous.'

'It's true! And I genuinely am sorry, Flora. I won't do it again, ever. It was only for half an hour or so, just to break up the night. I mean, the Candy Crush is a bit more of an addiction, to be honest, but the headphones, well that's more because I just don't like silence and I–'

'Okay, okay. Go and get me a hot chocolate and I'll think about it,' Flora said shaking her head.

'Where will I find a hot chocolate at this time of night?' Nick asked.

Flora merely stared at him, an expression of incredulity on her face.

'Right. I get it. Just go and do it, right? Just find somewhere and get one.'

'Exactly,' Flora answered.

'And you'll be okay here?' Nick said. 'On your own?'

Flora shrugged. 'Who knows. But I've survived so far so I guess I'll just have to take my chances.'

Nick checked his pockets and gave her a brief nod, then headed for the main door. 'One hot chocolate, coming up.'

'Wait a second,' Flora said, her mind working overtime now. Nick stopped and looked back questioningly. 'Do you listen to music every night?'

'Look, it's only for a short–'

'I know, and I'm not interested in having a go at you again. I just really need to know.'

'Well, yeah. I guess. Most nights. Sorry.'

'And the night before last, when you were here on your own. Did you have your earphones in then?'

Nick pulled a face, thinking. 'I guess I must have done. It was deathly quiet that night too.'

'So, when you called me to say that you hadn't heard the noises again – the seven chimes or the bangs or the footsteps or the woman screaming – you wouldn't have heard them anyway, would you?'

'Oh, I'm sure I would,' Nick said confidently.

'No. You wouldn't. You didn't hear me calling your name when I was this far away from you. And I wasn't whispering it.'

'I guess.' Nick shifted awkwardly and glanced at the door. 'Do you still want that hot chocolate?'

Flora gestured for him to go, then she took up a position on the bench to think. The seat was still warm from Nick's behind, and she couldn't decide whether this was a good or a bad thing. In the end she figured it was silly to move to a cold part of the bench just for the sake of it, so she hunkered down to wait for her chocolate, and hopefully for some kind of clarity.

It was almost certainly five nights in a row, Flora noted. It definitely couldn't be written off as a coincidence. Someone – a living breathing person, not an ancient curse – must be doing this. But who? And, more to the point, why? Could it be … No. Surely Marshall wouldn't stoop so low. Flora shouldn't even be thinking it.

But then again, who knew what went on in the mind of that crazy American hunk.

She went to dial Marshall's number, but realised that her phone was still recording. Interesting. So now she had the whole thing on video. That would be something she'd look at very carefully later. Marshall answered groggily. Flora mumbled an apology for waking him and said she'd explain in the morning. Not a practical joke from him, then. Not that she had really thought it was.

Next, she called Jasmin, who answered on the first ring.

'Has it happened again?'

'The noises? Yes, it has,' said Flora warily, feeling uneasy at the tone of panic in Jasmin's voice.

'Oh god no.'

'What?' Flora insisted. 'What is it?'

'I can't say over the phone. We'll talk tomorrow.'

'No.' Suddenly Flora was angry again, a well of frustration boiling inside her. 'If there's anything I need to know you'll tell me now. Or me and my staff will pack up and go home and you can find someone else to look after this crazy mess of a job.'

There was silence on the line, and Flora listened to the beating of her heart, her eyes wide with shock at her own temper. That was no way to speak to a client. Jasmin would most likely tell her to get lost, and then they wouldn't get paid and an entire week's worth of work, not to mention Nick's wages and all the research they'd put into this, would be wasted.

'Okay,' Jasmin said quietly. 'I'll tell you.'

Flora let out a soft sigh of relief. 'Is it about the curse?'

'Yes.'

'You know that I don't believe in curses, don't you?' Flora said. 'My theory is that someone is doing this. I'm pretty sure I heard someone in here tonight.'

'That's just not possible, Flora. No one could get in there. Security is so tight, and only you and I have keys.'

That was true. Flora felt a shiver go down her spine. Those footsteps, so strange, almost ... yes, almost otherworldly.

No, it couldn't be. The one thing that Flora was sure of was that everything had a logical explanation.

She was just really struggling to find one for this.

Jasmin was speaking again, her voice strained in Flora's ear. 'There is more to the curse than I told you earlier. If the tablet is taken away from its rightful home, the spirit of the Lamassu will stalk the guardians until the tablet is returned. They will have seven nights of unrest, and on the seventh night death will strike.'

'I know this already,' Flora said, hugging herself in the cold of the lobby. Where was Nick with that hot chocolate? She needed some normality, something to bring her back down to earth.

'This is the fifth night,' Jasmin said ominously.

'I know,' Flora repeated.

'And you, my dear, are the guardian.'

For a moment the silence was so absolute it seemed to suck all the breath out of Flora's body. She felt weightless, as though she could float right up to the painted ceiling. She actually gripped the bench with her free hand, digging her nails into the wood.

'Are you still there, Flora?' Jasmin said.

'Mm-hm.' Flora could only respond with a murmur.

'So you see, it really is imperative that you find out what happened to the Tablet of Lamassu – and you only have two more days to do it. You were the appointed guardian of the collection, Flora. The curse recognises you. If you don't find it by the seventh night your life is in mortal danger.'

Flora ended the call, her goodbye automatic and distant, then she sat for a while, staring at the floor. When Nick returned, proudly clutching a steaming hot chocolate in a takeout cup, Flora took it from him without a word.

'Hey,' he said, 'you're shivering. Did something happen while I was gone?'

She shook her head.

'Nothing happened,' she said. 'Not yet. But it will, Nick. I have a feeling that something will happen, and when it does, apparently it's going to be all my fault.'

Chapter 12

There was always something incredibly reassuring about a new notepad. A new unlined notepad with a hard cover, a little larger than A5 size, and a really good pen. Black ink, never blue. Blue just felt wrong. And the notepad shouldn't be too garish, but it shouldn't be boring either.

This one, thought Flora now, unpacking her tote bag after her stationery shopping spree in town, was just right. A beautiful jade green cover, nice creamy off-white pages, not too thick, not too thin. She laid her haul on the kitchen counter: pens, post-it notes, pastel highlighters, a set of pencils and a cute little rubber – or eraser, as Marshall would insist on calling it with an eye roll and cheeky wink – in the shape of a plant pot.

Thank goodness for Paperchase.

Flora made coffee, then settled down in her favourite spot under the skylight. She opened up the notepad to the first page and began to sketch out a mind map. Since high school, this was her preferred way of organising her thoughts, and it worked better than trying to figure it out in her head. First she wrote *White & Co. Museum* in the centre of the page. Next, she drew lots of lines radiating outward from the circle, with labels like Jasmin White, Lamassu missing, Lucy Akopian, noises at night. After a few minutes, Flora sat back and looked at her diagram. And then, with a lump in her throat, she added John Hopper's name in the top right corner.

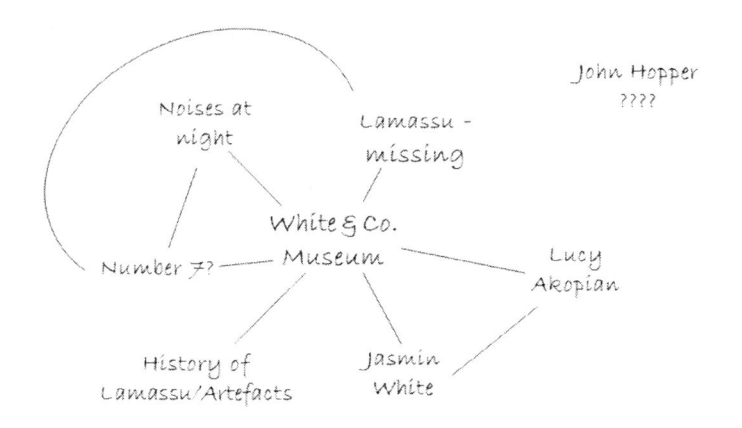

Diagram (mind map centered on "White & Co. Museum"):
- Noises at night
- Lamassu – missing
- John Hopper ????
- Lucy Akopian
- Jasmin White
- History of Lamassu/Artefacts
- Number 7?

Was it just a coincidence that a man claiming to be her birth father had turned up at the exact same point all this craziness had kicked off?

Flora didn't know, but she resolved to be more circumspect with him for the foreseeable future. At the very least, until all this museum business was sorted. She sighed and tapped the pen on her teeth. Please, she thought, don't let Marshall be right about this.

Turning to a fresh page, Flora began to write all that she could remember about the strange and scary sounds that had been occurring each night. Her memory of that awful first night was as clear as day. The scream came first, that was a definite. Followed by a second terrifying scream.

The lights had gone out that first night directly after the screams. And then, the footsteps. Those horrid sounding steps, so unnatural and slow. Flora thought for a minute, then wrote:

After footsteps stopped, the clock began to chime midnight.

But midnight never came, did it? At least, not in terms of chimes.

She quickly scribbled down what she could remember about the second and fourth nights, annoyed afresh at Nick and his earphones. No way to know for sure whether the noises occurred while he was on watch alone, but it was fairly safe to assume that they had.

And last night. Total blackout, then the footsteps again, and the feeling – so strong and so creepy – that someone was watching her. That feather-like touch to her scalp. But no one, not even the sign of someone, in the building at all. Just a shadowy sense of fear, lurking in the darkness.

'Okay,' she said out loud, flicking her hair out of her eyes and trying to focus. 'Ideas.'

Flora began to list all the ways in which those creepy noises could have happened. First, natural causes. Old pipe work for the banging. Rats for the odd footsteps? She laughed at this, then grimaced, imagining huge rats with heavy boots on. What about creaking beams? Sounds were magnified at night, especially in an empty old building with strange acoustics. For the screaming woman, Flora wrote: *foxes*. It was entirely possible. Foxes were known to come into towns and cities at night, searching for food. And she'd heard foxes at her Uncle Max's house in the countryside – they were pretty loud.

If you've heard foxes before, Flora, then you know that what you and Marshall and Nick all heard was not a bloody fox. Uncle Max's sensible voice resonated in her head, but Flora shrugged it away and added *cats fighting* to her list.

The chiming clock was easier to explain. It was obviously broken, chiming normally most of the time, but only seven at midnight. This would be a mechanical problem, nothing sinister.

Flora sat back with a deep sigh of satisfaction. Okay, so here was progress. Nothing so spooky after all about the night-time happenings at the museum. It was amazing how your mind could get carried away and play tricks on you. Especially after spending your daytime hours packing up and cataloguing strange and freaky exhibits.

She turned her attention now to the death of Lucy Akopian. This was more difficult. There was a link with Jasmin, obviously, but no other reason for Lucy to be in Shrewsbury at all. Had she been planning to come and see her old friend? The most likely explanation for Lucy's presence was that she'd come for the Lamassu – this was backed up by its disappearance on the same night Lucy died. So, Flora reasoned, Lucy may have had an accomplice, who helped her break into the museum – while Flora and Nick were in the office, most likely – to steal the Lamassu. And then, the accomplice had killed her, opened a crate, placed her on top, and then taken the priceless artefact for himself. But the time of death didn't fit this explanation. Annoyingly.

Why had he opened the crate? Perhaps the Lamassu was inside it. But here, Flora paused, her pen hovering over the paper. She had packed that crate herself, and was absolutely certain that no stone tablet with a carving on it had found its way into that particular box. It was her first day, and she'd been extra careful with the artefacts, examining each one with fascination.

For now, anyway, Flora had a reasonably plausible narrative for what had happened that night, and she found that it made her extremely happy. There was no curse, no spooky mystery. Just a bad, greedy person willing to commit theft and murder to get what he wanted.

Which, when you thought about it, wasn't actually good news at all. Because that person was still out there. And Flora and Nick were, in effect, witnesses to the crime.

Flora swallowed hard. She hadn't thought of that until now. Should she tell the police what she had figured out? She shook her head, glancing up at the skylight where clouds drifted lazily past. No way. She had no intention of being laughed at and ridiculed again.

The police could figure it out on their own, or not. Meanwhile, Flora would just have to keep on digging.

***

By late afternoon, Flora and Marshall had transferred the packed contents of the museum to the inside of their lorry and driven it to Shakers Removals headquarters. Headquarters was perhaps a slightly glamorous description; the office and small warehouse, inside which the lorry was now parked up, were sited by the railway arches close to Shrewsbury station. Decidedly unsalubrious.

Glad to be out of the museum at last, Flora had been in a buoyant mood initially, but Marshall seemed tense, and it was beginning to get on her nerves.

'Are you okay?' she asked him as he jumped down from the cab and dragged a set of wooden steps across the floor of the warehouse.

'You've asked me that at least ten times today,' he responded.

'That's because it's perfectly clear to me that you are not okay,' Flora snapped.

'Well, Missy, if you know I'm not okay why do you keep on asking me if I am?' Marshall answered with a sarcastic smile.

'Jesus,' Flora muttered under her breath. She reached up into the cab to relieve her tote, then headed towards the back of the van and climbed the three steps.

'Hey,' Marshall called, jogging to catch her up. 'Whatcha doing?'

'What does it look like?' she said.

'It kinda looks like you're planning to stay here tonight, on your own, being a hero or something,' Marshall said tiredly. 'Jeez, Flora. Can you not just let this rest?'

'Let what rest?' she said. She took a thermos flask and

a book out of her bag and set them down on the floor. On one of the crates, Flora laid a thin knitted blanket that she'd also pulled from her oversized tote bag. She sat cross-legged on the blanket and smiled. 'I've no idea what you are talking about?'

Marshall grinned at her, and ran his fingers through his hair. 'Some set up you got here.'

'It is.'

'Planning on spending the night?'

'Sure am,' Flora said, mimicking Marshall's accent. She flashed him a challenging smile, then picked up her book and pretended to read it.

'You ain't reading that, are you honey?'

Marshall stood close to her, casting her in his shadow. Flora inhaled his scent. So warm and masculine and just ... lovely. She tipped her head and looked up at him.

'Wanna join me?'

'Sure do,' he said huskily.

'Okay then.'

She closed her eyes as Marshall leaned in and kissed her. With one smooth movement, he laid her on her back on the blanket, stroking the length of her legs, his face close to her ear.

'Sexy you,' he whispered. 'But these jeans were a bad idea.'

Flora tried to relax into it. His kisses were gentle, but she knew well enough where this would lead. Those strong hands were on her waistband now, and now they were unbuttoning her Levis. Marshall in full seduction mode was intoxicating, insistent. And very, very sexy. Flora stretched out her hand, feeling the soft texture of the woollen blanket. She smiled as her boyfriend began to tug down her jeans. What was he like? And here, of all places. The inside of a lorry. Very romantic. Her hand strayed further as she allowed herself to sink deeper into Marshall's kisses, which were now moving down to her throat. She touched the rough wood of the packing crate. Her fingers snagged on a clip – the kind she used to secure the boxes before she sealed them.

She opened her eyes. Lucy Akopian's face sprung into her mind. Lucy, who had been found lying in a crate just like this one, in almost the exact same position as Flora was lying now.

'No,' she said, pushing Marshall away with both hands. 'No, stop it. This isn't right.'

'Don't worry, baby. There's no one around to hear us. They've all gone home for the day.'

'I'm serious, Marshall. Just stop, okay.'

She gave him a shove and sat upright, fumbling to do up her jeans. Her face felt flushed, her skin hot and sticky. What the hell was she thinking, messing around in here, surrounded by their client's priceless antiquities?

'What?' she said. Marshall was looking at her, his expression unreadable. His eyes had darkened, but other than that there were no signs of annoyance.

'What?' Flora said again, standing. She brushed herself down, as though she'd been for a roll in the hay, rather than a quick fumble on a wooden crate. 'For goodness sake, say something!'

Marshall opened his mouth as if to speak, but then he shook his head and gave an almost imperceptible smile. Picking up his coat from the floor, he turned around and jumped right out of the container.

'Well, thanks a lot, big guy,' Flora shouted after him. 'What, I don't want to do it just one time, and you're gonna get the sulks with me?'

She slammed the lorry door shut and turned around to lean her back against it. Damn Marshall. Impenetrable man. *Impossible* man.

'Knickers to you,' she said out loud. And then she smiled. Way to go with the insults, Flora. Is that the worst you can do?

When she heard the knock on the warehouse door,

Flora was drinking her first cup of tea from her flask. She'd fired up an electric heater and positioned it next to her camping chair. She was planning to sleep in the cab, but for now was content to sit in the warehouse, enjoying the safety of a familiar space. Finally the collection was under her control, not scattered around in a spooky old building. Walking toward the entrance, she wondered whether to be annoyed at Marshall for leaving, or happy that he'd come back to keep her company.

'Hey handsome,' she said as she unlocked the smaller personal door, smiling out into the night. But the person standing outside, peering in uncertainly, wasn't Marshall.

It was Jasmin.

Chapter 13

Flora stepped back to let the older woman inside. 'Hi. What are you doing here?'

'Do you mind,' Jasmin said, ducking her head as she entered, even though there was plenty of space above her small frame. 'I just thought I'd check on you. I mean, check you are okay.'

And check on your collection, Flora thought. But why not? The poor woman must be out of her mind with everything that has been going on.

'It's all going great,' said Flora. 'As you can see.'

She stepped back so that Jasmin could see into the back of the lorry, and together they surveyed the stacked crates and smaller boxes. Some of the artefacts had been wrapped in packing blankets, like the suit of armour and some of the larger paintings.

'It's crazy to see it all here,' Jasmin said wistfully. 'It looks so … small.'

Flora nodded. 'I know what you mean. People say that when they move house. Years and years of buying stuff, all that clutter and layers upon layers of memories. And it takes them weeks, sometimes months, to pack it up. Then they look at it all crammed into our van and say, "Is that all we own?"'

'Are you staying here alone tonight, Flora?' Jasmin asked.

'Yeah. I think it's best. I don't feel right about leaving it. I'll be fine, though. Don't worry. I have everything I need, and it's warm and snug.'

'I am grateful for the extra trouble you're going to,' Jasmin said softly. Flora thought she might have had tears in her eyes, but it could have just been the light.

'Well, it's all part of the job.' Flora didn't add that she would much rather be looking after the collection here, on her own turf, than in the museum in town. She would be very happy if she never had to set foot in there again.

'Your young man not with you?'

'Which one?' Flora asked, laughing.

'The tall, handsome one,' Jasmin said with a wink. '*Your* young man.'

'Oh, he's gone off in a huff.' Flora leaned against the crate with her blanket laid over, pulling a disappointed face. 'Maybe I should get on Tinder like you,' she added with another laugh. 'Find myself a new model.'

'Pardon?' Jasmin returned her smile, but looked confused. 'Tinder?'

'Yeah, you know. Like how you met your date.'

'Date?'

For a couple of seconds Jasmin's face was completely blank. Then her expression cleared and she nodded. 'Oh, yes of course. My Tinder date. Sure, you should. Definitely.'

'Have you seen him again?' Flora asked.

'Who my dear?'

'Your date!' Flora said, laughing. 'Wow, he was either really bad or completely forgettable.'

'Ha, yes.'

Jasmin stood up and smoothed down her skirt. Today she was rocking the white look with a silk two-piece and a fine-knit long cardigan. She was incongruously glamorous, juxtaposed with the rust-touched container. Hell, she'd look glamorous next to the Queen.

'I should be going,' Jasmin said. 'Would it be possible to have a glass of water before I leave? I feel a little faint.'

'Oh, I'm so sorry.'

Flora told her to sit down, she'd only be a moment.

She ran to the Shaker's office, clattering up the metal stairs. In the tiny kitchen, she rinsed out a glass and filled it with water from the tap. She paused at the window, glancing out across the yard. There were five businesses currently occupying the small industrial area under the railway. All the other buildings were in darkness now, with the only light coming from the warehouse below.

Back downstairs, Flora was surprised to see the chair empty. She heard movement inside the lorry, but found the door latched from the inside. She knocked gently. 'Jasmin? Are you in there?'

'Oh, gosh, yes. I'm fine,' Jasmin said from behind the metal door. 'Hang on. Oh now, how do I open this.'

'There's a sliding lock thing just by the–'

But the door swung outwards before she could finish, and Flora climbed in, a little anxious. 'What's wrong?' she said.

'Nothing my dear. Why do you ask?'

'The door,' Flora said. 'You were locked in. I thought …'

Jasmin laid a cool hand on Flora's arm. 'I'm not like you, my dear little Flora. I'm not tough or streetwise, neither am I young. And I don't have a nice man to look after me. Not anymore. I have to take whatever precautions I need to take.'

'Of course,' Flora said, feeling both relieved *and* more anxious than she was before.

I will be fine here tonight, she told herself. Of course I will.

Flora saw Jasmin outside, casting surreptitious glances around the car park.

Jasmin called to her from inside her car. 'Lock the door, Flora. *All* the doors. Don't take any chances. You are the guardian, remember. The curse has its eye on you.'

'Thanks,' muttered Flora. 'That really helps a lot.'

Back inside the warehouse, Flora locked the personal

door and shook it a couple of times. She checked the roll-down shutters. All safe and secure. She shut her eyes briefly, trying to calm her breathing.

Damn that stupid curse. She didn't believe in it anyway.

But despite that, she took extra care to latch and bolt the lorry doors as well, before climbing into the cab.

She checked her phone, then settled herself down for the night. Flora was exhausted. Broken sleep and keeping odd working hours was having a decidedly negative effect. She snuggled into her blanket and pulled her poncho over her legs. It would not be long before sleep took her. And then, there was only one more day to go until they were rid of this job completely.

Investigation or not, Flora had to admit that she couldn't wait to see the back of this collection, and of Jasmin too.

She woke to the sound of a train passing overhead. Another glance at her phone told her it was two minutes after midnight. The goods train chugging by was soothing, and Flora smiled contentedly. The light on the tiny electric heater out in the warehouse cast an orange glow in the semi-darkness. What a strange thing to be doing, Flora thought dreamily. To be lying in a container full of ancient antiquities – just her and hundreds of artefacts from all over the world. She imagined them watching over her, keeping her safe. Were they also glad to be out of that creepy museum? Their new home at the British Museum would be modern and well lit, clean and ordered. Flora had seen pictures a planogram of the room where the White & Co collection would be displayed to the public. No creepy noises there. No banging pipes or foxes or huge rats wearing boots. No screaming cats.

Suddenly, her eyes opened wide. That was a cat, surely? Something had interrupted her dream-state – something loud and sharp and wild. And then she heard it. The wail was ethereal, shocking; Flora was frozen inside it. Her skin prickled, a shiver running down her spine. It was impossible. She sat upright. Eyes wide, she turned to look behind her. The sound was coming from inside the lorry. From inside the collection itself.

The wailing stopped. Flora held her breath, waiting. What would come next? Banging? Footsteps? The chiming of a ghostly clock, counting down to seven – the curse of the Sign of Seven?

'No,' Flora said out loud, her voice hollow. 'No, I will not have this!' A surge of anger welled up inside her, fear turning into fury, fury turning to resolve. She fumbled for her phone, selecting her music app and turning up the volume as loud as it would go. With her hands over her ears, Flora curled up inside the cab and sang along with the Kings of Leon. The world had gone crazy. But singing was a damn sight better than crying.

***

'Well isn't this the cosy little picture?'

Flora opened her eyes, squinting into sharp white light.

'Marshall?'

Silhouetted in the doorway, Marshall's form appeared larger than normal, and he was certainly giving off some seriously forbidding vibes. Flora stretched out her legs and arched her back a little, reaching instinctively for her phone …

And then she remembered.

There was a warm body behind her, providing comfort and support. Quite a lot of support. But not the kind Marshall would approve of.

'It's not remotely what it looks like,' she said, struggling to her feet.

'Really?' Marshall responded with a cool smile. 'That's interesting.' He moved out of the doorway, flooding the van with light. Flora heard a groan by her side. Oh dear. This was about to get awkward.

'Because from where I'm standing,' Marshall continued, 'it looks very much as though you and Mr Muscle here spent the night together.'

'Absolutely not,' Flora said firmly. 'That *is* what it looks like, I can see that–'

'Oh, can you? Well, that's something.'

'But it's not like that at all.'

The groan turned into a yawn, and Nick emerged, bleary eyed, from behind Flora.

'Hey, mate,' he said. 'What's up?'

'What's up?' Marshall echoed. Flora lowered her head to her hands. 'What's *up?*'

'Look,' she said, 'I called Nick in the night. I heard those noises again – here, inside the van – and I was freaked out, okay? And you'd gone off in a huff because … Well, you know why. I didn't think you'd want to come back here. So I called Nick. He *is* our security guard. We came in here to check out the collection. By this time it was really late, and Nick said he'd stay to keep an eye on things. I don't see that I did anything wrong, to be honest,' Flora finished, hotly.

'To be honest.' Marshall repeated her words slowly. 'Well, Flora, it sure would be nice if you managed to be honest. And you could start by being honest with yourself.'

'What's that supposed to mean?'

'I'd better be going.' Nick slid past her and picked up his backpack. He shot Flora a sympathetic glance. 'See you later.'

'Later?' Marshall drawled at Nick's departing back. 'Got a date have we?'

'Nick's doing the night watch,' Flora answered tiredly. 'The final one before we move the collection for good.'

'Alone? Or are the two of you bunking up again?'

'Oh for goodness sake!' Flora rounded on him. 'I was scared. You left me here on my own, to fend for myself–'

'I *left* you? Seems to me you pushed me away. And now we know why, don't we?'

'The noises, Marshall. I heard them – right here inside the van. It was … it was insane.' She looked around the interior of the lorry, taking in the crates and the boxes and the shrouded artefacts. 'There was something *in here*. I was terrified.'

'Well, Flora, at least now we know who you turn to when you're terrified.'

'Oh my god, you are the worst!' A sob choked off the last of her sentence, and Flora turned away so Marshall couldn't see her face. She began to stuff her things back into her tote, furious tears stinging her eyes.

A shadow fell over her. She could smell Marshall's scent, and something else. Like an animal, she sensed danger.

'You know what I think, Flora?'

His voice was cold, his words jagged pieces of ice thrown down upon her.

'No,' she mumbled. 'But I'm sure you're going to tell me.'

'I think you are full of shit. I think you pretend to be so sweet and cute, and you try so hard to keep everyone happy, but it's all a front. You're just a needy little girl waiting to get attached to anyone who's nice to her. Look at the people you drag into your life! First there was Joy – you latched onto her like she was your own grandmother – then Celeste, who you insisted was your best friend even though she blatantly hated you, and now Nick. Is he your latest project, Flora? Jeez, you're even willing to believe some stranger who pretends to be your dad. It's crazy, is what it is.'

Slowly, Flora got to her feet. She placed her bag over her shoulder and carefully slipped her feet into her battered Converse. It felt as though all the air had been sucked out of the inside of the van. Outside their warehouse, the car park was filling up; she could hear voices and faint music, car doors slamming, a man shouting at someone that he'd be inside in a minute.

'So you're just gonna leave now?' Marshall taunted as she climbed out of the back of the lorry and walked towards the open warehouse door. 'You got nothing to say to me?'

Flora glanced back at him. His handsome face was twisted into a snarl. She shook her head.

'Not really,' she said quietly.

'That doesn't surprise me.' Marshall jumped down and was next to her in two angry strides. 'You got plenty to say to everyone else – you just love to explain things, don't you? You think you know better than anyone, even the police. Until it comes to explaining something like this.'

'Marshall, I just did explain it to you.'

'That was hardly an explanation.'

'Well it's all I've got, okay?'

She waited for him to respond, but his mouth took on that set expression she knew so well. He was probably annoyed at himself now, for showing too much emotion, for taking it too far.

It wasn't their first row, but it was shaping up to be one of their worst. Flora sighed deeply.

'Look, Marshall, I'm tired. All I want is to go home, take a long shower, get some sleep, and then think about what is going on with this bloody museum.'

He shrugged. 'You do what you like. Just like always. I suppose you want me to lock up here? Tidy up your little love nest for you?'

Flora shook her head in exasperation and began to walk away. Outside, the sun warmed her face. She stopped for a moment and closed her eyes. Then a thought occurred to her.

'Marshall, what did you mean about knowing better

than anyone else, "even the police"?'

He was standing right where she'd left him, a study in self-righteousness.

'That was another dig, right?' she said. 'Another way to hurt me because you're jealous of Nick, and you can't stand the thought that I might be right about John Hopper – that I might actually have a family after all.'

Was that it? she thought. Was Marshall really so insecure that he'd resent her finding her father in case it took her away from him?

'It's got nothing to do with that,' he said flatly. 'I just can't stand it anymore, is all.'

'Stand what?' Flora cried.

'You making a fool of yourself, Flora. Over and over again. It's embarrassing. I told you before. My girlfriend pretending to be some kind of private investigator.' He ran a hand through his hair, then laughed. It was not a nice laugh. 'First you got yourself involved in all that retirement village stuff, then you dragged us into the thing with the film set. I was arrested. Did you ever think about how that made me feel?'

'I thought about nothing else! And you weren't arrested,' she added. 'You were taken in for questioning.'

'Oh well, that's alright then. Flora, honey – when are you gonna get it into your head that you are not a real investigator? Sure, you've figured a few things out and helped the police a bit, but it's been nothing but luck. A combination of luck and being in the right place at the right time. You see that, don't you? You're not so deluded as to think that you are a real P.I.?'

'Jasmin thinks I am,' Flora retorted. 'She hired me specifically to solve the case of the missing Lamassu.'

'*The case of the* ... Flora, you are crazy! She only "hired" you so you wouldn't walk out of the job once there was a dead body involved, which any reputable company or normal person probably would. Or maybe – have you even thought about this – maybe she did it herself, like the police believe. Meanwhile she's got you running around in circles trying to figure it all out and cover for her, just by playing to your ego.'

Stunned, Flora stared at him. 'I feel like I barely know you, Marshall Goodman. Have you felt like this all along?'

He shrugged.

'Well.' Flora could not think of a single thing to say.

'I've got stuff to do in the office,' Marshall mumbled, then he turned and headed for the stairs.

Flora walked home in a bubble of astonishment and hurt. She felt numb; she didn't notice the warmth of the morning, the bustle on the streets. His words rang in her head, and stung at her heart. He was cruel and dismissive; he was jealous and mean. But worse of all – what if he was right?

Chapter 14

After a shower and a steadying cup of coffee, Flora decided to go to the one place she had always been able to turn to for answers: Shrewsbury's beautiful library. It was here that Heston – good old Heston – had helped her solve the Maples mystery, and it was here that she would seek comfort and information, and – most importantly – a refuge from Marshall.

Her confidence was at an all-time low. No matter how Marshall chose to frame it, Flora did indeed have a genuine client, and her client needed her to find a missing relic. So far, Flora had made very little progress in that area. So far, all she'd managed to do was allow herself to get sidetracked.

Walking through the revolving doors of the massive library, Flora acknowledged that she had to complete the rest of the museum job perfectly, or Shakers' reputation would be ruined: a dead body placed inside packing crates on her watch; the murders on the film set last year; her link to the Maples scandal – people only remember these things in a positive light if you're on the *winning* side, bathed in glory. One mishap and Shakers was going down.

She also knew that Marshall was right about one thing: her so-called powers of detection to date had owed more than she liked to admit to luck and timing.

If she could solve this mystery, and pull off a perfect re-installation of the collection of antiquities, all would be okay. As for Marshall, who knew? Maybe working together just wasn't going to pan out if their relationship was going to survive. But would it survive anyway? John

Hopper had thrown more than a spanner in the works. Flora had always felt insecure about her family, and now she had a chance to get to know her father she couldn't let Marshall get in the way of that. She just couldn't.

She checked her phone, then turned it to silent, noting the time and resolving not to spend more than a couple of hours cooped up in here. There was too much to be done, and at some point she would have to face Marshall again. She also needed to call Nick to check he was okay for tonight's watch. With a heavy sigh, Flora realised that tonight was the seventh night of the curse of the Sign of Seven. Time might indeed be running out. She had to find some answers, and she had to find them fast.

**

'Flora? Is that you?'

'Heston! I was just thinking about you. How are you?'

Flora smiled at her ex-boyfriend. He hadn't changed a bit. Still smart and buttoned up, that public school coolness with just a touch of delicacy. You could not find more of a contrast to Marshall if you tried.

They caught up in hushed tones, Heston leaning gracefully on a trolley of books, Flora fidgeting nervously, wondering if it would be an imposition to ask for Heston's help again.

Never mind the effect enlisting her ex would have on Marshall's current levels of jealousy.

'I'll be taking my break in ten minutes if you'd like to join me for coffee,' Heston said finally.

Flora sighed in relief. 'I would love that,' she gushed. 'Just coffee, though,' she added. 'And perhaps a bit of advice. As a friend.'

He smiled and nodded.

Best to be crystal clear from now on, Flora decided. She had enough going on in her life, without muddying the waters any further.

While she waited for Heston at the little cafe around the corner, Flora took out her notes and made a list of her most pertinent questions. She ordered cappuccino for herself, and a cortado for her ex. Silently, she ran through how she was going to convince Heston to help her.

She needn't have worried. Heston was game – enthusiastic, even. And it turned out he was another of the few residents of the town who not only knew about the museum, but had been a regular visitor.

Flora smiled. She shouldn't have been surprised, really.

'Will you help me research Lamassu?' she asked, finishing her coffee and wiping the froth from her upper lip. 'There's all sorts of stuff online, but I need to get at it from a different angle, if you know what I mean.'

Heston nodded solemnly. 'I know exactly what you mean. And I think I might know of someone else who can help us. An expert.'

'You're a good friend,' Flora said.

'I know.' Heston grinned. 'Hey, whatever happened to that Neanderthal American you used to work with? Didn't you date him after we split up?'

Flora groaned. 'Don't even ask.' She pushed back her chair. 'Come on, let's get to work.'

***

The melodic tones of a new Skype call filled Flora's small lounge. She checked her face quickly in the mirror, then settled down on the sofa in front of her laptop and accepted the call.

Professor Paulson's round, pleasant face immediately filled her screen. Heston had dug up his name from the library's list of industry experts. Then he and Flora had unearthed some copies of academic papers written thirty years ago, put out a request to a university in Switzerland, and received an email response from the eminent professor within the hour.

Flora could not be more grateful that the author of those papers was still alive, let alone that he was Skyping her from his Geneva home at three o'clock on a Saturday afternoon.

'Miss Lively, is it?' the professor said, smiling broadly. He was a distinctive looking man in his late sixties or early seventies, with a shiny balding head, black-rimmed glasses, and a thick white moustache.

'Thank you so much for agreeing to chat to me,' Flora said, reflexively raising her voice. 'I appreciate you're a busy man.'

'Not so much these days,' he answered, smiling ruefully. 'So, what can I help you with? You mentioned in your email that you need information about some Assyrian artefacts?'

'Yes,' Flora said, pulling her notebook onto her knee. 'That's your area of expertise, isn't it?'

'That and other things,' the professor replied, laughing. Flora laughed politely. 'Sorry,' he continued, 'just my little joke. Since they hung me out to dry I've become quite well known locally for my appreciation of fine cigars.'

'Ah,' Flora said, smiling. She assumed that by "they", the professor meant the university where he'd worked for over twenty five years.

'So, Miss Lively, what is it that you need to know?'

Flora explained, as succinctly as she could, the situation at the museum. She told the professor what she knew about the tablet, including the fact that it was currently missing. She had decided not to mention Lucy Akopian's death, preferring to stick to the pretext that she was simply working for Jasmin White, the museum's owner, and trying to track down a priceless artefact. Which was, in any case, the truth.

The professor listened carefully. He appeared to be making notes off-screen, which Flora found reassuring. For the first time since all this had started, she was finally beginning to feel like she was getting somewhere. Doing some proper investigating. Gathering the evidence.

Marshall's disparaging words rang in her ears, but Flora pushed them away.

'Ah, the Lamassu,' the professor said, sitting back in his chair with his fingers laced behind his head. What Flora assumed was his study appeared dark and musty, with a wall of bookcases and an old globe on a side table. Flora tried to imagine the view out of his window – the Alps, perhaps, or a shining blue lake. What she wouldn't give to be in some glamorous location right now, instead of trying to unravel an impossible knot of ancient mysteries and stolen treasures.

The professor spoke slowly, pausing occasionally to puff on a small cigar. Flora rested her chin in her hands, elbows on knees, and listened to his story of explorers and expeditions, a world occupied by the privileged elite, a relic of colonialism and the British Empire, and the fundamental belief in finders-keepers.

'The word antiquities itself is a much-debated term,' Professor Paulson said, after giving Flora a brief tour of the world's most popular archaeological sites. 'A museum's Department of Antiquities will most often include items from the dawn of civilization up until the Dark Ages, from Western Europe to the Caspian Sea, embracing the cultures of Egypt, Greece, Rome and the Near East.'

'The Near East?' Flora cut in. 'I've never heard of that.'

'Originally it described the Ottoman Empire, but that's only a rough guide. The term has fallen out of use in recent years – think Western Asia, Turkey, Egypt. You get the picture.'

Flora didn't, but she nodded anyway. 'I wasn't great at geography in school,' she confessed.

'The key thing,' the professor continued, 'is to remember that most antiquities have been recovered through archaeological pursuits, while antiques have not. The cut-off dates for antiques is roughly three hundred years, although they are often far newer.'

'And the Lamassu originates from Assyria?' Flora said. 'And is officially an antiquity?'

The professor chuckled. 'We are getting a little off track, aren't we? You'll have to forgive an old man with a new audience. But your main interest here is the Lamassu. Well, the first recorded Lamassu comes from three thousand BC. It's also known as Lumasi, Alad, and Shedu. The human-headed, eagle-winged bull or lion is a frequent figure in Mesopotamian art and mythology – they were believed to be very powerful creatures, and served as symbols of protection. Every important city wanted to have Lamassu protect the gateway to their citadel. They were also known as the guardians who inspired armies to protect their cities. The Mesopotamians believed that Lamassu frightened away the forces of chaos and brought peace to their homes. *Lamassu* in the Akkadian language means "protective spirits".'

'Guardians,' Flora repeated. 'That's interesting.'

'Why so, my dear?'

'Just something that the owner of the museum said about a curse.' Flora laughed nervously. 'About me being the guardian or something.'

The professor's expression grew grave. 'You're not talking about the Sign of Seven?'

Flora nodded slowly. 'You've heard of it?'

'Why, of course! It's infamous in the world of ancient Assyrian culture.'

'You don't say,' Flora commented flatly. Any hope she'd had that Jasmin had made the whole thing up suddenly evaporated.

'And you say that you – you yourself – are the guardian?'

'Apparently. And that's bad, right?' Flora added with a sigh.

'Has the curse been set in motion?' asked the professor, reaching for something off-screen and then opening up a thick, ancient-looking book.

'Erm, yes.' She paused, watching the top of his head as he consulted his text. His scalp reflected the light from his computer screen. Any shinier and she'd be able to see her own face in it. 'But come on, these old myths and legends – there just stories, right?'

Professor Paulson looked up and smiled. 'Oh, of course they are. No truth in them whatsoever.' But his smile didn't quite reach his eyes.

'Is there anything else you can tell me about the Lamassu that has gone missing?' Flora asked, suddenly keen to bring the call to an end. She knew more than she would ever need to know about antiquities in general, but felt no nearer to understanding the mystery at hand.

'You say it is a tablet?' The professor thought for a moment, stroking his chin. From this angle, Flora could see that under his moustache curled a distinct hair-lip, and she felt momentarily embarrassed that she'd noticed something he clearly went to some lengths to disguise. 'It the tablet engraved or carved in relief?' he asked, gazing back directly at the screen.

'What's the difference?'

'Engraved is where the carving is indented,' the professor explained with only the slightest edge of impatience. 'Whereas in relief means that the image is proud of the surface. It's the background that is cut away.'

Flora shook her head. 'I never saw it. Does it make a difference?'

'It might. Lamassu were protectors not only of kings

and palaces, but of every single human being in the ancient world. People felt safer knowing that their spirits were close, so Lamassu were engraved on clay tablets, which were then buried under the threshold of their homes. A house with a Lamassu was believed to be a happier place than one without the mythical creature nearby. But there were some Lamassu where the effect was reversed. Legend says that there were certain tablets where the Lamassu was not engraved, but carved in relief. And these Lamassu had to be treated very carefully indeed.'

Flora reached for a drink of water, her mouth suddenly dry. The professor continued.

'It was considered bad luck to remove a Lamassu from its home. As you can imagine. But for the reverse-Lamassu, bad luck turned into a deadly curse.'

'The Sign of Seven?' Flora whispered.

'You know that seven is considered an unlucky number by many, don't you?'

Flora put down her glass. 'Not really. I thought it was lucky.'

'In some cultures, perhaps. But the so-called seven year itch is the point at which many marriages end, and of course there is said to be seven years' bad luck if you break a mirror.'

'True. So it can be good or bad luck?' Flora said, silently counting how many years she had known Marshall.

'Here's where it gets interesting,' Professor Paulson said excitedly. 'Mythology says that one's reflection is part of your soul, so if your reflection – be it in a pool of water, a mirror, or any surface – is disrupted, damage would be done to the soul. The ancients considered such an act to mark the end of a life and, supposedly, it takes seven years for renewal and growth to occur. So, if your soul is damaged, you have seven fragmented years before becoming whole again. Of course, on a cellular level a human being does indeed become a new person cell-by-cell in increments of about seven years. So the myth has legs, so to speak.'

'And the curse?' Flora prompted.

'Ah, yes. Well, if a Lamassu is taken from its home, the image of the great beast is disrupted. Its very soul – and therefore its power to protect and inspire – is damaged. For a normal Lamassu, the remedy is simply to bury the tablet for seven years and wait for it to be restored. But for a Lamassu that is carved in relief …'

The professor paused, glancing at something Flora couldn't see. He appeared to be listening. When he turned back to his computer he was frowning.

'Is everything okay?' Flora asked.

'Yes, yes. But I must go soon. I'm afraid something has come up.'

Flora tried to hide her disappointment. There was so much more she wanted to ask.

'May I email you with a few more questions?' she said, relieved when he nodded and smiled. 'By the way, you didn't finish,' she said quickly as she saw his hand reaching to end their call. 'You were talking about the number seven, and Lamassu that are carved in relief.'

The professor smiled sadly. 'So much needless destruction occurred on archaeological digs, my dear. You go to a museum today, you gaze at the exhibits, and all you see are the relics of dead societies, accompanied by a typed explanation of where it came from and when. Who truly knows the damage that was done when that piece of pottery or bone or metal was ripped from its resting place? The great Francis Bacon said, "Antiquities are history defaced, or some remnants of history which have casually escaped the shipwreck of time". There are myths and legends and curses aplenty. But none of us know which are made up to terrify thieves and plunders, and which exist to this day.'

'But I need to understand–'

'Do let me know if you find your Lamassu, my dear,' the professor said abruptly. 'Goodbye for now.'

And with that he was gone, his image replaced by a plain blue screen, and Flora was left with his final words that hung in the air like a warning.

Chapter 15

Her faith in the power of research restored, Flora made coffee and a doorstep cheese sandwich, then plugged herself into the world wide web, notebook by her side. Professor Paulson had been such a help in pointing her in the right direction, and Flora resolved to send him a proper thank you note just as soon as she was on the other side of this.

It was his comment about Francis Bacon that had given Flora her first proper clue. History defaced, he'd said, and that triggered the memory of Jasmin's impassioned plea for Flora to find her missing Lamassu. There had been something in her eyes that day; Flora refused to believe that she'd been played, no matter the about-turn her employer had made later. She knew truth when she saw it, especially when it was linked to personal pain. Jasmin cared too much, and down in the basement when she had first confided in Flora, she had been unable to hide just how much.

'There you are,' Flora whispered, zooming in on the image on her screen. 'Not so much plunderer as plundered,' she said to herself, bookmarking yet another website before she finally sat back, satisfied. She glanced at her watch, wondering where Marshall had got to, then jumped when her phone beeped.

An unknown number appeared with a text, and Flora opened it with a frown.

Dear Flora, it read. I have to go away for a short time. I will be back, I promise. Yours, John Hopper.

She pursed her lips. Such a formal text message. And so frustrating – leaving too many questions unanswered.

Why was he going away? Where to? Why didn't he come and tell her himself, in person?

She was composing a reply when she noticed the little red dot indicating other messages she'd missed while she'd been on the call with Professor Paulson. Five messages, all from Marshall. Flora sighed and opened them up. Each text was a single word, sent in quick succession.

Sorry
For
Being
A
Dick

Flora smiled and shook her head. It didn't seem to matter what he did, she couldn't stay mad at him for long. And nor could he, it seemed, stay mad at her.

***

'Hey you.'

'Hey yourself.'

Flora grinned and leaned back against the wall of her building. She was headed to the warehouse to check on Nick, but seeing Marshall hanging around outside wasn't a total surprise. In fact, it wasn't a surprise at all – she'd watched from her vantage point in the window of the penthouse as he crossed the bridge, half hidden by the enormous bunch of flowers he was now gripping awkwardly, as though he had been caught stealing candy. He was still wearing the same clothes he'd been in that morning, but as well as buying flowers he'd also found time to get a haircut. He looked handsome, and more upbeat somehow. Like a weight had been lifted. His stride over the bridge had been purposeful, and Flora, after only a moment's hesitation, had quickly changed her top and thrown on white sandals, finishing with a spray of Marshall's favourite perfume.

'What you got there?' Flora said. On her way down the stairs she'd added lip gloss and fluffed up her hair. Now though, she feigned disinterest, glancing at her nails then looking up at the darkening sky.

'Nothing,' Marshall said, then he looked at the flowers like he was seeing them for the first time. 'Oh, these! I found them. They looked like they needed a home, thought you might want to oblige.'

'I guess I could,' Flora said nonchalantly. 'If they're going spare.'

Marshall shrugged, kicking at a stone. 'I could bring them upstairs if you like.'

'Are they heavy? Do you think I need help carrying them?'

'I think you might, yeah.'

'Oh, well. In that case.'

In a heartbeat, Marshall was in front of her, lifting her off the ground into his embrace. Flora breathed in his scent, allowing herself a full minute of bliss. She kissed him on the lips, then wriggled a little to signal her desire to be put down.

'Those flowers are ruined,' she observed, pulling a sad face. Marshall had dropped them in his haste to pick her up, and at least two of the larger roses had been crushed underfoot.

'I'll buy you some more,' he countered.

'Damn right you will.'.

'Look, Flora, I need to say something.'

'You didn't say enough already?'

Marshall gave her a wry smile. 'I guess I didn't. I'm sorry, sweetheart. The stuff I said last night, it was unforgivable.'

'That's probably why I don't forgive you,' Flora smirked.

'Can we go inside?' Marshall asked. 'It's kinda hard to do this out here. I can feel at least five pairs of eyes on me.'

'My neighbours are fascinated by you, you know. You're what passes for exotic around here.'

'After we get these in water, I'd like to take you out to dinner,' Marshall said, holding open the entrance door.

'And I'd like to eat dinner. But I need to go check on Nick first. And I think we owe him an apology. Oh, and by "we", I mean "you".'

'Already done, my tiny little piece of dynamite.'

Flora stopped halfway up the stairs and gazed at her boyfriend, wide-eyed. 'You apologised to *Nick*?'

'Sure did. He took it well. Better than you. Far more graciously.'

Flora laughed out loud. It felt good.

'Oh my god. Marshall Goodman finally learns the art of humility.'

'Wanna see what else I can do?'

'Sure,' Flora said, shrugging. 'Knock yourself out.'

Marshall grinned. He came towards her in a low crouch, grabbed her upper legs and threw her back over his shoulder. Flora squealed in delight as he carried her on up the stairs to her apartment.

'It's just like in a film,' she laughed. 'My neighbours will think you're truly crazy now.'

'Crazy for you, Miss Lively,' Marshall said, setting her down gently outside the peacock blue door.

And for a short while Flora forgot their differences, and forgot all about Lamassu and murders and plundered antiquities. It was just her and Marshall, doing what they seemed to do best.

***

Dinner in a fancy restaurant wasn't their style, but takeout pizza washed down with a nice bottle of red in candlelight definitely was.

'Have you made any progress on your case?' Marshall asked as he threw the discarded pieces of crust inside the pizza box and folded it shut. Flora all but choked on her wine.

'Seriously?'

'What? I'm interested.'

Flora regarded him doubtfully, but Marshall insisted.

'My mom used to say, "If you can't beat em, join em". I figure that applies as much here as anywhere.' He grinned. 'Come on, you're dying to tell me, ain't ya?'

He knew her so well. Wrapping herself in a throw and snuggling into Marshall's side, Flora recounted her session with Professor Paulson in as much detail as she could remember. She even told him about meeting up with Heston, watching closely for jealous Marshall to re-emerge, ready to bolt at the first sign of trouble. But his body language remained relaxed, and he merely smiled at the mention of her ex. Flora should have known better. Marshall might be thrown off by a guy like Nick, but Heston was no threat.

'I did a bit more digging after I came off the Skype call,' Flora continued, nodding for Marshall to top up her wine.

'And?'

'Well, it wasn't that hard to find out more about Lucy Akopian.'

'She was the lady that got herself murdered, right?' Marshall interrupted.

'Exactly. Well, Lucy's husband Fed Akopian went missing in nineteen-eighty-two on an expedition to Peru. There's no mention of him being with either Jasmin or a young assistant in the records. Lucy divorced him in his absence, and he was presumed dead. But in the list of Fed's fellow explorers on the Peru expedition is the name Yasemin Beyaz. Interesting, don't you think?'

Marshall looked confused. 'Erm, yes? But hang on, what did you mean about a young assistant?'

'Oh, sorry. I forgot you're not completely up to date with Jasmin's story.' Flora quickly filled him in on the information she'd gleaned from their employer to date, including the conflicting stories about the provenance of the Lamassu tablet. 'First off, she told me that it had been in her family for hundreds of years. Then, after she'd been interviewed by that detective, she claimed that she'd lied to me and it was an artefact that she and Lucy had stolen together. Acquired, was how she described it, and not entirely legally.'

'Why would she admit that?' Marshall said, still frowning.

'I have a theory,' Flora said with a heavy sigh. 'It pains me to admit it, but it is starting to look as though our Jasmin isn't the innocent party she's made herself out to be.'

Marshall gave her a consoling hug. 'Not everything is how it seems on the surface,' he said gravely. Flora wondered if this were a veiled reference to John Hopper, but if it was, Marshall kept the rest of his thoughts to himself for once. 'Tell me more about this name you found,' Marshall prompted. 'Yasemin, did you say? That's similar to Jasmin, right?'

'Right!' Flora grabbed her notebook and quickly rifled through the first few pages. 'Not only is it similar, it's actually the Turkish version of the name. And …' she paused for effect, but it wasn't necessary: Marshall was hanging on her every word. 'The surname Beyaz – Beyaz is Turkish for white.'

'Okay,' Marshall said slowly. 'So you think Jasmin White's real name is Yasemin Beyaz. And this Yasemin was on the expedition to Peru when Lucy's husband went missing.'

'Fed Akopian,' Flora put in.

'Who Jasmin, or possibly Yasemin, was having an affair with.'

'I think it had moved on from a mere affair by then,' Flora said. 'Lucy was long gone. Fed and Jasmin were an item. There's more,' she added.

'Go on.'

Flora allowed herself a fleeting smile. She'd never seen Marshall so entranced before.

'You remember the night that I stayed in the museum on my own? It was the fourth night, and I was convinced that the noises were just an anomaly because Nick hadn't heard them on his watch. Of course, we now know that this was just because he'd had music blaring in his ears and was feeding his Candy Crush addiction.'

Marshall rolled his eyes at Nick's fecklessness, but thankfully resisted any urge to comment.

'I took the opportunity to do a bit of investigating,' Flora continued, 'and had a look through the filing cabinet in Jasmin's office.' Noting Marshall's smirk, Flora added, 'Well, I found keys in the desk. I only had to break into one of the drawers.'

Marshall laughed out loud and planted a kiss on Flora's head. 'You are adorable,' he said. 'There really are no lengths you won't go to, are there?'

Flora tried to unpick this double-negative, while also wondering what had brought on Marshall's change of heart. He had gone from embarrassed to cheering in less than twenty-four hours, and nice though it was, Flora couldn't entirely trust it.

'And what did you find in the filing cabinet, honey?'

Flora brought herself back to the present. 'I think it was in the personnel files, but I'm not completely sure. It was very soon after that I heard the screaming sound again, and that threw me. But I am sure I saw the name Beyaz in Jasmin's records. I remember the elaborate Z. There's no doubt in my mind doubt that Yasemin and Jasmin are the same person.'

'What does it all mean, sweetheart?' Marshall said, pulling her into his chest and stroking her hair. 'Do you think Jasmin is guilty?'

'She's guilty of something, I'm sure of that,' Flora murmured. 'Maybe not murder, but possibly something worse.'

'Worse than murder? What could be worse than murder?'

Flora closed her eyes, thinking about Professor Paulson and Francis Bacon. 'There are other ways to be responsible for a death,' she said softly. 'Or even many deaths.'

'That's very cryptic,' Marshall whispered, kissing her face gently.

'Do you believe in curses?' Flora said, tilting her head to meet his lips full on.

In lieu of an answer, Marshall took her into his embrace. The converted school building was quiet at night; up here in the penthouse apartment you could be anywhere. Safe and sound, far removed from all the strangeness and danger in the world. In the distance, the clock tower above the Market Hall began to strike midnight. She smiled as she sank further into Marshall's kisses. This was them at their best, connected and happy, all conflict forgotten. She allowed Marshall to lift up her arms and slide her T-shirt over her head. But part of her mind was still counting the chimes. She just couldn't help it.

Chapter 16

The following morning, Flora and Marshall left early to relieve Nick of his night duty. They took a brisk walk across town, hand in hand, sharing smug glances when each remembered the passion of the night before. Flora felt a new bounce in her step, and Marshall seemed more relaxed than she'd seen him in weeks. She had already forgiven him for his harsh words. Sticks and stones – her parents had always believed in forgiving words spoken in anger. Flora was wise enough to know that if she and Marshall were to have any future together, they would both have to learn to let a lot of disagreements go. Their relationship would consist of nothing but conflict otherwise.

Outside Shaker's warehouse, a young woman was banging on the metal shutters.

'Can we help you?' Flora said. Marshall took out his keys and unlocked the smaller door to the side.

'Are you Flora?' the woman said, glaring over her shoulder. 'Is my Nick is in there? He's not answering his phone.'

'Oh, hi,' Flora said. 'I didn't know … I mean, are you Nick's …?' She tailed off, hoping the young woman would fill in the blank. Sister? Girlfriend? Personal trainer? The latter was certainly possible: Nick's early morning visitor rocked her cropped bra top and skin-tight leggings, paired with a loose-fitting windbreaker and designer running shoes.

'I'm Cady,' she said, banging a fist on the shutters again, even though Marshall was now standing holding open the personal door. 'Nick's girlfriend.'

Flora and Marshall exchanged a glance. He had never mentioned a girlfriend.

'Hey, buddy,' Marshall called, walking into the dimly lit warehouse. 'You decent?'

'He's probably gone home already,' Flora said, following him inside.

'My Friend Locator says he's here,' Cady replied definitively, hot on Flora's heels. 'And he always answers when *I* call him.'

'What's a Friend Locator?' Flora asked while Marshall checked the cab, then joined them at the rear of the lorry. Cady held up her phone and pointed to a little arrow on the screen.

'It's a tracker. And it shows that he's still here, with his phone.'

Another glance passed between Flora and Marshall. A tracker? Really?

'Well, he's probably just fallen asleep,' Marshall said, rattling the metal doors at the back of the van. 'Hey, Nick mate. Open up. You've got a search party out for you.'

There was no sound from inside. Flora began to feel uneasy.

'Are you absolutely sure he's still here?' she asked Nick's girlfriend, who merely held up her phone and pointed once again at the screen. 'Right,' Flora nodded. 'The tracker. Okay, well we're gonna have to get inside the lorry somehow.'

'I'm on it,' Marshall said, jogging to the back of the warehouse. 'Gonna grab a crowbar. Those doors are latched from the inside.'

'What if he's ill?' Cady cried. 'What if he had another heart attack?'

'*Another* heart attack?' Flora echoed.

'He has a weak heart.'

This was news to Flora. Marshall returned with the crowbar and slid it into the narrow gap between the lorry doors. He grunted, then dragged the set of steps over, before trying again.

'Need more leverage,' he said through gritted teeth. And then, 'Ah, there she goes.'

As Marshall stepped down, the lorry doors swung slowly outward. Light penetrated the interior of the container a little at a time, first showing the stacked crates near the entrance, then illuminating further inside, as Flora and Cady craned their necks to see.

'Oh!' Cady exclaimed, her hands flying up to her mouth. 'Oh, Nick! Oh my god, no!'

Lying face down with his upper body slumped on top of a crate lay their night guard. The back of his head appeared sticky, as though some kind of red-brown gel had been thrown over him. It only took a second for Flora to realise this was blood. As if in slow motion, she took in the entire macabre scene. The suit of armour, uncovered now and leaning over Nick in a mock-menacing pose; the footprints in the dust; the heavy metal sword, also smeared with blood, lying with its hilt right next to Nick's unmoving head.

It seemed as though Flora was hearing the screaming sounds again, and she wondered through her confusion how it could be that the noises from the museum had followed them here. It wasn't midnight. It wasn't dark. But then the world came back into focus and she realised the screaming was coming from a source right by her side. Cady, her mouth stretched open, her eyes wide, threw herself forwards and began to scramble into the van, her fingers clawing for purchase.

'You need to stop her,' Flora said to Marshall, who stood immobile, still gripping the crowbar. She was surprised at how calm her voice sounded. 'She mustn't touch anything. And we need to call the police.'

Marshall nodded and moved to Cady's side. She fought him off at first, but then collapsed against him, still crying Nick's name. Flora pulled out her phone and began to dial. But then something close to Nick's body caught her eye.

'Emergency. Which service?'

'Police,' Flora said. And then, focusing in more closely, she added, 'And an ambulance. Yes, we definitely need an ambulance.'

***

'Thank heavens he's okay.'

Flora nodded, but then remembered she was on the phone and Jasmin couldn't see her. 'Yes. You've no idea how frightening it was. I thought–'

'You thought it was the Sign of Seven?' Jasmin interrupted.

'He was just lying there, with his head all smashed in.'

'My dear. That must have been awful.'

'It looked as though the suit of armour had come alive and killed him!' Flora said with a shudder.

'Oh, that old thing wouldn't hurt a fly,' Jasmin exclaimed. 'Now, if it had been the Ötzi mummy, that would have been another story all together.'

Flora looked at the phone, then shook her head.

'The important thing is that Nick is alright,' she said. 'He's stable, anyway. The police think that the armour fell on him knocked him out. He had a really bad gash on his head.'

Nick was yet to wake up fully; Cady had gone with him to the hospital, agreeing to call Flora as soon as she had news.

'He'll likely have a concussion, and a hell of a headache when he does wake up,' Flora added. 'But at least we know it was just an accident. Not the so-called curse.'

She had been so relieved to see Nick's fingers moving – just the tiniest movement, barely perceptible in the dim light, but enough to galvanise them all into action. Flora knew that if it hadn't been for the curse, and Lucy Akopian's murder, she and Marshall would have dived into the lorry at once to check for a pulse. It had been too easy to assume that Nick had met with a similar fate.

Jasmin made a strange scoffing noise on the other end of the line. She said, 'Well, it wasn't just an accident, Flora. We both know that.'

'What are you talking about?' Flora threw Marshall a look – he was casually chatting to Detective Inspector Sarah Buxton, laughing at something she'd said and leaning with one foot up on the steps, knee bent, in that showy masculine way men had when they wanted to impress.

'The Sign of Seven, Flora,' Jasmin continued. 'This happened to Nick on the seventh night. That means the curse is satisfied. You have nothing else to worry about. It makes sense, of course it does,' she added as though to herself.

'What does?' Flora asked.

'Well, I assumed that you were the guardian because you were in charge of the collection when the Lamassu went missing. But I'd forgotten about your young night guard. He was the guardian after all! And now the Lamassu has had its revenge.'

Flora shook her head in irritation. 'But you said that someone would die on the seventh night. Nick didn't die, and nobody tried to kill him. It was just a stupid accident.'

'If you want to believe that, Flora, I can't stop you. But we both know that the curse is real.'

Jasmin rang off before Flora could reply.

'Ugh, she is so annoying,' Flora exclaimed. Then she bit her lip, momentarily puzzled. Marshall glanced over, quickly stepping away from the attractive young detective when he saw Flora's expression.

'You okay?' he asked.

'Yeah. I think so. I just heard ... No, it must be a coincidence.'

'You're not making any sense.' Marshall told her.

'I thought I heard a man's voice when I was on the phone to Jasmin just now,' Flora said. 'But it might have just been the radio or the TV or something.'

'A man's voice,' Marshall said. 'That's interesting.'

Flora shot him a look as Sarah Buxton joined them, shoving her phone into the pocket of her navy jacket. In jeans, white shirt and boots, she didn't look like most plain-clothed police Flora had met. The D.I. was positively stylish.

'Was that your esteemed client on the phone?' she asked Flora, who nodded in response. 'And I suppose she's still claiming to know nothing about the incident at the museum?' The detective frowned when Flora confirmed that yes, this was indeed Jasmin's position. 'You seem like nice people,' Sarah Buxton said, looking from Flora to Marshall and back again. 'You shouldn't get mixed up in stuff that doesn't concern you.'

'Jeez, how many times have I heard that?' Flora huffed when the detective had left the warehouse.

'Not enough to take any notice,' Marshall joked. 'Hey, I'm kidding!'

'Ha. Very funny. What did you mean just now?'

'What's that honey?' Marshall said, running his fingers through his already tousled hair. 'What a day. And it's not even lunchtime yet.'

'Just before. You said something about the man's voice, that it was "interesting".'

'Ah.' Marshall's expression became grave. 'Look, Flora, you're not going to like what I've got to say, but just hear me out. I know that this is a touchy subject for us, but I wouldn't be doing my job – and by that I mean caring for the woman I love – if I didn't say this. Is that okay with you?'

Flora nodded mutely. She was both anxious and

touched. Marshall didn't often use the L-word. He must be really worried about her reaction.

It was obviously going to be about John Hopper.

'It's about the man who claims to be your dad,' Marshall began.

'He says he's my birth father,' Flora corrected. 'Not my dad.'

'Right. Look, has it occurred to you that the timing here is a little off? He turns up just at the point when you're doing this museum job and someone gets murdered and a priceless artefact goes missing?'

Flora had stayed awake nights thinking about this very thing. She said, 'No. That hasn't occurred to me at all. Because there is no connection.'

Marshall nodded. 'Sure. I understand. It's not nice to think of it. But, Flora, you need to be careful. You're practically a public figure – it wouldn't be difficult for someone to find out about your past if they wanted to gain your trust. There is the possibility that this man might be involved somehow. He could be the man Jasmin was with on the night of the murder, have your considered that? Or, I don't know, perhaps he saw the murder while he was hanging around. Or saw something else important.'

'If that was the case, he would have told me,' Flora countered.

'Not if he was there for reasons he wants to keep secret. Say, for example, to steal something from the museum. It could even have been opportunistic. Maybe that's where your missing Lamassu went, and now he's checking that you haven't yet tracked it down.'

'Well, he's not doing a very good job of checking because he's gone away,' Flora said, sounding more triumphant than she felt.

'Oh. Has he? I'm sorry, Flora.'

Flora didn't want to have this conversation again. Things were good, despite the drama of the morning so far. She gave Marshall a hug and told him thanks for being concerned, but there was no need to worry.

There *was* no need to worry.

But throughout the rest of the day, no matter what she was doing her mind kept returning to Marshall's theory. What did she really know about John Hopper? Was it a coincidence that he'd appeared for the first time on the night of the murder? He *was* vague about his past – and also about his present. Could Marshall be right?

And there was also the thing that Marshall didn't know, that Flora couldn't bring herself to mention. The voice she'd heard in the background while talking to Jasmin had sounded distinctly familiar. Flora could not be certain where she'd heard it before, but she was pretty sure she had. She didn't *think* it was John Hopper, but she had to consider the possibility.

Flora was convinced that this man was indeed her birth father. But what if her birth father was also a thief? Or worse?

Chapter 17

Marshall locked the office door, then jumped down the metal steps two at a time, filling the warehouse with an echoing clatter.

'Easy tiger,' Flora laughed. 'Anyone would think you were eager to get going.'

He swung her into a happy embrace, planting her down again next to the passenger door of the lorry.

'Hop in, sweetheart. Next stop the big smoke.'

Flora creased up at his attempt at a London accent.

'What's up me love?' he said, the mock-cockney even more pronounced. 'Sum fin wrong with me noggin?'

'Oh my god. You'll be the death of me. Clearly you watched too much Mary Poppins growing up,' Flora said, grinning. 'No one in the whole of the UK sounds like that.'

'Are you sure?' Marshall said, his usual drawl back to normal.

'Quite sure.'

'"Quite sure",' Marshall mimicked in clipped English. 'I do not speak that way!'

Marshall just winked at her.

A voice from the warehouse door called their attention. Flora turned, her heart sinking when she saw the elegant figure in white hovering by the entrance. It was only natural that Jasmin would want to say goodbye to her collection, but she was the last person Flora wanted to see today.

'Hi,' Flora said weakly.

'Wotcha,' Marshall said. Flora elbowed him in the ribs.

'Any news on your young man?' Jasmin asked, walking delicately across the dusty warehouse.

'He's right here,' Marshall joked. Flora elbowed him again and said, 'If you mean Nick, then no, there isn't much news. He woke up briefly earlier, but that's all I know.'

'Poor boy,' Jasmin cooed, her big brown eyes doleful.

'He'll be fine,' Marshall assured her. 'Big strapping "young man" like that – he'll bounce back in no time.'

Flora rolled her eyes. 'Anyway, thanks for asking after Nick. His girlfriend said he'll be out of hospital in a day or two, and he'll make a full recovery.'

'And did he say anything?' Jasmin inquired. 'About what happened?'

'You mean how he managed to knock over a suit of armour and get himself knocked out?' Marshall joked. 'I think he's gonna want to say as little about that as possible.'

'Hmm. Quite.' Jasmin gazed at her hands. 'Well, Flora, I'm sure you'll be perfectly safe now. There's absolutely nothing to worry about.'

Until the older woman said that, Flora hadn't been worried. But now she was imagining the collection coming to life on the motorway; visions of that horrible little doll possessed and climbing into the driver's cab filled her mind.

Well, okay. We'll be setting off in a few minutes,' she said, giving herself a brisk shake. 'The collection is all packed up, safe and sound.'

Jasmin eyed the padlocked lorry. 'May I go inside for a few minutes? I would really like to be alone with my beloved friends just one last time.'

'No can do, sorry,' Marshall said. He didn't sound sorry at all. 'She's locked and loaded and ready to roll.'

Jasmin took a step closer to the container and laid a gloved hand on one of the doors. She whispered something under her breath, but it was in a language

Flora didn't understand.

'Do you have time for a quick coffee before you set off?' Jasmin said. She seemed to be directing this at Flora alone, but Flora answered for the two of them.

'We really do have to get going, sorry.'

'Can't let this one have too many liquids or she'll be wanting to stop at every gas station from here to London.'

'Marshall!' Honestly, she almost preferred him when he was grumpy.

'So,' Flora said, feeling a little awkward now that it was time to say goodbye. She wondered what would happen now that she'd failed to find the missing Lamassu. Would Jasmin be forced to report it to the police? Or maybe she already had. You couldn't really keep something like that quiet, not when there had been a murder. Flora remembered Sarah Buxton's words during that first meeting: *You're being played.* Was that true? But if so, why? What exactly had Flora's role in all of this been?

'You know,' Jasmin said, stopping by the door and turning back with the serene smile still in place. 'I think I've changed my mind.'

Marshall and Flora stared at her with identical expressions of confusion. For a horrible moment, Flora thought that the woman meant she'd changed her mind about London. That she'd want them to reinstall the entire collection back in that awful spooky old museum, with night shifts and crazy noises and clocks that never chimed midnight. She imagined herself stuck in a loop of endless packing and unpacking for the rest of her life.

But then, she thought, wasn't that the very nature of owning a removals firm? A continuous loop of packing and unpacking. She sighed, her shoulders drooping.

'What do you mean?' Marshall said warily.

'I mean that I plan to come to London after all,' Jasmin said. 'Yes! It's decided. I'll pay a visit to the capital before I leave – there's somewhere I've always wanted to visit, so I'll be able to kill two birds with one stone, as you say. So, I'll see you there, Flora. Marshall.'

'Ah, Jesus,' Marshall muttered. 'Just what we need. Her breathing down our necks for the next two days.'

'Yeah,' Flora said, distracted. She watched Jasmin pick her way carefully over the lip at the bottom of the warehouse door. A gust of wind caught the immaculate white coat, billowing it out behind her like a superhero cape. 'But the real question is, why did she suddenly change her mind?'

'Search me. She's bat shit crazy to be so attached to this old heap of rubbish, if you ask me.'

Flora stared at her boyfriend for a moment. She nodded once, then turned on her heel and jogged to the door.

'Jasmin, wait!' Flora called. Wow, she sure moved fast for an older lady. Panting heavily, Flora caught her on the far side of the car park. 'About that coffee,' she said. 'I think I can make a bit of time after all.'

***

Jasmin insisted on taking Flora to the museum, grabbing takeout coffees on the way. Flora had no choice but to agree, annoyed at herself already for acting on impulse, and she was impatient and snappy in the line at Costa, while Jasmin waited outside in the car.

'A man is coming to check the electricity,' Jasmin said by way of explanation, and she drove at lightning speed through Shrewsbury's narrow streets, jerking the car into its tiny parking space behind the museum so swiftly that Flora barely had time to balance their cups.

Inside, they sat where the ticket area had been, sipping in silence for a few minutes. Flora steeled herself. It was time to get this done.

'Jasmin,' she began, 'there's something I need to ask

you.'

'What's that, my dear?'

'Is your name really Yasemin Beyaz?'

As soon as the words were out of Flora's mouth, she knew she was right. More than that, she knew that the name was something Jasmin had hoped to keep secret. It had been no more than a theory, but the look on Jasmin's face confirmed it. The expression of confusion that now clouded her features had replaced an initial reaction that was impossible to miss.

Jasmin's first reaction had been one of unmistakable fear.

'How did you find that name?' Jasmin said quietly. 'Were you prying? Have you been looking into my personal information?'

'I was investigating,' Flora said. 'Like you asked me to.'

'I asked you to find a missing artefact, not to pry into my private heritage.'

Flora didn't answer. She reflected that the two now seemed to be one and the same thing. Instead she asked the burning question that was foremost on her mind. 'Why did you change your name?'

'It is not unusual to change one's name,' Jasmin replied coolly. She threw back her long hair, a curtain of silk over one elegant shoulder. 'Was that why you ran after me today? To ask about my given name?'

'Not just that,' Flora admitted. 'I wanted to talk to you about something else as well.' Now it would get really awkward. But it had to be done. 'It's about the Lamassu,' she said quietly.

'Have you found it?' Jasmin shot upright, nearly spilling her coffee over her long white skirt.

'No. No, I haven't. But I think I know why.'

'Go on.'

Flora took a deep breath. 'I think I haven't found it because ... because it isn't missing.'

She watched the older woman's face closely, but this time her composure didn't slip for a second.

'Not missing? I don't understand.'

Flora folded her hands calmly in her lap. 'Well, I haven't figured out all the details yet, but here is what I think I know. I think you used the death of Lucy Akopian to fake a burglary and say that the Lamassu was now missing. That's what my gut tells me, and the facts seem to fit. You didn't do this for insurance money, obviously, as you chose not to declare it. Instead, you asked me to investigate. I'm guessing that this was some kind of protection in case you were found out, exposed. You could claim genuine innocence by pointing to the fact that you hired me to find the tablet.'

'"Faked a burglary"?' Jasmin echoed, her confused expression turning to one of disbelief. 'I don't know what you are saying, Flora. Why are you saying this to me?'

'Look,' Flora began, 'my feeling is that the Lamassu wasn't necessarily in the museum to begin with. At least, it wasn't on display. You had it somewhere safe – somewhere very safe. Safer than being in a flimsy glass cabinet for anyone to see, and potentially steal. I'm thinking that maybe somebody else was after it, someone who knew that you had it and shouldn't have had it, and that you knew the Lamassu was at risk of being stolen. Maybe it was your old business partner, or someone else from your past. So, when Lucy was killed, and the museum broken into, you decided to take the opportunity to claim that the Lamassu had been taken. Even though it hadn't.'

'That makes no sense,' Jasmin asserted hotly. 'If, as you say, I wanted the world to know that the Seventh Tablet of Lamassu was stolen, why have I kept it a secret from everyone except you?'

Flora frowned. This was something she hadn't worked out yet, and it irked her that Jasmin had got there so fast.

'I don't know,' she confessed, 'but I'm sure you have a reason. The thing is—'

Jasmin cut Flora off with a wave of her hand. 'This is how you repay me? I give you a job, a well-paid job, and I give you the chance to investigate a real mystery, and you repay me my blaming it on me, your employer? I am too shocked to look at you.' Dramatically, the woman turned away, her chin tilted towards the ornate ceiling.

'I'm sorry,' Flora said. 'It's just that none of this makes any sense unless the Lamassu is really—'

'I do not want to hear any more of this nonsense. I think you should leave.' Standing, Jasmin added, 'I'm afraid I won't be giving you a lift back to your warehouse. I find that I am far too angry.'

Flora couldn't help admiring the woman for her composure under stress. 'I'm happy to walk back,' she murmured. She placed her coffee on the window sill and took a step towards the door. 'Look,' she said. 'I'm sorry if I've caused offence, but you did ask me to investigate this and—'

'And I'm beginning to see that this was a mistake,' Jasmin stated, her brown eyes cold and narrow. 'The sooner Shakers Removals is out of my life the better – it is you who are responsible for the missing Lamassu, and as far as I'm concerned you are also responsible for the murder of dear Lucy. If you'd been doing your job properly, none of this would ever have happened.'

'That's outrageous,' Flora cried. 'You can't blame this on us. We've been on the back foot from the start – you haven't been honest with us, Jasmin. You've held onto essential information that could have really helped me get to the bottom of things.'

'Honest? I've been nothing but honest and everything I have done is completely correct.'

'Oh, really?' Flora was very close to losing her temper now. She began to tick items off on her fingers. 'Your real name, that fact that you did know who the murdered woman was, the true history of the Lamassu – one minute it's your precious heritage, the next it's just something you and a Lucy stole together. Telling me it was in the collection all along when there is no record of it in my inventory, the identity of the man you were with on the night Lucy was killed ...' Flora tailed off, thinking again about John Hopper and his mysterious appearance that night. Nick has seen him outside the museum, hadn't he? So John couldn't have been the man Jasmin was with. That, at least, was a huge relief.

Jasmin's composure was also beginning to slip. 'I want you out of here right now,' she hissed. 'And if there are any more mishaps with my collection then the whole world will know just how incompetent Shakers Removals really is. I will sue you, I will go to the newspapers, I will smear your name everywhere I go.'

Horrified, Flora almost ran out of the museum, blinking back tears of frustration. She thought about her dad, the only dad she'd ever known, who had built up this business from nothing. If she single-handedly brought it to ruination because of her vanity and her crazy ideas about being an investigator, it wasn't only Marshall who wouldn't forgive her. Letting Peter Lively down was the worst thing Flora could do. She would never forgive herself.

She was halfway across town before her breathing returned to normal. Her stride slowed and she ran a hand through her tousled hair. Ugh, that woman! She was so slippery it was almost impossible to get a handle on what was really going on. Flora thrust her hands deep into her pockets and clenched her teeth. They had to finish this job, she mused, and they had to do it perfectly. Absolutely without a hitch. And there must be no more run-ins with Jasmin, no mix-ups or mess-ups, and no conflict whatsoever.

Which was not going to be easy, however you looked

at it.

As Flora weaved her way through Shrewsbury's busy town centre, dodging shoppers and pushchairs and bicycles and groups of languid teenagers, she reflected that she really wasn't cut out for this investigating malarkey at all. Packing and unpacking people's houses was so much easier, even with all their emotional baggage and stresses and finicky requests.

'I'll go back to it, dad, I promise I will,' she whispered under her breath. 'Just let me get through this intact. And then, it'll be back to the old Shakers. Domestic moves all the way.'

And then her thoughts turned to John Hopper again; the other dad, the one who may have started it all. She clenched her fists inside her pockets and leaned in to climb the steep hill ahead.

Chapter 18

'Are you ready to talk about it yet?'

Flora shook her head. She slumped even further into the passenger seat and gazed hard out of the window. Marshall drove on in silence.

The English countryside drifted past, flat and indifferent. They'd left Shropshire behind a while back, speeding through a bit of Staffordshire, flying past the West Midlands, and now this featureless stretch of fields flanked by banks of trees. An hour into their journey and Flora hadn't said a word. She watched the scenery, glanced down into people's cars, and tried hard to forget the horrible scene at the museum with Jasmin.

'You're gonna have to tell me sooner or later,' Marshall said in a sing-song voice. 'Flora Lively can't keep anything in for long.'

Flora pulled a face. He was right. But every time she opened her mouth, she just about shrivelled up with shame. Ugh, it was a nightmare. The whole sorry affair, from beginning to end, was a complete and utter …

'Look, honey. That license plate spells BUM.'

Flora looked up and smiled. Marshall cuffed her cheek gently, not taking his eyes off the road.

'Ah, I knew that'd cheer you up. You Brits, you can't resist words like bum and poo. It's a cultural thing.'

'It is not!' Flora exclaimed. Then she caught his grin and smiled despite herself. He was so good at getting her out of a funk. Good at getting her into one as well, of course, but equally good at getting her out.

'Grab a drink and then tell me what happened,' Marshall instructed, gesturing to the flask he'd brought along for the journey. Flora did as she was told, grimacing at the bitter coffee but finishing her cup regardless.

'So?' he prompted. 'Spill the beans. Last I saw you

were running after old Jasmin there like you had ants in your pants. Then you turn up an hour later balling your eyes out saying you've ruined our lives. Or our livelihoods. Or some such rubbish. Come on, sweetheart.' Marshall reached over and rubbed her leg. 'Tell your fella all about it.'

Flora took a deep breath, then sighed it out. 'Sure. Okay, fine.' She shuffled until she was sitting more upright, quickly checking her hair in the visor mirror. God, she looked a mess. Her eyes were puffy and her skin looked like it hadn't seen the sun in months.

'Why did you go after her, is what I want to know?' Marshall said, indicating to pull out of the inside lane after coming up behind a car doing little over thirty miles an hour. 'Hey, you should walk, you'd get there faster,' he shouted at his rear view mirror.

'It was what you said about how attached she was to this old heap of rubbish, actually,' Flora began. 'And something that had been bothering me from the very start.'

'What was that, honey?'

'Well, this Lamassu tablet was super-important and super-valuable, right? At first, I wondered why she wouldn't just take it overseas with her, if it was that special, but then figured you can't really, can you? You can't just stick something like that in your underwear drawer and hope for the best.'

'Is that where you keep your priceless valuables? Your underwear drawer?' Marshall winked.

'Funny. The thing is, when Jasmin first told me about the missing Lamassu, I swear she was completely genuine. She was scared and confused and desperate. She reached out to me, not just because of my background – as she saw it – in helping solve crimes, but most likely because I just happened to be there. The right place at the right time,' Flora mused. She turned to him and shook her head. 'I'm telling you, Marshall, the story she told about the tablet being in her family for generations – I believed her.'

'Even though she's admitted since that it was a lie?'

'I told you, she did that to throw me off.' Flora settled back, getting into her stride. 'You know I did some research after speaking with that professor? I remembered something that Jasmin had said when she first told me about Lamassu. Not *the* Lamassu, but them in general. She'd told me about an ancient statue being defaced by Isis a few years back. I decided to look that up. And guess what I found?'

Marshall shot her a puzzled frown. 'That Jasmin is a member of Isis?'

'No, dummy!' Flora laughed. 'I found a news report from when it happened. It was pretty shocking, actually – these men with power drills just hacking away at the face of this majestic winged bull creature.' The smile fell from her face. 'Imagine if that was your heritage. This wanton destruction of something that had stood there for thousands of years, surviving wars and storms and every kind of change possible.'

'It's stupid, is what it is.'

Flora nodded. 'It was all over the news at the time, and I looked at the articles for a bit, just shocked really. But then I saw it.'

'What?'

'A photo taken by someone on the ground. And there, in the crowd, clear as day, is Jasmin.'

Marshall looked across at her. 'So?'

'So, she was there! She saw it happen. It wasn't just something that took place on the other side of the world, that she read about in the papers. It happened *to her.* In this photograph you can see the expression on her face. She looks devastated. And something else. I want to say outraged, but it wasn't quite that. There was a bit of fury, but also something else. She looked like she wanted to … Oh, I don't know …'

'Get revenge?' Marshall offered.

Flora sat up, her eyes wide. 'Yes! Yes, that's it exactly. Jasmin was there, watching that happen, and she looked completely devastated, but also vengeful. This Lamassu business, it's personal to her. Marshall, I'm telling you, this was not just some artefact she "acquired" when she hung out with Lucy Akopian. This thing, whatever it is, means *everything* to her.'

'Then why would she give it to the British Museum?'

'Not give, sell,' Flora said. 'That was something else I found out. People "gift" things to museums all the time, but they don't really. Money changes hands. It was a taxi driver tipped me off to that, actually. He was going on about fakes, about how a big museum had bought one and there was a huge scandal. I looked it up. It was called the Amarna Princess. Some bloke sold it to a museum in Manchester for four-hundred-and-forty-*thousand* pounds.'

Marshall whistled. 'Nice work if you can get it.'

'He got four years in prison for it,' Flora said.

'Ouch.'

'Good at forgeries, bad at not getting caught,' she quipped. 'But that got me thinking about the reason Jasmin might be willing to give up the Lamassu tablet. I mean, she's in a right mess financially. She's got bills going back years, and–'

'She told you all this did she?' Marshall interrupted, pursing his lips. 'Or did you find out by snooping?'

'Not snooping, investigating. And you're gonna have to admit soon that I am quite good at it. Anyway,' Flora continued when Marshall said nothing, 'once I had that little inconsistency cleared up, the rest was easy to slot into place. Jasmin pretends to everyone that the Lamassu tablet is part of her collection, just another artefact that she's acquired on her travels – and no one asks questions, because everyone in the art and antiquities world knows that trade was completely unregulated before the nineteen-seventy UNESCO convention, and–'

'You really have been doing your research on this one, haven't you?' Marshall cut in, sounding impressed.

'Like you would not believe. The law on "Ownership of Cultural Property" is pretty tight now, but trade in illicit antiquities carries on, they just keep it under the radar. Hence all the so-called gifts to museums. Well, that's one theory, anyway. I'm not an expert. But one thing that bugged me was why the Lamassu wasn't in the collection when we did our initial inventory. I guess it's because she didn't ever want to display it, publicly. She couldn't take the risk that a visitor would recognise its value and it would be stolen. Security at the museum wasn't exactly tight.'

'So Jasmin gets to sell her collection to the British Museum, including a priceless Lamassu, and live happily ever after off the proceeds. She knows it's safe, being looked after properly, and can visit whenever she likes.' Marshall thought for a moment. 'And Lucy Akopian, her old business partner, gets word of this deal? Comes to Shrewsbury to confront Jasmin, and to claim a share of the cash.'

'Well done, Marshall,' Flora grinned, patting his knee. 'We'll make a detective out of you yet. I imagine it would have been quite the scene – their first meeting after Lucy's husband ran away with her best friend.'

'You sound like you don't think that meeting ever took place.'

'How could it? Lucy was killed before Jasmin even knew she was in town.'

'For someone so switched on, Flora, you can be incredibly dense sometimes. The thing with you is – no, hear me out – you're great at working out the background stuff and doing the research and putting a puzzle together. But your Achilles heel is this – you think people are fundamentally good. You can never point the finger at someone you like. Not when it comes to murder.'

'Well, I can and I have,' Flora protested hotly.

'Yes, but only at the eleventh hour, when that person has pulled the wool over your eyes again and again. This time, why don't you just admit that it was most likely Jasmin who did away with her rival? It's the obvious solution.'

'One,' Flora counted on her fingers, 'Jasmin has an alibi for the night Lucy was killed. Two, there is no evidence whatsoever that Lucy had been in touch with Jasmin or that they had met before that night. The police let Jasmin go, Marshall. They suspected her, but they couldn't prove anything. And, three ...' she paused, biting her lip.

'Go on. Three?'

Flora shrugged. 'I looked into her eyes. The day she was taken away by the police. She swore she hadn't done it. And I believed her.'

Despite all the other lies, Flora was sure of this. She'd seen anger, she'd seen fear – she'd seen all kinds of emotions in the older woman's eyes. But she hadn't detected even the slightest sign of guilt.

Surely Jasmin wasn't *that* good a liar?

'Oh, well. There it is, your honour. Flora Lively looked into her eyes – she must be innocent.'

'I know it sounds stupid. But this time ... This time I'm sure I'm right. Whoever killed Lucy Akopian, it wasn't Jasmin.'

'You'll stake your reputation on it, right?' Marshall said, chuckling.

Flora closed her eyes. She tipped back her head and allowed the rumble of the road to fill her ears. Despite everything, she knew she was right. She didn't know how she knew, she just knew. Jasmin had lied and misled them, and was almost certainly capable of stealing valuable antiquities and selling them on for her own gain. But murder? Not a chance. Flora was sure of this.

Just like she knew that John Hopper was her birth father. It was something she felt inside. Marshall didn't understand. Women learned early on to trust their intuition. Sometimes it was the only weapon they had.

'You're not gonna tell me about your beef with Jasmin, are you?' Marshall said. His voice seemed to come at her from far away, and Flora realised she was sleepy. Deliciously sleepy. For the first time in days she relaxed her shoulders fully and allowed her mind to wander. In a few hours they would be in London, and the whole nightmare would continue. But for now, she could drift away on the rumble of wheels, her thoughts easy, her head nodding and dropping with every undulation in the road. In her dreams, women in white hid mysterious objects behind their backs and Lamassu came to life and trotted down the steep streets of Shrewsbury. Flora followed them, a huge magnifying glass in her hand. *I know your secrets*, she seemed to be saying, but no words came out of her mouth. The Lamassu dipped their bearded heads gracefully and continued on their way.

Chapter 19

'Good sleep?'

Flora opened her eyes blearily. Marshall's handsome face was right in front of hers; she realised that they had stopped and he'd already got out of the cab. He was now perched on the step, passenger door open, a mischievous smile playing on his lips.

'I wasn't asleep,' she murmured.

'Tell that to the drool,' he laughed, jumping down onto the pavement.

Flora wiped a hand across her mouth, grimacing at the sliver of wetness that snaked down to her chin. 'Where are we?' she asked, changing the subject.

'Why, we're in your fine capital, my lady,' Marshall quipped, the terrible English accent back again.

'Give it a rest, idiot.' Flora groaned and stretched out her stiff back, before climbing down to join Marshall outside. 'So, this is the place?'

'Sure is. Grand, ain't it?'

'Very.'

Side by side, they surveyed the exterior of the museum.

'It looks more Greek than British,' Marshall observed.

Flora nodded. 'Greek Revival style, apparently. The columns are like a Greek temple, and that pediment up there – see it? The long triangle thing with statues carved into it? That's supposed to represent the progress of civilization. From the Stone Age all the way to philosophy and education.'

Marshall whistled. 'You know a lot about museums, Flora.'

'More than I ever wanted to know,' she replied with a rueful smile. She yawned and stretched again. 'Too many hours keeping watch over Jasmin's treasures and reading her dusty old books and magazines.'

'Well, I'm guessing we don't go in the grand entrance. You can't get near it – looks like pedestrians only.'

'And we can't stay here long either, someone is going to lynch us,' Flora agreed as another angry driver beeped their horn. The lorry wasn't blocking anyone's progress down the busy Bloomsbury street, but stopping anywhere around here was clearly the worst kind of crime.

'Look for the trades' entrance then,' Marshall said, giving her a quick peck on the head, before jogging round the front of the van. Flora climbed back in and pulled the museum's website up on her phone.

'Right,' she said, tugging her seatbelt across her chest, 'we have to go to the other end of Great Russell Street – there's a turning there.'

'I'm on it, madam.'

Getting into the museum was a palaver on a grand scale, involving security searches, identity checks, and an admonishment for not phoning ahead. Flora's protests that the vehicle access had been booked for weeks fell on deaf ears. But after a lot of head shaking and mumbled conversations, Flora and Marshall were finally allowed inside and shown into a small storage space where they could offload the crates. Tomorrow they would set up the collection to Jasmin's exacting requirements, under the watchful eyes of museum staff. It wasn't a task either of them were particularly looking forward to.

Two hours later they were back in the van, this time navigating London's streets in search of their digs.

'I'll drop you at the front and then go find the lorry park,' Marshall said. Flora didn't answer – she was too busy scanning the tall Victorian buildings for their hotel. 'It's just over the river,' Marshall continued. 'Shouldn't take me long to get back. Are you okay honey?'

'I'm just … Ah, there it is!' Flora pointed to a slim, white-fronted guest house with a wrought iron sign swinging slightly in the breeze. Marshall eased the van to a gentle stop and passed Flora his rucksack.

'I'm excited,' Flora said, leaning over to kiss him. 'It's like having an actual mini-break together. Shall I look for a nice restaurant so we can eat out tonight?'

Marshall smiled. 'Sure. But can you get out already? There's a tailback about a mile long behind us and that guy looks like he's gonna have an aneurysm.'

Flora noted the angry-looking man who was halfway out of his car and shaking his fist at them. 'Got it,' she grinned. 'See you in a few hours.'

She jumped down from the lorry, pulled her bag after her and caught Marshall's as he tossed it over. With a cheery wave to the red-faced man, she dashed across the road and up the steps to their hotel.

Two nights in the capital with her fella. The job from hell nearly over. And, best of all, she felt that she was pretty close to solving this crazy mystery once and for all. Something told her a breakthrough was imminent.

Things were finally looking up.

* * *

Albert was the team member assigned to work with them on Jasmin's collection; in Flora's opinion, they could not have been given a nicer person to help out. Marshall wasn't so convinced.

'You're homophobic,' Flora whispered while Albert's distinguished back was temporarily turned. 'And it's not a good look on you.'

Marshall bristled. 'I am not. And how do you know he's gay, anyway?'

'Come off it. Your face when he walked in! I know you, remember. You couldn't be more uncomfortable if they stitched you into a suit made of tiny needles.'

'Shut up, Lively. You don't know what you're talking about. I think it's you that's got the problem. Stereotyping, that's what I'd say.'

Flora gave up and turned back to her folder with a little shake of her head. Baiting Marshall was fun, but even that couldn't drag her out of her current mood. Damn but this work was tedious. The pictorial guide she'd made while packing up the Shropshire White and Co. Museum of Antiquities should have made the job easy; they could see how each item had been displayed in its original location, and recreate it here. That was the plan. But for some reason, the artefacts hadn't been packed in the order they needed to go on display, something Marshall insisted on pointing out every five minutes. And to make matters worse, the cabinets and wall spaces here were completely different, meaning almost every item needed to be re-evaluated and discussed before being set into place.

Boring, boring, boring.

Albert, however, was in his element, exclaiming delightedly over every artefact they unpacked, regaling Flora and Marshall with detailed descriptions and extended history lessons. Flora listened dutifully, even though she'd heard most of the stories before from Jasmin, but Marshall didn't even feign an interest. He busied himself now, shifting another crate closer to the display cabinets. The morning was almost over and they were only on their third crate. At this rate it was going to take a week, not a couple of days, to get shot of this damn collection.

'Do you have anywhere we could grab a coffee?' Flora asked Albert, who was adoringly stroking a grubby clay pot.

'Oh, the coffee here is disgusting,' Albert told her cheerfully. 'You'd have to pop out for anything decent. And it's ridiculously expensive. I shouldn't bother, to be honest. I have a flask of peppermint tea, though. I'll pop and get it right now.'

Despondent, and now caffeine-deprived, Flora sighed and took another look at the photographs in her folder. It seemed like a lifetime ago that she'd begun this job. How she wished she hadn't bothered. Her buoyant mood from the night before had dissipated during dinner, when she finally told Marshall about her argument with Jasmin, and he'd pointed out, quite reasonably, that there was every possibility they wouldn't even get their full fee for this contract.

'And she might sue us to boot,' Flora had agreed glumly.

Marshall thought that was unlikely, but what did he know? Marshall had the annoying habit of being pessimistic when things were going well, and optimistic when everything was crashing to the ground. The most contrary man she had ever …

'Flora? Where does this want to go?'

She shook herself back to the present. 'That looks early Mesopotamian, so over there with that stuff.'

'And this?' Marshall held up a large brass vase with elongated handles and an ornately shaped neck.

'I …' Flora stopped, momentarily confused. 'Hang on.' She rifled through her folder, searching the images. Some were of individual items, others of groups of artefacts as they were about to be packed. She reached the last page, then flicked through the photographs again.

'I can't find that,' she said, biting her lip.

'You can't?' Marshall set the vase down on the polished floor and crossed the room.

'No,' she said. 'I don't get it. I logged everything. Hang on, help me up a minute.'

Marshall held out his hand and Flora jumped to her feet. 'What's the vase in there with?'

'It was in this crate here.'

Together they leaned over and peered inside the box.

'There's some other brass stuff in here, a couple of clay heads,' Marshall reported, lifting and replacing each item as he did. 'More bits of pottery.'

'Marshall,' Flora said quietly. 'I've never seen any of this before. Except that vase. I'm sure I recognise that. Did you pack this crate?'

'I don't think so.'

'This is so weird.' Then she noticed the tape around the edge of the lid. Marshall had sliced it carefully with his Stanley knife, but it was so obvious Flora couldn't believe neither of them had noticed it before. 'Oh, Marshall, look. Look what crate this is.'

'What?'

She swallowed hard and gazed up at him, her eyes wary. 'This is the crate that Lucy was found in. Don't you remember? The police, they took it away for forensics or whatever, but all they needed was the top layers of tissue she'd been found on. When they'd checked it over they repacked it and sent it back to the museum.'

'How do you know it was this crate?'

'Because of the tape, look. They resealed it with ordinary packing tape, not the special stuff that Jasmin made us buy. But if you look closely, you can see the original tape underneath.' She stopped, a frown clouding her eyes. 'That's where I saw that vase, Marshall.'

'Where?'

'It was in the crate where they found Lucy Akopian's body. It was right by her side.'

'Are you sure?' Marshall crouched down next to her, sitting back on his heels. 'Well, that explains it then. You said that she was found on the crate that you'd packed earlier that night.'

'But no, that's not right,' Flora said. 'I mean, yes, that was the crate I'd packed. It was in that exact position, right where I'd left it after I sealed it up. But that vase – I remember it so clearly now. I remember seeing it in the crate when Nick and I ran into the room. The handles, you see, and the way her hands were flopped over ... It looked ... it looked as though she was holding onto it.'

'Hey, it's okay honey. Don't get upset.'

Flora shook her head. 'I'm not upset. Not now. I was then, of course I was. And it made everything so confusing. I remember screaming when I saw her there, and running out of the room. And then when we were being questioned, it was all hidden from view. Thankfully.' She shuddered at the memory.

'I remember that,' Marshall said, stroking her back. 'But you were absolutely certain that you'd packed that very crate. Are you saying now that you hadn't?'

'I don't know what I'm saying,' Flora admitted, offering him a sad little smile. 'But that vase isn't in this folder here, and I know for a fact that I photographed and logged everything. And I don't remember seeing any of this other stuff at all. Do you?'

Marshall returned her smile. 'It was a difficult job, honey. We got bored, maybe we got a little bit sloppy–'

'No.' She cut him off. 'Not me. And especially not that night. It was our first proper night of packing. I was excited. Believe it or not, I felt happy to be there. Until it all went so disastrously wrong.'

'What's gone wrong?' Albert said, standing in the doorway, a flask in one hand and three paper cups in the other.

Flora forced a smile. 'Nothing. It's all fine.'

'Come on,' Marshall said, offering her his hand. 'On your feet, girl. We can switch for a bit.'

'Good idea. But I think I'll pass on this particular box, if that's okay. I just can't ...'

'Sure, honey. That's fine. We'll leave this one till later.'

For the next half an hour, Flora unpacked and Marshall checked items off their list. After an hour or so, she began to feel better – the physical work was absorbing and gave her a feeling of satisfaction. When she found the spooky doll with the wonky eye it was almost like finding an old friend. Although even Albert admitted it was pretty unpleasant to look at.

Flora turned her attention to the suit of armour, carefully unrolling the bubble wrap.

'Can you help me with this?' she said to Marshall. 'The wrap seems to be stuck inside his leg.'

Marshall lifted the armour so Flora could loosen the lower section. 'It might not be a *he*, you know. It's kinda small for a man.'

'People were tiny back then,' Albert said, coming over to help. 'Compared to now, anyway.'

'Marshall, just pull it up a bit there ... Careful now ... Oh, no!'

Flora jumped back with a cry as the suit of armour came apart in her hands and crashed to the floor. Limbs lay upside down and back to front, the body face down and the helmet by its side and facing upwards.

'That looks painful,' Marshall quipped.

'Great,' Flora sighed. 'That is going to take us ages to reconstruct.'

'I'll do it,' Albert said happily. He reached down and grabbed the stand. 'There's a knack to these things.'

'What's that?' Flora said, pointing to a small red cube that lay amongst the wreckage.

Marshall frowned. 'It looks like one of those Bluetooth speakers.'

'Yeah, it is.' Flora picked it up. 'But what on earth is it doing here?'

Albert shook his head. 'Does it belong to Mrs White, perhaps?'

'I don't think so.'

'It might have been Nick's,' Marshall suggested.

'I guess.' Flora stared at the speaker, then set it aside gently. 'He loves his music, doesn't he? He must have put it down somewhere and it's accidentally been packed. Although how it ended up in the armour I do not know.'

'Another mystery,' Marshall said, getting to his feet and stretching. 'Time for a break? We could do with some fresh air.'

Flora put the speaker in her bag and followed him out, smiling goodbye to Albert and promising to be back within the hour. She made a mental note to take it with her when she went to visit Nick in hospital later that week. She should also call Cady and find out how he was doing.

Had he heard something that night? He must have gone into the back of the lorry for a reason. She shuddered at the memory of seeing him lying there, fearing the worst.

'Marshall?' she said.

He stopped and turned, holding the door open for her. Behind him was the main hall of the museum. A buzz of voices and laughter hung in the air.

What was it that was tugging at her mind? Was it something to do with the speaker, or with the image of Nick slumped on the floor? Damn, but it was so frustrating when a thought refused to be pinned down.

'Give those brain cells a rest for an hour, eh?' Marshall said, grinning. 'Let's go and get some proper London coffee.'

Flora nodded and smiled up at him. 'Sure,' she said.

Just for an hour, though. The germ of an idea was starting to form, and she wasn't about to let go of it – not even for the best coffee in the world.

Chapter 20

It was later that afternoon that they found the missing Lamassu.

Flora had resumed her role of checking through the folder, ticking off items as they were unwrapped, and showing Marshall and Albert how they should sit in the display boxes. Most of the larger items were set up now, spaced around the perimeter of the room: the Ötzi mummy, the repaired suit of armour, the strange sad painting of the woman with the white veiled hat. Other paintings were stacked against the wall, along with the African death mask and various items of ancient weaponry. They still made Flora shudder. In fact, the entire exhibition made her uneasy, even though here it was displayed in a white room with white shelves and sparkling glass cases. A far cry from the dark, dank, dusty rooms of the old museum.

Marshall had overcome his initial wariness of Albert and even had a bit of good-natured banter going. Just like men, Flora thought. They always found a way to make a situation into a joke. She'd often suspected that she was too serious; Marshall forced her to lighten up occasionally, however much she resisted.

And then, Albert whistled.

'Now this,' he said, 'this is something really special. I never thought to see one so well preserved. And this is coming here? We are lucky.'

Flora glanced up, not fully paying attention; Albert exclaimed enthusiastically about pretty much everything.

He held aloft a piece of stone, about a foot in length and half as wide. Carved onto the surface was the image of a Lamassu. There was no mistaking that majestic head, and even from six feet away, Flora could make out the intricate wings and the long, shaped beard.

Jasmin's voice drifted into her head: *Carved in relief, onto a small stone slab* … Flora swallowed hard, not trusting herself to speak.

'But isn't that …?' Marshall looked at Flora, his eyes wide.

She nodded, getting to her feet.

Albert was examining the tablet closely. 'Ah, just look at this. The delicacy of the work is astonishing. Did you know that the Lamassu were the most powerful of all mythic beasts.' He sighed happily. 'I'm holding in my hands one of the greatest mysteries of all time.'

If only you knew, Flora thought. Clearly Jasmin hadn't told the museum anything about the break in *or* the murder; she wouldn't want to jeopardize her deal.

But the Lamassu had been there all along.

'We have some full-size Lamassu right here, you know,' Albert said, still gushing, 'and they are magnificent. But the smaller tablets, now they were–'

Flora cut him off. She already knew more than she'd ever wanted to about the winged creatures. Right now she had more pressing things on her mind. And she was tired of keeping Jasmin's secrets for her. It was time to get all of this out in the open. Shake it up and see what fell to the floor. It was the only way they were going to get to the bottom of this mystery.

'Albert,' Flora said gravely. 'We need your help. There's something you should know about that Lamassu.'

'What is it?' Albert said, holding the tablet to his chest like a baby.

'You better sit down, mate,' Marshall said, shaking his head. 'This is gonna be a long story.'

***

'I take it she was happy,' Marshall said as soon as Flora hung up the phone.

Calling Jasmin with the news had been a surreal experience. After accusing the woman of lying about the Lamassu all along, Flora didn't know whether to feel vindicated or apologetic. In one sense she was proved right: the Lamassu never had gone missing. But she was also dead wrong – the supposedly cursed tablet clearly *had* been in the collection, packed by either Flora or Marshall, and somehow missed when the crates were checked.

Flora sighed. Marshall looked up from his phone and gave her a sympathetic smile. They'd come outside for a phone signal, and were now standing by the museum's staff entrance, enjoying some late October sunshine. At least, Marshall was enjoying it. Flora was lost in the details, the frown on her face turning into an unhappy scowl.

'What's up honey?'

'It just doesn't feel right,' Flora complained.

'Oh, no.' Marshall pocketed his phone and took hold of Flora's shoulders. 'Don't do this. It's over, it's sorted, everyone is happy. The mystery is solved. You solved it.'

Flora gave him a stern look. '*I* solved it? Are you delusional? For one thing, what was there to solve? The mystery of why someone didn't look properly for their precious missing artefact? Or the mystery of why a competent removals company failed to record packing said precious artefact? Give me a break.'

'Stuff goes wrong,' he shrugged. 'Get over it.'

'And what about the noises, Marshall?' she demanded. 'What about Lucy Akopian's death? Something is wrong here, and I'm absolutely sure it all fits together. Jasmin White is in it up to her neck.'

'You've changed your tune.'

'I know bullshit when I hear it,' Flora retorted.

Jasmin's tone just now had been off, somehow. Flora

couldn't pinpoint how or why, but her radar was finely tuned, and she just *knew*.

She leaned against the cool stone wall and closed her eyes. The low sun was turning everything pinky-golden; it would have been a beautiful evening if her mind wasn't in turmoil. They had planned a visit to Soho, a meal in a Chinese buffet-style restaurant, a movie cuddled up in their cute hotel room after. But Flora knew she wouldn't enjoy any of that now.

'Someone,' she said, her eyes still closed, 'must have put the Lamassu into that crate after we'd packed it. It's the only explanation.'

'There's no way, honey. That crate was sealed tight when I opened it earlier. They all were. And don't forget, there were other things inside it that you don't remember packing, like that vase. We must have been having an off day.' Marshall shrugged. 'Or else Jasmin packed that one herself.'

Flora's eyes sprung open. 'What did you just say?'

'Erm, that Jasmin maybe packed it herself?'

'No, the other thing.' Flora bit her lip. Her body was buzzing now, an energy building inside, flowing up from her feet. 'The part about the vase. Are you saying that the Lamassu was inside the same crate where they found Lucy Akopian?'

Marshall nodded. 'Now, Flora, don't start going off on another tangent. Let's stay focused here. Everything has worked out for the best. We're off the hook, Jasmin is hap–'

'That's it!' Flora cried. 'Oh my god, I can't believe how stupid I've been.'

'Well, maybe a little over-eager, but I wouldn't say stupid.'

'Marshall,' she grabbed his arm so tightly he winced. 'We need to get the rest of those crates open right now.'

'What, all of them? But that's gonna take hours.'

'Then we'd better not stand around discussing it,'

Flora said over her shoulder. She was already holding open the door, impatiently tapping her toe. 'Come *on*, slow coach.'

'Flora, what's going on?' Marshall spoke tiredly, his shoulders drooping. 'I thought this was over.'

'Far from over, my love,' Flora answered, her eyes bright. 'What was it Sherlock Homes used to say? Come on, Watson. The game is afoot.'

* * *

Albert was a little put out at the idea of opening all of the remaining crates at once and sifting through them haphazardly, but Flora insisted.

'Trust me,' she said, her smile brilliant and ever so slightly wild. 'It will all work out in the end. But we have to do this now. There's no time to waste.'

Cajoled into line, Albert and Marshall unpacked quickly, stacking items by the side of their respective boxes after showing them to Flora, who sat on the floor in the centre of the exhibition space, furiously checking and ticking the pages in her folder.

'Is that everything?' she said after Marshall had presented her with a colourful statue of a Japanese Samurai warrior.

'That's it,' he confirmed, his voice muffled as he leaned inside the last crate to do a final check.

'It's a varied collection, isn't it?' Albert commented, surveying the array of artefacts. He rubbed his hand over his perfectly shaped beard and smiled. 'Eclectic. That's the word. It really speaks of the post-colonial culture and of collectivism in general.'

'Whatever you say,' Flora murmured. Personally she thought that the collection, seen together now for the first time in one room, and without the gloomy – but somehow more authentic – atmosphere of the Shropshire White & Co Museum, resembled nothing so much as a pile of old tat. She checked one final page, then jumped to her feet, satisfied.

'Right. That's as much as we can do here. Albert, we'll be back in the morning to help you set it up as per instructions. Marshall, time to go.'

'Yes madam,' Marshall said, rolling his eyes at Albert, who giggled. 'Whatever you say.'

But outside, heading west on Montague Place and trying to keep pace with Flora, he said, 'Do you have to speak to me like I'm the hired help? Ordering me around like that. It's embarrassing.'

'Get over yourself, Goodman. This is more important than your fragile ego.'

'Fine,' he said, 'but why are we practically running? Our table isn't booked until eight o'clock. We've got loads of time to get ready.'

Flora stopped so suddenly Marshall nearly knocked her over. 'Ah,' she said. 'About that. The thing is, I don't think I can go out for dinner. I've got too much to think about.'

'What?' Marshall's mouth dropped open.

'Sweetheart,' she began.

'Don't you *sweetheart* me. This was your idea, Flora. All of this. Make the most of a trip to the capital, you said. Go out to Soho, you said, find somewhere nice to eat. And now you're gonna bail on me?'

Flora shrugged and took off again, calling to Marshall over her shoulder. 'Okay, fine. We can go. But there's something I need to do back at the hotel first.'

'What?' Marshall said, this time allowing his frustration to creep into his voice. 'What do you need to do?'

Flora smiled and grabbed hold of his hand, pulling him along with her.

'I think I've cracked it, Marshall,' she told him breathlessly. 'And when I tell you, you're going to have to admit that I'm the best private investigator you know.'

'Flora, you're the only private investigator I know,' he replied, exasperated. But Flora just blew him a kiss and grinned.

'I knew you'd admit it one day. I really am a proper investigator. You just said so yourself.'

***

'Flora.'

'Mmm?'

'Flora!'

'Oh, for goodness sake. What now?' Flora dragged her gaze away from her phone. She had been glued to the internet most of the evening, much to Marshall's obvious annoyance.

'Are we going to choose a film to watch?' he said, the hectoring tone that Flora thought she'd stamped out at the restaurant now creeping back in.

'I'm happy to watch anything, sweetheart,' she said calmly, forcing herself to smile. No point risking another argument. That wasn't going to achieve anything. 'Whatever you like.'

Marshall regarded her sceptically. 'And you'll actually watch it with me? Or will you have your nose in that thing?'

Flora held up her phone and made a show of turning it off and placing it with elaborate care on the polished mahogany desk. 'Happy now?'

The hotel room was large and, in Flora's opinion, luxurious. King size bed, bouncy pillows, wide-screen TV on the wall. Marshall bemoaned the lack of a mini-bar, but Flora thought the ultra-modern drench shower in the en suite more than made up for it. The best feature by far, however, was the tiny balcony that looked out over London's towering skyline. Not that Flora had had much opportunity to enjoy the view. Last night they'd been too exhausted to do anything other than sleep, and tonight, after being marched around Soho and all but force-fed Chinese food, Flora wanted nothing more than to sit quietly and think.

Marshall, unfortunately, had other ideas.

'Come and sit over here,' he said, patting the soft white duvet.

'Marshall, I don't–'

'Just come here, Flora-bloody-Lively. Your man is feeling neglected and we've got this room and all … Might as well enjoy it. Tomorrow we're heading back to boring old Shropshire and our romantic break will be over.'

Flora grinned at his downcast expression, even though she knew it was feigned. She climbed onto the vast bed and snuggled into his arms.

'That's better,' he said, the smile evident in his voice.

He'd chosen a rom com for them to watch together, but Flora couldn't follow the story at all. It seemed to involve a rich, obnoxious man lusting after a girl half his age, while his attractive assistant masqueraded as his wife for some inexplicable reason. Flora allowed her mind to drift. When Marshall kissed her head a short while later, Flora was astonished to see the credits rolling on the TV screen.

'Did you enjoy that?' Marshall was asking, his fingers smoothing back her hair.

'Mm-mm. It was really funny.'

'That bit where he dressed up as a lion,' Marshall laughed. 'That was hilarious, right?'

Flora faked a giggle. 'Oh god, yes. So funny, right?'

'Honey?'

'Yes?'

'No one dressed up as a lion.' He drew back and looked at her, pursing his lips. 'You didn't take any of that in, did you? Where is your head tonight?'

Flora scooted up and sat back on her heels. 'Marshall,

you know where my head is. Okay, I'm sorry I couldn't concentrate on the film, and I'm sorry I wasn't paying attention at the restaurant.'

'No, it was fine. I enjoyed talking to the top of your head while you stared at your phone.'

'Fair point,' Flora admitted. 'But I've had a lot on my mind.'

'And you still don't want to share it?' Marshall asked with a sigh. He swung his legs off the bed and headed to the bathroom.

In fact, Flora desperately wanted to share what she had discovered. But she was worried that Marshall wouldn't see it the way she did, or that he'd dismiss her idea, or ridicule her deductions. As he had so many times before.

If only Marshall really could play Watson to her Holmes, she thought ruefully. Just her luck that the only sidekick she had was usually looking for ways to unpick her, not build her up.

In the bathroom, Marshall was cleaning his teeth. Flora made a decision. She jumped off the bed and stood by the open door.

'Okay,' she said. 'It's like this. *Everything* in the crate where they found Lucy Akopian was different to the stuff I packed into it. And yet, how could that be? I saw that it was in the same place, right in the middle of the atrium on the night Lucy was found, with the African mask lying next to it and all my rolls of tape and paper. No one else had been in there and the crates hadn't been moved. But even on then I felt something was off. At the time I had no idea what it was, but now I'm sure I do. Take a look at this.'

She grabbed their folder off the desk and flipped to a page she'd marked with a yellow post-it. 'Look. On this page is the stuff I packed into that crate. I remember this bronze pendant so clearly – I thought it must have been so uncomfortable to wear, for one thing! I packed it into that exact crate, along with Jasmin's collection of Japanese antiques, including this little wooden monkey.'

The mizaru's eyes were hidden by its tiny carved hands. Flora pulled the Polaroid out of its plastic sleeve and passed it Marshall.

'See no evil,' he said, wiping his mouth on a fluffy white towel, then dropping the towel into the sink. 'My mum had a set of those when I was a kid.'

'I'm telling you, Marshall, this is the stuff I packed that night. We went through the entire collection today, the monkey and the angel pendent are present and correct, but they weren't where they should have been. Which can mean only one thing.'

'That you're losing your mind?' Marshall ventured, pushing the bathroom door shut gently. 'Some privacy please?'

Flora looked at the photograph in her hand. 'It means that the crates were moved,' she said. 'Or, more specifically, that another crate was brought into the museum that night. And inside it, was Lucy Akopian's body.'

The door swung open and Marshall's astonished face appeared. 'Are you serious? I mean, are you for real? Aren't things complicated enough without you using your imagination to invent all of this?' Astonishment gave way to incredulity, followed quickly by annoyance; Marshall walked past her and jumped onto the bed with a grunt. 'Let's just go to sleep. I am beyond tired.'

'I am not imagining it,' she insisted, rounding the bed and hunkering down by his side so he couldn't pretend he wasn't listening. 'I checked the inventory. That's partly what I was doing tonight. None of the things in that extra crate were listed. Not a single one of them. The clay heads, the pottery. The Lamassu. And,' she said quickly before he could interrupt, 'there's something else. Based on that inventory, and on Jasmin's advice, we ordered in twenty-eight crates for this job, and fifteen rolls of acid-free tissue paper, and ten rolls of tape.' She paused now, making sure she had his full attention. 'Today, I counted twenty-*nine* crates, Marshall. Twenty-nine. Now, why don't you tell me where that extra box of antiquities came from?'

Chapter 21

Frank Sinatra immortalised New York as the city that never sleeps, but Flora figured London had a pretty good claim on that title too. Sitting outside on their little balcony, she had yet to notice a significant drop in activity, even though it was now two o'clock in the morning. Groups of people walked by every few minutes; most of the buildings in the street had lit up windows; the hum of traffic continued like the roar of a distant river in full flow. Every few minutes a car or van swept along the street, headlights illuminating the banks of trees and the railings and the uneven pavements. It was exhausting, but Flora loved it. Sleepy Shropshire was nothing like this. She wondered whether she and Marshall might get along better if they lived in a city. More to do, more to see. Less time to focus on each other's flaws and irritations.

Although, to be fair, it was mostly she who did that.

Marshall was fast asleep in the enormous bed, contented and oblivious. He'd listened until his eyelids began to droop, and then had begged her to let them carry on putting it all together in the morning. How could she refuse? But Flora knew that sleep was a long way off for her. Now that she was beginning to understand what had happened – and had some inkling of why – she had to figure out what the hell she was going to do about it. Because one thing was certain: they had been played. D.I. Sarah Buxton was right She and Marshall had been used and taken advantage of, lied to and blamed, *and* had been made accessories to a cold-blooded murder.

Jasmin was not getting away with it.

Flora just had to figure out how on earth she was going to prove any of this before the woman hot-footed it out of the country to live happily ever after on the proceeds of her looting.

She leaned her elbows on the balcony railings and placed her chin in her hands. Her poncho kept her body warm but her face was starting to feel the cold. Briefly, she closed her eyes, allowing the buzz of the city to wash over her. Here she felt small and insignificant, but it wasn't an unpleasant feeling. In a strange way it was comforting.

She opened her eyes and looked down into the street. A movement, a man in dark clothing, turning and quickly walking away. Someone had been watching her. Flora pulled back on instinct, but then leaned over the railings for a better look. All she could see was a retreating back, shoulders hunched, as the man hugged the shadows then rounded the corner and disappeared from view.

Flora sat back, puzzled. What she thought she'd seen was impossible. She had imagined it, conjured him from her imagination. For a moment there she had been absolutely sure that the man on the street was John Hopper. Was he watching over her, even now so far from home? Of course not. But the thought of him soothed her, and Flora smiled, partly at her own silliness and partly at the knowledge that when all this was over, she had this to look forward to. Getting to know her birth father. An unexpected but entirely welcome distraction.

Inside their room, Marshall was snoring softly. Flora dropped her poncho to the floor and lifted the heavy duvet. Slipping into the covers, feeling Marshall's warmth radiating towards her, she experienced a moment of pure contentment. And then she fell into a deep, dreamless sleep.

***

'What I don't understand is, how could Jasmin have managed all this? She must be near on seventy, and she's a tiny little thing. Bringing in a crate, moving them around, leaving a dead body in the atrium ... It just sounds a bit far-fetched.'

They were on their way back to the museum, hand in hand, the early morning sunshine turning them into long shadows. Well rested, Marshall was in a buoyant mood, but had no idea what Flora was planning, and she was keeping him talking so that he didn't think to ask.

'I've been thinking about that,' she told him, swinging his hand a little. 'She must have had an accomplice. Probably the man she said she was on a date with. And those crates aren't really that heavy, packed full of tissue paper.'

'So what you and Nick heard that night was them moving the crates? What about the woman screaming? Didn't the police say Lucy couldn't have been killed there?'

'I have a theory about that too,' Flora said.

'Of course you do.' Marshall smiled and squeezed her hand. 'Go on then.'

Flora beamed. 'Well, I think that Jasmin made up the whole curse of the Sign of Seven thing to cover up the noises we heard that night. They were different that first night – the order things happened, the sounds themselves. So my theory is that we *did* hear something, but a lot of it was to distract us from what was really happening.'

'And then she somehow managed to make those noises again every night?'

'Exactly. To create the impression of the curse.' Flora paused and frowned. 'And to get us all running around like idiots every night, frightened out of our wits.'

Marshall sidestepped a small group of tourists taking

a long-armed selfie outside the museum. 'Frightening you and Nick out of your wits,' he said. 'I wasn't bothered by it at all.'

'Sure you weren't,' Flora said, laughing.

'So what you're saying is, there never was a curse.' Marshall raised a quizzical eyebrow as they slipped through a towering iron gate, showed their passes to the security guard, and headed to the staff entrance.

'I guess not.' Flora frowned again. 'But ...'

She stopped suddenly, her hand slipping out of Marshall's. All around her, slowly filling the vast courtyard outside the museum, people chatted excitedly, consulting guidebooks, calling to their friends, herding their children closer, gazing up at the carved stone pediment with awe. Marshall walked a few more steps before he realised he'd lost her.

'Hey, Lively. What's up?'

'Marshall,' she said slowly. 'That doesn't fit.'

'Fit what? Come on, honey. Let's get inside.'

'No, wait. Listen. There is a curse. Professor Paulson confirmed it.'

'So Jasmin knew about the supposed curse and just used that to explain the noises.' Marshall shrugged and took hold of Flora's hand again. 'Come on inside. Let's get this thing finished and get back to normal life. Won't that be nice?'

'Mmm.' Flora wasn't listening. Thinking about the professor, with his kindly face and authoritative glasses, had given her an idea. 'Marshall,' she said urgently. 'Where in the museum do they have the best mobile reception?'

'Nowhere. It's a black spot. Which is pretty annoying because–'

'It'll have to be out here then,' Flora interrupted, looking around. 'Yes, over there.' She ran over to five large green bins and pulled out her phone. Marshall followed, a smile hovering on his lips.

'Is this the part where you seem like you've lost your mind and I'm left looking like an idiot?' he asked. 'Or are you going to tell me what you're doing?'

'The professor,' she said, flipping through her contacts. 'Here it is. Right. I hope he answers.' She looked around distractedly and nodded to herself, then she held her phone in front of her face and waited.

Marshall sighed and leaned against a whitewashed stone wall. 'You'll tell me when you're good and ready I suppose. Like, why are we hanging around the bins? And why are you Skyping someone at eight-thirty in the morning?'

Flora flicked her gaze to Marshall, then back at the phone. 'I'm calling Professor Paulson, dummy. We Skyped, so I've got his number saved in my … Hang on, I think he's answering.'

The melodic tones stopped and the professor's smiling face appeared on Flora's screen. 'Well, hello again. Miss Lively, isn't it? How nice to hear from you.'

Flora fixed a radiant smile on her face. 'How are things in Switzerland? It's nice and sunny there.'

'Ah, we are lucky with the weather. And how is it in rainy old England?'

Flora could see that he was outside, the sun glinting off his spectacles. She smiled. 'It's not raining today. In fact, it's quite sunny here too. I hope I didn't disturb you. I'm not sure of the time difference. I was worried you might still be asleep.'

'Not at all, my dear. We're only an hour ahead of you here. So to what do I owe this pleasure?'

'Do you remember the Lamassu I asked about when we last spoke?' Flora said, feeling breathless under the weight of her idea.

'Of course I do!' The older man's double chin wobbled in consternation. 'The majestic winged bull is my life's work. I'm hardly likely to forget.'

Flora ignored Marshall's *what the hell are you doing*

expression, and ploughed on. 'I have some news about the missing tablet, and I'm afraid you aren't going to like it at all. In fact, I think it's going to make you pretty angry.'

The professor's eyes narrowed and his face moved even closer to the screen. 'Tell me, Miss Lively. Tell me everything.'

Flora took a deep steadying breath, and then she began.

***

'So your plan is what, exactly?' Marshall pressed as they finally entered the museum. His voice dropped to a low murmur; the quiet inside the building was like a suffocating blanket.

'Didn't you hear?' Flora whispered.

'You told me to go and keep lookout,' Marshall reminded her. 'Those were your exact words. *Keep lookout*. What for I do not know.'

'Right. Sorry. Well, he's furious that the Lamassu has fallen into the hands of – his words – someone so unscrupulous,' Flora said in a low voice, 'and he'll do anything to make sure she doesn't get away with it. He's going to call the museum right now and tell them it's a fake.'

'But it isn't a fake,' Marshall pointed out. 'Or is it? I'm confused.'

'Of course it isn't,' Flora said, rolling her eyes. 'Do keep up, sweetheart.' She typed a code into the keypad by a large grey door and pushed through it ahead of Marshall. 'The professor is going to say that he's just authenticated the real tablet in Switzerland. He's also going to call that detective, Sarah Buxton. I gave him her number.'

'And then?'

'Then, the big wigs at the museum call Jasmin and tell

her that *her* Lamassu is a fake. She comes racing over here in a panic and I confront her with the evidence of the boxes being switched. If I do it in front of the museum staff, and if D.I. Buxton does her bit and calls in the police here, Jasmin should crack and admit everything.'

Marshall pulled a face. 'That has more holes than one of your favourite teabags, Flora.'

'I know,' she sighed. 'But it's the best I can do. We don't have much time. Jasmin said she was coming to London but she might already be on her way to the airport for all we know. The museum is *not* going to want the collection to open to the public with a potential fake included. The scandal would be awful.' She shrugged. 'I don't know what else to do.'

'It's a good idea,' Marshall said, hugging her. 'You have a devious mind, though. I never would have thought of that.'

'Thank you. So,' she said, looking around the exhibition space. 'We can relax for a bit I guess. The calm before the storm.'

'Albert has been busy,' Marshall observed.

'He must have stayed late last night finishing off.' Flora looked around approvingly. 'It looks great, doesn't it? He's got everything just right.'

'I like what he's done with the Lamassu.'

Flora followed Marshall's gaze. The Seventh Tablet of Lamassu had been pinned between two sheets of glass and mounted high in a lit cabinet. Beneath it, as though worshiping the great beast, clay figurines and other carvings had been arranged in a semi-circle. The information note, fixed to the wall nearby, stated the history of Lamassu, and referenced the giant statues in rooms 6a and 6b.

'I'd like to go and see them before we leave,' Flora said softly. 'I believe it's quite sight.'

'No time like the present,' Marshall suggested.

It was still early, but the flow into the museum's grand entrance hall was already a steady stream. Flora and Marshall rounded the cafe and the impressive white staircases, then slipped past the gift shop and entered room six.

Flora was immediately awed. The vast space opened out in three directions: Egyptian sculptures stretched out to the left and the right; ahead was a room filled with Greek statues.

'Now this is something,' Marshall said, letting out a low whistle. 'And look, they must be the Lamassu.'

A pair of winged beasts stood to one side. Flora approached, taking in the noble human heads and carefully carved bodies. 'I thought they'd be bigger,' she said.

Marshall laughed. 'You're hard to impress, Miss Lively, that's for sure.'

On closer inspection the pair weren't identical. One was a winged lion, the other a winged bull. Flora scanned the information panel on the wall.

'These are replicas of statues from the gates of Balawat.'

'These won't disappoint you, Flora,' Marshall called. 'Come and look at this.'

Flora followed his voice. Off to the side of the Greek statues stood two enormous Lamassu. The light was dimmer in here, with relief-carved panels lining the walls. More than twice Marshall's height, the beasts towered over them, imposing – almost forbidding – and completely majestic. Flora drew in a breath.

'You like?' Marshall said, laying his arm across her shoulder.

'Built for the Assyrian king Sargon,' she read.

'Magic guardians against misfortune,' Marshall added. 'They haven't been done much for our Jasmin, have they?'

He wandered away to inspect a half-naked statue of

Venus. Flora looked up at the Lamassu.

'Marshall,' she said, 'how did Albert finish of the exhibits on his own?'

'Huh?'

'We were supposed to do it today, ready for the opening later. And we had the folder with us at the hotel. Unless he has a photographic memory there's no way Albert could have known where everything was supposed to go. Marshall!' she snapped. 'If you could tear yourself away for one second.'

Marshall grinned at her. 'Venus isn't a patch on you, honey. You'd look great draped in a sheet.'

'I'm serious. Think about it for a minute. Jasmin's collection had been laid out perfectly – it was an exact replica of her museum in there.'

'What are you thinking?' Marshall said, joining her by the giant winged statues.

'You know what I'm thinking,' she said quietly.

'Jasmin?'

'She's the only other person who could have set the entire collection up like that.'

'So she's here,' Marshall shrugged. 'That's what you wanted isn't it?'

Flora nodded. 'But isn't it strange that she'd come in and do the rest of the job herself, without even contacting me? It just doesn't feel right.'

'She said she wanted to say goodbye to her precious pile of junk,' Marshall explained. 'She probably just popped in and then got carried away. Or maybe Albert was still here and he asked her to help him.'

'Maybe.' Flora moved nearer to one of the Lamassu and reached up to touch the cool stone.

'I don't think you're meant to touch the exhibits, Flora.'

'I don't think the Lamassu mind much,' she said distractedly. 'We need to find Albert,' she announced, turning abruptly. 'And I want to call the professor again, see if he's spoken to anyone here yet.'

Flora strode purposefully past the Greek statues, casting Venus a withering glare. The goddess of love gazed down on her, oblivious.

Chapter 22

Flora clung to Marshall's hand as they weaved their way through the growing crowds of museum visitors, heading towards the entrance. She had a nagging, sickening feeling in the pit of her stomach. 'I'm sure I've missed something,' she murmured, but Marshall didn't hear.

Near the entrance, Flora's pocket vibrated. 'Hang on,' she said, stepping to one side and pulling out her phone. 'I've got a signal. I'm gonna call Jasmin.' She dialled, but then her face paled. 'Marshall, the number isn't recognised. It must have been disconnected.'

'It's probably not going through. The signal here is terrible.' Marshall pulled her into a nook near the cafe.

'No, look – I've got three bars and loads of notifications came through.'

'How many messages do you get in a day, Flora? All those little red numbers!'

'Just because you don't have any friends,' Flora retorted. 'Can we focus here, please?'

'Sorry. Maybe try the professor?'

Flora nodded and opened Skype. She chose the audio only option, and pressed call.

'He's not answering.'

'Try him again.'

'Still no answer.'

'Shall we go look for Albert, then?'

'Marshall, did you hear that?' Flora's eyes narrowed. 'That's so weird.'

'What is?'

'When I called Professor Paulson just now, both times when it rang out I heard the Skype tone.'

'Erm, yes. On your phone.'

'Not only on *my* phone. On another phone. Out there.'

They looked across the crowded entrance hall. Tourists filed in and milled about, getting orientated, checking bags, heading to the little coffee shop at the side of the museum or making directly for the imposing white atrium. The hum of conversation was low, reverential.

'You're not the only one with Skype, Flora,' Marshall pointed out.

She lifted her phone and pressed the icon next to Professor Paulson's name again. The familiar melody rang out, and at the same time was faintly mirrored by another phone somewhere in the throng.

'Weird,' Marshall stated.

'Very weird,' Flora agreed.

'Try it again.'

'It's just a coincidence, right? I mean, I spoke to the man in Switzerland less than two hours ago. He can't be–'

'Miss Lively? Mr Goodman?'

Flora and Marshall swung around. Standing behind them were two uniformed security guards and a tall grey-haired man in a loose-fitting tweed suit.

'Yes?' Flora answered, warily.

'Would you follow us please?' the smaller of the security guards said. His voice was thin and reedy, with a slightly Scottish burr.

'I don't … what for?' Flora looked at Marshall, who said nothing. 'Is this about the Lamassu?' she asked. 'Is Jasmin here?'

The professor must have come through for them, she thought. She squared her shoulders in preparation.

The tall man stepped forward. His face was gaunt, and his smile didn't reach his eyes. 'We don't want a scene. If you could just come with us, I'm sure we can get this cleared up in no time.'

'And you are?' Marshall's words came out like a growl.

'I'm the assistant to the director of the British Museum. Now, please–'

'Clear what up?' Flora said, bristling as the second guard tried to take her arm. She pulled away and sidestepped him. 'Can't you just tell us what's going on? Did you call Jasmin White yet? Is she on her way here? This is about the Lamassu, isn't it? Have you heard from Professor Paulson? Hey, you don't have to manhandle me!'

'Get your hands off her.'

'Marshall, it's okay. Can we all just calm down? I can explain everything, I just need–'

'People are staring,' the assistant director said, his voice low. 'We need to do this with minimum fuss.'

'Do what, for goodness sake?' Flora cried, exasperated. People were indeed staring, and more than a few were pointing. A woman took out her phone and started to video the scene. A sea of faces, some concerned, others clearly enjoying themselves. And another face, familiar to Flora, watching calmly from the far side of the atrium, his eyes shaded by a low peaked cap.

John Hopper.

He was here. Flora blinked as a group of tourists jostled into the security guards and were sent on their way; by the time she refocused, the man had disappeared.

You're imagining him again, Flora.

But this time she was certain it had been him. So he *was* in London. Looking out for her, or for some other reason altogether? It could not be a coincidence that he was at the museum today. But what on earth was he doing?

Thrown off guard, Flora allowed herself to be

shepherded into a small office just past the gift shop. She was aware of Marshall arguing and generally trying to throw his weight around, but it didn't seem to be doing him much good. Before long they were sitting side by side on a low plastic sofa, with the short security guard perched on an small wooden desk, his hands clasped loosely in his lap. The other guard stood by the door, presumably in case they made a run for it, and the assistant director hovered behind the desk, sighing heavily.

'This is all very unfortunate,' he said. 'I do so hate a scene.'

'Maybe if you gave us a head's up, there wouldn't be a scene,' Marshall said gruffly.

The guard seated on the desk said, 'We've had a complaint.'

'I know all about that,' Flora interrupted. 'It was my friend, Professor Paulson, who called you. He told you about a fake artefact that is being passed off as the real thing, right here in the museum.'

The assistant director's face paled at the mention of the word fake.

'Well,' Flora continued hesitantly, 'it isn't actually a fake. The professor made that up, so that you would bring Jasmin White here and confront her. The thing is, the woman you've bought this collection from, she faked a burglary and pretended that the Lamassu tablet had been stolen. But it hadn't. It was there all along, packed up with the other artefacts. Except, we didn't pack it. We know now that it was brought in with a box of other stuff, and in that box was also the body of–'

'Flora.'

She stopped. Marshall had his hand on her arm. He shook his head slowly. She swallowed.

'I think,' Marshall said, his smile as cold as ice, 'that you should tell us what this complaint was about.'

'Sure.' The security guard eyed Flora curiously.

'Although I'm sure your story is far more interesting. But for now, all we need to do is look inside your bag.'

'My ... my bag?' Flora looked around the room, puzzled. 'What on earth for?'

'There was a report of a woman matching your description, with a man matching your description, Mr Goodman, showing an unhealthy interest in one of the exhibits. The person who called us said he had seen you take the exhibit from its case and put it inside your bag. Now, this is a sensitive and highly unusual item, and we didn't want to embarrass you, or the assistant director here, by doing this in the middle of the great hall.'

'I'm sorry, I literally have no idea what you're talking about.' Flora tried to imagine fitting one of the enormous winged bulls into her tote. 'Who said this?'

'Your bag please, madam?'

Flora handed her bag to the second guard wordlessly. She turned to say something to Marshall, but he shook his head again and put his finger to his lips. His eyes were wary. Flora snaked her hand into his, and found his reassuring squeeze hugely comforting.

They watched as the guard emptied Flora's tote. Out came the knitting bag with its tangle of wool and needles sticking out of the top, then her oversized purse, lipstick, hairbrush, notebook, pens, the key to their hotel room. Nick's red Bluetooth speaker. Her house keys, a small fabric bag containing a variety of painkillers and plasters. A bottle of perfume. Another lipstick. A few receipts and other scraps of paper. Earphones. Each item was looked at carefully then placed on the desk. Eventually, the man reached the bottom of her tote and all but stuck his head inside to check it was empty.

'That's pretty much it, I think,' Flora snapped. 'You might find the odd dust ball in there. Maybe a tampon or two.'

His head emerged quickly. 'Nothing,' he said to his colleague, who nodded sagely.

'Did you take the item, Miss Lively?' the first guard asked.

Flora threw up her hands in exasperation. 'I genuinely have no idea what you're talking about.'

'And if you don't start talking soon, there is going to be trouble,' Marshall added. 'You've brought us in here, probably just carried out an illegal search, and now you're detaining us with no explanation or cause.' His tone matched the casual timbre of the security guard, but his eyes said danger.

'It was an ancient bronze phallus,' the assistant director said pompously. 'From the Roman era. An amulet, actually, worn as a fertility symbol by–'

Marshall burst out laughing. Flora glanced at him angrily, then noticed that both security guards were also trying to suppress smiles. The assistant director huffed.

'It's hardly funny. These phalluses were hugely important to the culture of the–'

Now Marshall was roaring with laughter, and the smaller guard could barely contain his smirk.

'Marshall, what's got into you?'

He wiped a tear from the corner of his eye and grinned. 'An ancient bronze phallus, Flora? Really?'

'I don't get it,' she said. The taller security guard began to laugh now, but quickly stopped when the assistant director threw him a stern look.

'A phallus is a penis,' Marshall whispered.

'A what?' Flora's eyes widened.

'And someone has accused you of showing a – what was it you said? An unhealthy interest in it.'

'And putting it in your bag,' the first security guard confirmed. Even he looked dubious now. He jumped down from the desk and turned to face the assistant director. 'Do we have anything on CCTV confirming this?'

'Erm, no. I don't think so. Not yet, anyway.'

'It is definitely missing, though?'

The taller man baulked. 'Well, we haven't checked as yet. We had the complaint and Miss Lively and Mr Goodman were pointed out to us and then–'

'It clearly isn't in Flora's bag,' Marshall stated, more sombre now, 'and we haven't been outside of the museum since nine this morning. Nor did we look at any ancient phalli.'

'The plural is actually phalluses,' the assistant director said. Marshall grinned again.

'Look.' Flora was desperate to take control of the situation. 'Who exactly made this allegation about me?'

'I'm afraid I'm not at liberty to say.'

Marshall's expression turned sour and he rounded on the assistant director. 'Mate, you're gonna have to do better than that. You've brought us in here, insulted my girlfriend's honour, and illegally searched her bag. Come up with some concrete evidence or get out of my way.' This last was directed at the security guard by the door, who was twice Marshall's size but still recoiled.

Flora smiled to herself. Insulted her honour, indeed. Marshall was great to have around in a crisis – he could ramp it up to eleven in seconds.

'Is it possible, do you think,' the smaller security guard said, 'that someone could be playing a joke on you?'

'You think?' Marshall answered.

'Marshall,' Flora said quietly, 'I don't think it's a joke. I think someone wants us out of the way.'

'Me too,' he whispered. 'Which is all the more reason for us to get out of this room.'

'We need to get hold of the professor and see what's going on.'

Marshall nodded and stood up.

'So if there's nothing else?'

Flora followed Marshall's lead and walked out of the tiny office. No one made a move to stop them. At the door, she stopped and turned around. 'Will you just tell me one thing?' she said. 'You're the assistant director, right?'

'The assistant to the director. But yes, essentially.'

'So if someone called the museum and reported that you'd bought a fake artefact, or one of the items on display was faked, would you hear about it?'

Again, the man's face paled at the mere mention of the F-word. 'I certainly would! And I would make it my business to investigate immediately.'

'And you've had no such call this morning?' Flora said, watching his expression carefully.

'Of course not.'

Flora nodded, then followed Marshall out of the room.

'We need coffee.' he said. But when he started to walk towards the museum cafe, Flora pulled him back.

'I totally need coffee' she said, grimacing, 'but please, can we just get out of here for a while? I can't breathe in this place.'

'Yes, my lady,' he answered, doffing an imaginary cap. 'Your wish is my command.'

Chapter 23

After Marshall had plied her with coffee and cake, he suggested they head back to the hotel to pack. A thorough debrief hadn't shed any more light on the situation, Professor Paulson still wasn't answering his phone, and Flora knew she had come to an impasse. More than that, she'd come to the end of the road.

'Cheer up, honey,' he said again. 'You can't win them all.'

Flora could have told him that she wasn't feeling down because she'd failed to solve the mystery, or even because Jasmin was potentially going to get away with murder. No, Flora's mood had started to plummet the moment she saw John Hopper at the museum. The incident with the bag-searching had been a diversion. In more ways than one. But now Flora had no choice but to face the truth.

John Hopper was in this up to his neck.

Turning up at the museum the night of the murder. Hanging around outside at midnight, just as the strange noises began. Being here, at the museum, on the day the collection was to go on display. Had it been him who had made the false complaint to get them out of the way? Was he the man Jasmin had been with on the night of the murder – her so-called alibi?

Flora was even starting to wonder whether John Hopper and Professor Paulson were one and the same. The professor clearly hadn't come through for them, which Flora couldn't understand for a second. He had been so keen to help. She had trusted him. Could that white moustache and those black-rimmed glasses be a clever disguise? But how did you fake a shiny bald head?

Worst of all was the sinking realisation that if John Hopper *was* mixed up in all this Lamassu business, then Marshall was right. He was not her birth father. The whole story had been made up. Which just about broke her heart.

Something else was bothering her too. She'd never truly believed that Jasmin could have killed Lucy Akopian. And if that was true, and Jasmin had an accomplice, then the accomplice must have been the killer. And if that man really was John Hopper ...

Has she been taken in by a cold-blooded murderer pretending to be her father?

'Honey? Are you okay?'

Marshall's new-found solicitousness was starting to get on her nerves, but it was enough of a novelty that Flora didn't want to burst the bubble just yet.

'Not really,' she sighed, snuggling into his shoulder briefly then pulling away. The chain coffee store was filling up for lunch now, and they were crushed together at one end of a long upholstered bench. Flora was beginning to feel just a little bit suffocated. 'I don't feel ready to go back to the hotel yet,' she confessed. 'In fact ... Marshall, would you mind if I just had an hour or two on my own?'

His hurt expression pierced her heart, but she stayed resolute. 'I just want to wander the streets for a while, maybe visit that little park over there. Collect my thoughts.'

'Time is getting on, sweetheart,' he reminded her. 'I have to get the lorry by six, and it's on the other side of the river.'

'I won't be long,' she promised.

'No more sleuthing, though,' Marshall said. 'Are we agreed?'

She nodded. Fat chance. She was going to write this one off as a disaster and learn her lesson. Solving mysteries was definitely best left to the experts.

Outside the cafe, Marshall held her close and kissed the top of her head. Flora forced a smile onto her face, and promised to follow him back to the hotel shortly. She watched him walk away, the familiar gait, the broad shoulders, the wavy, unruly hair. She stood in a shop doorway and watched until he was no longer visible, and then she let out a long, shaky sigh.

What now?

Flora decided to head towards Russell Square, drawn by the promise of trees and greenery in the midst of this city of concrete and brick and glass. She would sit for a while and let it all float away. And then she would get up and walk down Great Russell Street, taking one last look at the museum before going back to the hotel, and then back to Shropshire.

She might never come to London again.

Why had the professor promised to make a call, but then done the opposite? Flora pictured his kindly face, the white moustache, the glasses. Not a disguise, no. You couldn't fake that hair lip. It reminded her of something. Hadn't she seen a similar face somewhere else recently? She scanned her memory as she walked. It was there, she could feel it. The face of a man with a distinct hair lip. He was a younger man, and not unattractive. His curved lip had given the impression of mischief, a rakish air.

Flora stopped and gasped. The image came to her as clear her reflection in the window of the high-end shoe shop into which she now gazed, unseeing. A black and white photograph from long ago. A row of explorers smiling at the camera, the men dressed in light linen suits and straw panamas; the one woman in their group wearing a long white skirt, white buttoned-up shirt, and a smug smile.

Flora tried to place where she had seen the photograph. She was sure she'd seen it during her research online. She pulled out her phone again, and ran through her search history. There it was, just as she'd remembered. Eight men and one woman standing in front of a dusty jeep. And there, right in the centre, was a younger Professor Paulson, standing right next to the radiant Jasmin White. It's either him or his twin brother, Flora thought. So the professor had been on expeditions with Jasmin; he was a contemporary of hers. It made sense that they'd covered the same stomping ground back in the day, with their mutual interest in Assyrian artefacts. But why hadn't the professor mentioned it to Flora?

Yasemin Beyaz. Of course – he'd have known Jasmin by another name. He would have had no reason to connect the owner of a small museum in Shropshire with a glamorous woman he knew forty-odd years ago.

Was the professor in danger too, Flora wondered? Had she inadvertently put him at risk by contacting him? Perhaps that was why he hadn't made the call, and was now ignoring his phone.

Flora roused herself and began to move with the tide of people that flowed towards Russell Square. At the crossing, she waited for the green man to beep. She was on autopilot, head down, following the feet of the people in front, falling behind a little, her mind elsewhere. She didn't see the car until it was almost on top of her; if it hadn't been for a pair of hands yanking her out of the road she would certainly have been under its wheels, or thrown over the bonnet like a rag doll.

'Jesus!' A woman's voice said, and then, 'Are you okay, love?'

Reeling, Flora steadied herself against a nearby lamppost.

'That car was heading right for you,' said the man who very likely saved her life. Flora noticed only his reddish stubble, sandy blonde hair and prominent belly. A round woman with high heels clung onto his arm. Everything seemed to be coming to her in flashes. One minute she was crossing the road, the next ...

'Thank you,' she said, finding her voice at last. 'Oh my. Thank you so much.'

'S'alright. But you be careful, won't you?'

'Do you want to call the police?' the woman asked. 'I got a look at the car. Big black thing it was, going way too fast. Went straight through a red light! Man and a woman in it, the man was driving. Didn't get a butchers at him, but she was a sight for sore eyes. All long dark hair and dark skin, with a right snooty look on her face.'

Flora stared at the woman. It couldn't be. 'This woman,' she said, 'was she wearing white by any chance?'

'Well, she was as it goes! That's what made her stand out, like. Dressed as if she was going to a wedding or the opera something.'

'Jasmin,' Flora whispered. 'I don't suppose you got a good look at the man who was driving?' she asked.

'Nah. Not really. I think he had a grey jacket on, but I can't be sure. Will you be okay now? Be careful, love. Some drivers are crazy round here.'

Flora thanked them again, then stumbled to the nearest bench and sat down heavily. Too many coincidences belied the truth – she was pretty certain that Jasmin White had been in that car. Jasmin had tried to get rid of her and Marshall in the museum with that phallus stunt, and now this. Did that mean that Flora was near to the truth? But how could Jasmin possibly know what Flora was thinking?

John Hopper's face in the crowd ... Flora swallowed. Please, don't let him be a part of this.

An alternative explanation suddenly occurred to her. Maybe Professor Paulson *had* remembered Jasmin, and had contacted her instead of going along with Flora's plan. Some old loyalty, maybe an old crush that never faded. She pictured his face earlier, the white moustache, the sun glinting off his black-rimmed glasses ...

What did she know about the professor, really? She'd entrusted a whole load of information to some dusty old academic in Switzerland, but there was no reason for him to help Flora. On impulse, Flora Googled his name and scanned the resulting images. Nothing. It would help if she knew his first name. Where was it he used to work? Flora did another search, this time for Swiss universities. An information panel appeared at the top of her mobile search engine; Flora scrolled down the page, looking for something to jog her memory.

Then she stopped, frowned, and scrolled back to the top of the page. In Geneva, Switzerland it was six degrees and raining. Raining? She checked again, on a different site. Raining with heavy cloud cover, all over Switzerland.

And yet the professor had been standing in brilliant sunshine when Flora Skyped him earlier.

He could have been somewhere else, of course. But he'd answered her question about how things were in Switzerland by saying they were lucky with the weather. That had to have been a lie, whichever way you looked at it. Flora sifted through their two conversations, looking for inconsistencies. He knew a lot about Lamassu, most of which had been backed up by Flora's research. And he'd been nothing but helpful and open with her.

That was the problem with this business, she reflected. It made it impossible to trust anyone. Paranoia wasn't going to get her anywhere, and right now the one place she needed to be was back at the hotel with Marshall.

After scanning the busy street for large black cars, Flora set off, this time paying full attention to her surroundings.

The trouble was, with so many people about it was hard to get her bearings. She'd left Russell Square behind and had taken a left onto Keppel Street. She stopped and looked at the map on her phone. If she kept going this way she'd cross Tottenham Court Road and then be only a couple of blocks from the hotel. She pocketed her phone with a grimace. Blocks, indeed. She sounded more like Marshall every day.

But after walking for another thirty minutes, Flora was dismayed to find that she recognised nothing. Up ahead was the BT tower, looming over the buildings like a nineteen-seventies space station. She was certain their digs were nowhere near this landmark. She turned right into a narrow terrace and stopped to check her map again. Conway Street. There were fewer people here, and Flora began to feel uneasy. Should she retrace her steps? Or press on? You'd think, she mused, that with GPS and Google on everyone's phone it would be impossible to get lost. You couldn't, however, walk along with your phone in front of your nose. She didn't want to find herself being nearly mowed down by a car again.

The next street was even narrower and more deserted than the last. Flora jumped as a man called to her from a doorway. A rough sleeper, wrapped in a dirty blanket and sitting on cardboard, his eyes struggling to focus. Flora mumbled that she had no cash, and hurried on. Disorientated now, she turned right again, searching for a busier street, maybe somewhere with a cafe or a bar where she could stop and regroup. And call Marshall.

How he would love coming to her rescue. She'd never hear the end of it – the time she got lost walking four blocks in central London. But right now, Flora didn't care. She'd endure all the teasing just to be back in that cute hotel room, throwing their clothes into a suitcase, their banter easing the tension and guiding them back to normal life.

Another two streets and Flora found herself on a bridge overlooking the canal. It was busier here: there was a mooring below, and a steady stream of pedestrians jostling for position on the narrow pavement. She pulled out her phone. It was over two hours since she'd said goodbye to Marshall – he would be getting worried about her soon. But before she could dial, someone crashed heavily into her side; she threw out her hand to steady herself and dropped her phone onto the path.

'Sorry Miss.'

It was only a boy, no more than fourteen or fifteen, and he staggered on, the apology thrown over his shoulder. Flora crouched down to search for her phone. Panic rising in her chest, she scanned the pavement frantically. Someone nearly tripped over her, cursing and telling her to get out of the way. She stood up, her heart beating too fast. And there, on the other side of the road, a black car was parked. Its engine was running; the driver's window wound down, a man's arm visible. Flora turned away and began to jog, weaving between the oncoming pedestrians, trying to calm her breathing. She crossed the bridge and instinctively turned left, glancing back to see if the black car had followed, but the road had dropped down the embankment, and now Flora found herself on a narrow lane running parallel to the canal.

'Not a good idea,' she said, stopping to catch her breath. Worse still, the light was starting to fade. Soon it would be dusk, and she'd be here alone, wandering the streets with no phone and no clue where she was.

'Come on, Flora,' she said to herself sternly. 'Pull yourself together. You can think your way out of this.'

Her brave words, however, did little to comfort.

She decided to do a one-eighty and head towards the marina. She would ask for help, maybe borrow a phone, or at the very least get directions to their hotel.

The canal towpath was clean and well-maintained, with a row of benches overlooking the water and pretty houses on the other side. Flora began to feel better, smiling at a cyclist peddling towards her. The cyclist glared. London people, Flora noted, were not super-friendly.

She followed the towpath back under the bridge, glancing up and wondering what had happened to her phone. Someone must have grabbed it as soon as it fell out of her hands. A phone could be replaced, but all her numbers, her diary, her photos ...

Busy thinking about how she was going to get her data back, Flora didn't notice right away that someone was following her. But her senses were on high alert, and when she heard gravel crunching softly, she slowed, listening carefully. Should she turn and confront, or run? She took a deep, steadying breath. She was alone, there were likely two of them. She knew Jasmin was unlikely to be a threat, but who was the woman with?

Just who was this mystery accomplice?

Suddenly, Flora was mad as hell. She couldn't stand this for one moment longer. She'd lost her phone, she'd been humiliated at the museum, she was lost and afraid, and for what? If Jasmin or her accomplice wanted to do her harm, they were going to have to confront her face to face first. Flora summoned up all of her courage, clenched her fists tight, and swung around.

'What,' she screamed at the top of her voice, 'the hell do you want?'

Chapter 24

'Flora?'

John Hopper stood on the towpath, frozen in place. His eyes were wide, and he held out his hands, palms lifted. 'Flora,' he said again. 'Are you okay?'

'Don't come near me,' she hissed. 'You've been following me. I saw you at the museum.'

Her heart was beating so fast she could hear it above her own voice. Adrenaline coursed through her body, her legs felt like jelly and her stomach churned.

She'd thought she was such a good judge of character. She'd thought she could trust him. How wrong she'd been.

'Flora, you need to come with me,' he said. Flora laughed out loud, aware that her laugh sounded strange and a little unhinged.

'You've got to be joking,' she mocked, taking a step backwards. 'Come with you? The man who pretended to be my father? The man who has been following me, spying on me, trying to run me down.'

'That wasn't me, Flora. And I can explain, I promise. But please, I need you to trust me. You're in danger, and–'

'Yes, I know I'm in danger. From you and that crazy woman.' Flora backed away again. She risked a quick glance around her. It was even darker under the bridge, and there was no one else in sight. Faint music and voices from the marina seemed as far away as home. 'I'm not stupid. I have figured it out, you know.'

John Hopper took a step closer. 'Flora. Listen to your heart, not your fear. Remember our conversation over breakfast. Remember what I told you. You will never be in danger from me. Quite the opposite.'

Listen to your heart. It was such an incongruous thing to say, he took Flora by surprise. She allowed herself to look properly at his face. Without his cap his eyes were clearly visible and Flora could only see genuine emotion there. So much emotion. In fact, he was practically shaking. Her gaze travelled down to his hands. He was holding something out to her. A phone.

'It got kicked into the road,' he explained. 'I managed to grab it before a car went over it.'

'Why,' Flora said, her voice cracking, 'have you been following me?'

'To protect you.'

'From what, exactly?' When he hesitated, Flora cried out in frustration. 'You want me to trust you but you won't tell me anything! It's time to start talking. Else I'm going to run, screaming, towards those boats over there. Then we'll see if you really mean me any harm.'

He nodded. 'Fair enough. You are in danger, Flora. And I can protect you. Take your phone and call your boyfriend if you want to. Or call the police. It's up to you. But first, will you please come with me, just until we're somewhere safe. I'll tell you everything, I promise.'

'Tell me now,' Flora insisted. She didn't move as he approached her and held out her phone. Flora grabbed it and checked the screen. It didn't appear to be broken.

A red people carrier swung down into the narrow lane, its fan belt squealing in the damp air.

'We should get out of here,' John said. He dropped his hands to his sides. Flora was struck again by how solid he was, like an immovable object. But she didn't feel threatened anymore. Maybe it was the false security of having a mobile phone in her hand, but her breathing was starting to slow down as she thought more clearly.

'Where do you want to go?' she said.

'I'll walk you back to your hotel. We can talk on the

way.'

'You don't have a car?'

He shook his head. 'I can call a taxi though, if you don't feel up to walking.'

No car. So maybe it hadn't been him with Jasmin. Regardless, she definitely wasn't ready to be stuck in the back of a cab with him just yet.

'Walking is fine,' she said.

As they set off, Flora kept out of arm's reach and checked her messages. There was only one from Marshall, asking if she was okay. He would need to go and pick up their van from the lorry park soon. Flora texted that she was fine and wouldn't be long.

How to explain what had happened during the past couple of hours?

'So,' she said as they walked quickly up the embankment towards the bridge, 'what do you want to tell me?'

'First off, Flora, I'm sorry that I scared you. It's the last thing I wanted.' He laughed hollowly. 'I used to be a lot better at shadowing people. Must be losing my touch.'

Shadowing people? Flora shot him a sideways glance. Just who was this man?

'I thought you were with Jasmin. Working for her. Or with her,' Flora said, still watching him.

'I can see why you would think that, but no. Far from it.'

'Is Jasmin trying to hurt me? There was a car back there. It nearly ran me down.'

'I didn't see that. I'm sorry.'

'But I am in danger? You said you're trying to protect me ...?'

'Jasmin,' John said, his shoulders hunched, hands shoved deep into his pockets, 'isn't dangerous on her own. But the man she's with – now he's another story. Jasmin will do anything for him, anything he tells her.

She always has.'

'Who is he?' Flora asked, almost jogging to keep up with the older man's pace. 'And what do you have to do with all this? You're involved somehow, you must be. Is that why you were there in Shrewsbury, at the museum? Was it not for me at all?'

She could have bitten off her tongue as soon as the last question was out of her mouth. She did not want him to know how badly she wanted everything he had told her to be true. But John Hopper slowed his pace and looked at her, his eyes once again full of emotion.

'Flora, everything I have told you is true. Every word. I was there to see you, but I would probably have been there anyway, or someone would have. We've been watching Jasmin for some time.'

'So, you really are ... what you said you are? To me, I mean.' Flora couldn't hold it in any longer. The stress of the last few hours, never mind the last few days, had pushed her to tipping point.

'We can stop here for a moment,' he said, guiding her gently into a small cafe with steamed-up windows. Flora hesitated for only a moment, then followed him inside. They sat at a table covered in shiny fabric and John ordered two coffees in takeaway cups.

'We don't have much time, Flora. But I can see that you need to hear this now, not later. So bear with me, okay? Let me tell it in my own way.'

Flora nodded mutely. She tucked her hands under her thighs and began to listen.

***

'I found you last year, after a long search and calling in lots of favours from the agency I work for. You were working in this big country house, and it was hard to get the opportunity to talk to you on your own. I didn't know, you see, if meeting me would be embarrassing for you, or make you angry. I was going to approach you when you were out hiking one day, but I messed that up too. You seemed so anxious. I didn't want to make things worse. But then I got called away for work. It was terrible timing. I was in the Middle East for months. I tried to write to you, but I couldn't find the right words. Guess I'm more of a man of action.'

'So it was *you* who followed me at Stiperstones?' Flora said. She recalled the day she had gone out hiking alone while they were working on the film set, desperate for some space and a bit of clarity. She'd thought it was the murderer; she'd thought she was about to be attacked. 'You scared the shit out of me!'

'I know.' John grimaced. 'As I said, I used to be much better at shadowing people. But then, you are very sharp. Most people walk around oblivious. You, on the other hand, have a well-developed suspicious mind.'

Flora smiled. She couldn't deny it.

'When I heard about Lucy Akopian's murder I came back to England on the next flight. As first it was a good excuse to check in on you again, but then when I found out you were working for Jasmin White I was worried. I can't help but feel protective of you, even if I have no right to. I wanted to stay nearby but didn't want you to feel suffocated. And then of course, there's your hot-headed boyfriend. Although, to be fair, I did feel reassured that he would take care of you. He seems protective.'

'Some might say over-protective,' Flora sighed.

'It's not always a bad thing. I had to go away again to finish up a job, but I flew back as soon as I could, only to find that you and your fella had left for London that same day. So I tracked you down again and I've been keeping an eye on you.'

'I don't know why you didn't tell me all this when we first met. It would have saved me a lot of angst. I thought you were involved with Jasmin and the murder at the museum.'

'Well, your instincts weren't that far off. I suppose I am in a way.'

'Because of your job?' Flora said, leaning in and lowering her voice. 'Are you ... I mean, do you work for the government?'

John Hopper laughed. 'Not exactly. But we'll get to that later, I promise. For now, don't you think I should get you back to your over-protective boyfriend? Won't he be worried.'

Flora looked abashed. 'Actually he's been calling and texting the whole time we've been sat in here. But I wanted to hear you out. I do feel kind of bad.'

'Text him now,' John told her authoritatively. 'There's nothing worse than worrying about the person you love.'

Love. The word hung in the air as John paid for their coffees, then opened the cafe door for Flora. While they'd been inside it had started to drizzle; the road was slick with rain and smelt strongly of car fumes.

'I don't think,' Flora said, pulling her poncho over her head, 'that I will be able to call you dad.' She couldn't look at him, didn't want to see disappointment in his eyes.

John Hopper smiled at her and shook his head. 'I'm looking forward to finding out all about your dad. From where I'm standing, seems like he did a fine job of bringing you up. And John is just fine with me.'

'You're a private detective, aren't you,' Flora asked, taking his arm as they crossed the street. 'It's in the blood. I always knew it. Stuff just seems to happen to me, I can't help it.'

'I'm not a private detective.' John swapped her over to his other side, away from the road. Just like Marshall. She smiled to herself, feeling safe for the first time in days. She had two men protecting her. Nothing could hurt her now.

Chapter 25

'Where the hell have you been? And what is that asshole doing here!'

Flora made an apologetic face to John Hopper, then led Marshall back inside the hotel. Quickly, she told him what had happened that afternoon. When she got to the part about John finding her phone, Marshall interjected angrily.

'But if he was watching out for you, why did he let you get lost in the first place?'

'He's my father, not a mind reader! He didn't know where I was going, for goodness sake. It was only when I went down by the canal that he approached me.'

'You went where?'

'It's not important.' Flora blinked impatiently and ran her hand through her hair. 'Listen to me, Marshall. John overheard Jasmin saying there was one last place they have to go before they leave. It's our last chance to find them.'

'Find them? Find who? What are you talking about?' Marshall's face was turning an alarming shade of red. 'Flora, I missed the cut off time for the lorry park. Do you realise we're stuck here now, but we've been checked out of our room? We have nowhere to stay tonight. I had to pack for both of us, I've had nothing to eat, and I've been going out of my mind with worry. Meanwhile, you've been having adventures around Camden Town with your so-called father.'

Flora reached up and touched his cheek. 'Marshall,' she said softly. 'I love you. I don't tell you often enough, but I do love you. And I appreciate all that you do, and how you look out for me, and how you try to protect me.'

Taken aback, Marshall frowned. He opened his mouth to speak, but then closed it again.

'We can find another hotel,' Flora said. 'And we aren't going to argue so much anymore, Marshall. A bit of banter, like in the good old days, is fine. But this constant battling is just eroding our love. And I don't want that.'

'You've said love three times in five seconds,' he said sulkily. 'If you weren't looking at me like that I'd think you were breaking up with me.'

'Never,' Flora assured him. 'No matter how crazy you get me. But right now–'

Marshall groaned. 'Let me guess. Right now you need me to trust you, and go with the flow, right? Not ask too many questions, not go on about how annoyed I am at you. And probably come along on some wild goose chase across London to find someone–'

'Two people, actually,' Flora corrected, smiling.

'To find two people who may or may not be guilty of something or other and should really be dealt with by the police, not by an annoying woman from Shropshire. Is that fairly accurate?'

Flora stood on her tiptoes and kissed him on the mouth. She lingered just long enough to feel his response, then she pulled away slightly and looked into his eyes.

'Perfectly accurate,' she whispered with a mischievous wink. 'Now call a cab will you? We've got work to do.'

***

'I know where Jasmin is going,' Flora announced as soon as she, Marshall and John Hopper were inside the taxi. Marshall merely looked to the heavens, but John whistled.

'Where?'

'To Trafalgar Square, driver. As quick as you can.' Flora sat back, a proud smile on her face. 'I'm absolutely sure of it.'

'Ah. The Lamassu sculpture on the fourth plinth.' John nodded, clearly impressed. 'That makes sense.'

'Go on then, Miss Marple,' Marshall sighed. 'Tell us how you worked it out. You know you're dying to show off some more.'

'Well, it wasn't hard,' Flora admitted. 'I mean, she told me that she'd never seen it, but what it represents must mean so much to her. I found a news report of Isis destroying the winged bulls from the ancient city of Nineveh,' she explained to John. 'Jasmin was in the crowd, watching. This symbol of ancient protection, it's personal for her. I really wouldn't be surprised if ...' She tailed off uneasily. A thought had just occurred to her, but it was too outrageous to be possible.

'Jasmin's family hails back to the Iraq of old.' John took up the story. 'I think it's how she managed to convince herself that all the collecting she did wasn't really looting. She thinks of it as repatriation.'

'Excuse me,' Marshall said, leaning over to peer around Flora. 'How do you know so much about Jasmin White? I thought you were just along for the ride?'

'Ah.' Flora glanced at her father, then turned to her boyfriend. 'There might be a couple of other details I missed out.'

'It's okay, Flora,' John said. 'Let me. It's about time me and your fella got properly acquainted.'

Fifteen minutes later they arrived at Trafalgar Square, and Flora's neck was aching from flipping back and forth between the two men. She'd sat opened mouthed as John Hopper explained that he worked for a private security firm that specialised in tracking down and recovering lost treasures, returning them to their country or culture of origin.

The Middle East, Flora thought. It made sense now. That would be where he worked a lot of the time, and explained why Jasmin White had been on his radar.

'Hang on a minute,' Marshall said as they jumped out of the black cab. 'Are you saying you're some kind of treasure hunter?'

Flora's eyes widened. She hadn't thought of it like that. But John only shrugged.

'That's not my official job title,' he said modestly.

Marshall seemed to regard the older man with a little more respect. He threw his arm around Flora's shoulders. 'Well, it's not surprising that you turned out to be such a pain in the ass, then. Looks like a run of the mill existence was never gonna be your destiny.'

Before Flora could respond, John ushered them across the road. 'We'll wait over there,' he said, pointing to a set of long stone benches on the opposite side of the square. 'We'll have a good view of the plinth, but they won't see us. At least, they won't see us straight away.'

Flora agreed. It wasn't the obvious place to keep lookout – there were benches nearer to Nelson's column that gave a clearer view, and it was busier there, giving them more cover. But because of that, it would also be the first place that Jasmin was likely to check.

He was good. Flora grinned to herself, impressed. Her father, an international treasure hunter. Pretty cool.

'We all know what Jasmin looks like,' John said, scrolling through his phone, 'but you should see a picture of the man she's with. Just in case they turn up separately.' He passed the phone to Flora, tapping the screen to zoom. 'That's him. I've been on his tail for more years than I care to remember.'

Flora looked at the photograph and gasped.

'But this is Professor Paulson,' she cried.

'Who?'

'The expert who has been helping me. Well, I thought he was helping ...' Flora zoomed in closer. 'It's definitely him.'

The photo was grainy and taken covertly; the man was captured half-turning on a busy city street, his expression intense and focused. He was dressed in a navy pullover and white shirt, and was broad-shouldered and stocky. He was clean shaven, and there was no mistaking that sardonic tilt to his lips.

'You've spoken to him?' John Hopper said, visibly tense.

'Only on Skype. Hold on.' Flora pulled out her own phone and brought up the search history again. She showed John the black and white expedition photograph. 'It's the same person, isn't it?'

'That's him. I've seen that old clipping a few times. It was the last photo taken before he disappeared. He re-emerged a few years ago in Panama. I nearly caught up with him then, but he's a slippery character, that's for sure.'

'He disappeared?' Flora frowned. 'I don't get it. He was a university lecturer for thirty years. How could he have disappeared?'

'Flora,' John said, his eyes trained on the other side of the square. 'This man is not who you think he is. And his name is not Paulson.'

It hit Flora then like a hurricane. The final piece fell into place and her hands flew up to her mouth. 'Oh my god,' she cried. 'It's Fed Akopian, isn't it? That's the man Jasmin is with! He's not dead, or missing. He's been here the whole time!'

'Easy, tiger,' Marshall said. 'I thought we were on a secret stakeout.'

'Professor Paulson is Fed Akopian,' she whispered excitedly. 'I *knew* there was something off about him.'

Marshall laughed. 'Of course you did.'

'I did,' Flora protested. 'I remembered the old photo, figured out he knew Jasmin. I even looked up the weather in Switzerland.'

'You what?'

'It was raining there today. Not sunny. On the video call it was brilliant sunshine. Just like here.'

'Because he was here,' John Hopper said. 'You're right, Flora. It looks as though our man was posing as your professor.'

'So, hold on. Let me get this straight.' Flora could barely sit still. Connections were firing in her brain faster than she could think. 'Fed and Jasmin are working together. And it was Fed who killed Lucy? Of course it was, that makes sense now. But what I don't get is–'

'Flora?' John held up his hand, casting a quick but friendly glance her way before looking back at the fourth plinth. 'Why don't we do the debrief after we've got them both safely in police custody? Does that sound okay?'

Flora nodded, chastened, elbowing a snickering Marshall. Soon she would come face to face with not only Jasmin but also the man who had been working against her the whole time. Professor Paulson, indeed. Her mouth a thin line of displeasure, she settled back to wait.

***

An hour later, Flora's resolve was beginning to wear thin. She was freezing cold and bored out of her mind. *And* hungry and thirsty and tired of waiting.

'My bum is going numb,' she complained to Marshall. He glanced at her, shook his head, then went back to looking at his phone.

'I'm not here,' he said. 'None of this has anything to do with me.'

John Hopper looked like he hadn't moved a muscle since he last spoke. His breath was steady and even.

Flora sighed. This clearly wasn't a part of the whole detective thing that she was good at. Her strengths lay elsewhere. She turned her attention to the plinth; it was lit from below on all four sides, and even from this distance she was impressed by the detail. Made entirely from tin cans – Iraqi date-syrup cans, if her memory was correct – and constructed in response to Isis' vandalism, the sculpture was a riot of green and red and yellow.

'It's called *The Invisible Enemy Should Not Exist*,' John whispered. 'Fitting, don't you think?'

Flora nodded, although she wasn't entirely sure she understood. 'John,' she said, 'can I ask you a question about the Lamassu? Not that one, but the one Jasmin said had been stolen.'

'The Seventh Tablet,' John said softly.

'So that's a real thing? That's its name?'

'It is. It belonged to the daughter of an Assyrian king. Legend has it that the tablet was given to her as a promise of peace between two warring families. Originally it would have been painted similar to the statue over there. But it was more than a toy.' John paused, his eyes narrowing. Flora tried to follow his gaze, but there was no one around the plinth. Maybe, she thought with a tiny shiver, he was simply seeing into the past.

'War broke out,' he continued, his voice so low she had to strain to listen, 'and the young princess was snatched from her bed one night and never seen again. Each side blamed the other, one accused of murder, the other of faking her disappearance as an excuse to break the treaty.'

'And the Lamassu?' Flora prompted when John paused again.

'They said it was splashed with her blood, and from that day became irrevocably cursed.'

'Wow. Jasmin never told me any of this.'

'It's possible she doesn't know the whole story,' John conceded, returning his gaze to the other side of the square. 'Only that it was cursed.'

'Why the *Seventh* tablet?' Flora asked, rubbing her hands to try and warm them.

'It was the seventh gift given to the king that year. And the seventh promise of peace.'

'The noises at the museum,' Flora said, thinking of the clock and how it only chimed seven times at midnight. 'Do you think–'

'All Jasmin's doing,' John said quietly. 'We think that on the night you found Lucy Akopian, the sounds you heard were a crate–'

'Being brought inside,' Flora finished. 'And the Lamassu was packed into that crate, wasn't it, along with Lucy's body?'

John Hopper nodded. 'You are quite right, Flora. I'm impressed.'

'So Jasmin created the noises from that night on? The screams and the banging and the clock only chiming to seven?' When John nodded, Flora sighed. 'I suppose she did something to the clock so that it wouldn't chime midnight. She's a good actress. She had me completely fooled.'

'She had everyone fooled.'

'There's one thing that doesn't fit your neat little explanation,' Marshall piped up. 'If Lucy was already dead before she was put in that crate, then who did Flora and Nick hear screaming that first night?' He looked pleased with himself. Not so very clever, his expression said.

But John and Flora looked at each other and shook their heads in disbelief.

'Well, *obviously* it was Jasmin,' Flora said.

'She had no idea that Fed had killed his ex-wife,' John added.

'And when she opened the crate, probably eager to see what new treasures Fed had brought her ...'

'That he'd smuggled into the country illegally ...'

'She freaked out and went crazy.' Flora held up her

hand for a high-five, but John was looking at Marshall, a rare smile on his face.

'Ah, you guys are going to drive me crazy,' Marshall said, returning to his phone. 'And anyway, you're probably wasting your time. How do you know they haven't already been to see this stupid plinth statue thing? Or even if they are gonna bother.'

'When I last saw them, they were headed back to the museum,' John said firmly. 'They'll have a lot of loose ends to tie up before they can head to the airport. It explains why they needed you out of the way, Flora – you'd have recognised Fed from your Skype calls and raised the alarm.'

'They didn't have to run me down, though,' Flora said hotly.

'We don't know for sure it was them,' John pointed out.

'Hmm.' Flora wasn't so sure.'

'Anyway, there's no way they would have got here before us.'

'They'll be here,' Flora said, gazing at the tin-Lamassu, its message a warning across history. 'There's no way she'll leave the country without seeing this.'

Chapter 26

Flora woke up with a start. She couldn't have been asleep for more than ten minutes, her head on Marshall's chest, his arm warm around her shoulders.

'They're here.'

John's voice was low and steady, but Flora could hear the excited undertones. She rubbed her eyes and straightened her back. It was quieter than before, with only a few clusters of people crossing the square. She couldn't see Jasmin or Fed Akopian-slash-Professor Paulson. To their left, the stone lions guarded Nelson's column, and the spray from the fountains splashed onto the surrounding steps.

'What's the plan?' she whispered.

Marshall snickered. 'Some detective you are. You've been snoring for a half hour straight.'

She shot him a withering glare. 'Not the time, Marshall. Not the time.'

Abashed, Marshall nodded once. 'Sorry.'

'Okay,' John turned to Flora, his handsome face grave. 'You wait here. This could be dangerous and I–'

'Oh, no,' Flora said quickly. 'That's not happening. I've come too far to sit on the sidelines and watch.'

'Fed might be armed,' John Hopper protested. 'This isn't the place for heroics.'

'Did you hear that, Flora,' Marshall echoed. 'No heroics.'

Flora ignored him. 'We're in this together. Now, what's the plan?'

'We're wasting time,' John said, obviously realising it was pointless to keep arguing. 'Marshall, you walk around the perimeter that way. Stay near the wall. As soon as you start moving call the police. Give them my name and your location. That will be enough. Flora, you come with me. Stay close and–'

'No heroics. I got it.'

They circumnavigated Trafalgar Square, rounding the column to approach the fourth plinth from the west. John murmured instructions to her as they walked. He seemed to have a preternatural sense of what passersby were about to do, which way they might turn. Flora felt safe with him glued to her side. She also felt completely out of her depth.

'Where are they?' she whispered when John signalled for her to stop moving.

'There.' With the slightest nod of his head, he indicated a black range rover that was parked on the other side of a concrete barrier. Flora recognised it instantly.

'That's definitely the car that tried to run me down.' She felt suddenly sick. Fed might be armed, John had said. He had killed his ex wife; he was a wanted international trafficker of illegal antiquities. Fed Akopian was dangerous, Jasmin White was in thrall to him, and they'd already attacked her once in broad daylight.

What would they do under cover of darkness?

'It'll be okay, Flora,' John said. 'All we need to do is stall them until the police arrive. I have a contact in the Met, they'll be here soon.'

They crouched low behind a stone balustrade and watched Fed and Jasmin exit their car. Flora was surprised to see Jasmin dressed entirely in black, although it was obvious really that the woman wouldn't want to stand out tonight. Fed drew most of her attention, however. He was taller than she'd expected, and powerfully built. The white moustache was gone, along with the black-rimmed spectacles, and a grey beanie hat was pulled low over his head. But there was no mistaking that round face, the rakish curl of his lip, the piercing eyes. He let Jasmin walk ahead of him, his head pivoting, visibly tense and alert.

Jasmin ran across the road and approached the plinth. Flora watched, thinking about the history of the Lamassu, trying to put herself inside the woman's head. The invisible enemy should not exist, she thought. But it does. And maybe we are all our own invisible enemies. Jasmin had been the architect of her own downfall. The minute she read that newspaper report about a local woman solving crimes and decided to employ Flora's company, her fate was sealed. Despite all her attempts to confuse and obfuscate, to blame and deflect, here they were. Flora might have been on the back foot for most of the past two weeks, but she was one step ahead of them now.

Just then, Fed joined his partner by the plinth. He bent his head and said something in her ear. Jasmin pushed him away, still gazing up at the brightly coloured Lamassu. Flora thought that she could see tears in her eyes. Fed spoke again, then gripped her elbow. Jasmin gave out a little cry.

It was at this point that Flora spied Marshall. He was standing on the columned steps of the National Gallery building, about thirty metres away, trying to get their attention. Flora sucked in her breath. What was he thinking? He was going to ruin everything. She tapped John on the shoulder and pointed. Her father nodded.

'Wait here, Flora,' he whispered. 'I mean it.'

And then he stepped out from behind the balustrade and called out to Fed.

'Hey there, Mr Akopian. Long time no see.'

Fed whirled around as though he'd been shot in the arm. In one smooth movement he pulled Jasmin across his body and reached into his jacket pocket. Flora gasped. In his hand he held a shiny black pistol. He was pointing it not at John, however, but directly at Jasmin's head.

'Move any closer and I'll kill her.' Flora recognised his voice from their video calls, but he'd dropped the fake Swiss accent and was pure upper-class English. The smoothness of his voice in contrast to the swiftness of the escalation to violence left Flora reeling. Marshall had moved out of her line of vision. She just hoped he had the good sense to stay the hell out of the way.

John Hopper, however, seemed to be taking the turn of events in his stride. He stood solidly in front of Fed, his hands deep in his pockets, every part of him appearing completely relaxed.

'Ah, don't be like that, old chap,' he said casually. 'It's been so long since we caught up. Shame to pass up an opportunity like this.'

'I'm serious, friend,' Fed said warningly. 'This is not going to end the way you want it to.'

Meanwhile, Jasmin was struggling against Fed's grip, her cries muffled by his arm. She kicked him hard, her spiky heels hitting his shins, and he let go with a howl of pain. Jasmin ran, fast, heading for the gallery. For a moment, Fed appeared confused, unable to decide whether to go after her, shoot her, or deal with John Hopper first.

He made his decision and trained the gun on John. 'Just you and me then, old friend,' he said, smiling. 'The cards seem to be stacked in my favour this time, though.'

'I think we can work it out. My employers are willing to do a deal, in return for certain items being repatriated, naturally.'

'Naturally,' Fed agreed. He smiled and pulled out his phone, flicking his eyes to the screen, then back to John. 'Might that deal involve a significant sum of money?'

'It could. They do, as you know, have deep pockets.'

'Deep enough to send you all over the world tracking me down,' Fed laughed. 'I've led you a merry dance, don't you think?'

'And here we are,' John said mildly. 'Face to face at last.'

The sound of sirens filtered through the cold night air; Flora tensed, wondering what Fed would do now. He merely smiled even wider, his lip curling, his expression unreadable.

'Ah, I think you've been playing with me, all that talk of deals. Buying time? Waiting for the boys in blue to arrive?'

John Hopper shrugged. 'You would do the same, old chap. But it's still just me and you. Right here, right now. And I'm willing to talk.'

Fed's countenance changed abruptly. 'Cut the crap, Hopper. We both know who you work for. They'd rather see me hanging from this statue than pay me a penny.' He raised the pistol higher, then glanced back at his phone, his thumb working the screen. 'And as for it being just you and me ... Do you think I'm an idiot? I know you've got that meddling girl with you, and her great oaf of a boyfriend. And that, my friend, was your biggest mistake of all.'

Suddenly, the sound of screaming filled Flora's ears. It seemed to be coming from her, but her mouth was tightly shut; she had barely taken a breath these past few minutes. But the screaming got louder, and louder, and then it was replaced by the deafening chimes of a grandfather clock. She jumped up and saw John heading towards her, mouthing something she couldn't hear, his arms outstretched. How could the same noises she'd heard night after night at the museum be here now? Banging followed, and then more screaming. It was all merging together, a cacophony of sound, surrounding her, seeming to emanate from her own body ... From her own bag ...?

And then Flora understood. She threw her tote to the ground, tipping it up, letting the contents spill out. There it was – the little Bluetooth speaker they'd found in the crate yesterday. Fed must be transmitting some kind of recording, knowing that it would give away her hiding place, and that John would try to protect her, and ...

John stopped running and fell forwards onto the ground. It seemed to be after he'd fallen that the sound of the gun going off reached her ears, but that made no sense at all.

With a strangled cry, Flora ran to her father's side. She knelt over him, calling his name, trying to see his face. A shadow slid across them; Flora turned and looked directly into the barrel of Fed's pistol. She opened her mouth, more in shock than with intention to speak. It seemed so obscene, so ridiculous, to be here, facing this. Above them, the Lamassu looked down benignly. Flora looked into Fed's eyes. She saw nothing but hatred there.

'Get. Away. From. HER!'

Something threw itself at Fed, and pushed him to the ground. The gun clattered as it hit stone, and Flora kicked it away on instinct. It was Marshall – Marshall who had launched himself at her attacker and was now wrestling with the man, rolling further down the slope towards the column like a four-legged, two-headed beast.

'John?' Flora cried, turning back to her father. 'John, are you okay?'

She tried to turn him over. Had he been hit? She couldn't see a wound.

'Please, please be okay,' she sobbed. 'I've only just found you. You *can't* leave me again now. You just can't.'

'I think,' came a muffled voice from the ground, 'that it was me who found you.'

With effort, John Hopper eased himself onto his back and then gingerly sat up. 'And I'm not going anywhere. Don't you worry about that.'

Flora flung herself against him, not even feeling bad

when he winced with pain.

'You frightened the life out of me,' she said. 'I thought you'd been shot!'

'You thought right.' John tapped his chest with his knuckles. It made a hollow sound. 'Trusty old body armour,' he said, still wincing as he got up from the ground. 'Never leave home without it.'

'What *are* you?' Flora said, shaking her head in disbelief.

When John pulled her to standing, Flora saw that the police had surrounded them. Blue flashing lights reflected on the wet concrete and officers wearing hi-viz vests had cuffed Fed Akopian. An attractive policewoman with curly red hair nodded to John as she walked past.

'Your contact?' Flora smiled, noticing the look they exchanged.

John grinned. 'Fed had better watch out. If she's interrogating him, he won't be able to keep his secrets for long.'

'Hey! Does anybody want to know if I'm okay?' Marshall appeared behind Flora, only to be nearly knocked off his feet again when she threw her arms around him.

'You were the one who said no heroics,' she cried. 'But look at what you did!'

'You did great,' John told him. Marshall reached around Flora's back and shook his hand.

'It was a great plan,' he said.

'A what?' Flora pulled away from his embrace and looked from her boyfriend to her father and back again. 'You mean ... Did you two plan all that?'

'Sure did. We planned it all out while you were snoring your little head off.'

'Your boyfriend is an absolute gem, Flora. Carried it off like a pro.'

'So the waving at us, that was part of the plan too?

And diving on Fed out like that?'

John's eyes darkened. 'It went off pretty much as we agreed. Of course, I didn't know Fed would pull that trick with the speaker. That was clever, I've got to hand it to him. Finding out where you were hiding *and* distracting me in one move. But how did he know you'd have it on you?'

Flora thought for a moment. 'The museum. When they searched my bag. One of the security team, or maybe the assistant director, must have told him it was there.'

'He's good at getting people to trust him,' John agreed.

'Maybe that's what they were really looking for.' Flora hit herself on the side of her head with the flat of her hand. 'Of course! Nick must have heard the noises that night in the van. The speaker was hidden in the suit of armour, and when he tried to get to it–'

'It fell on him and knocked him out,' Marshall finished. 'See, I can do detecting too.'

Flora thought about Fed Akopian's other persona – the helpful professor – and frowned.

'How did Fed know I'd contact him about the Lamassu,' she wondered out loud. 'I mean, I dug up his name myself at the library.'

'Did you?' John said. 'Think about it. How exactly did you find him?'

'Well, it was my friend, Heston, who came up with him actually. But he got his name off a list of industry experts.' Flora shrugged. 'This professor had academic papers dating back thirty years.'

'None of that is hard to fake,' John told her. 'Fed most likely visited the library and offered to give a free talk or something. Got himself on the list that way. You have to understand, Flora, these people are criminals, and very successful ones. That kind of social engineering is second nature to them.'

Flora took this in, unhappy to have been so easily duped. 'Do you know why he killed Lucy?' she asked. 'Was it to do with the Lamassu?'

'You know I've been tracking Fed for years,' John said, adjusting his body armour and wincing again. 'The thing is, Fed needed to stay dead so that people like my employers wouldn't find him. Lucy had divorced him in his absence so had no claim on his estate – which is incredibly valuable and achieved entirely through illegal activity. Fed and Jasmin never really split up – the expedition to Peru and Fed's disappearance was all part of an elaborate plan to cover up their trafficking. Fed was too "hot" now, but as a spurned lover, Jasmin could turn her attention to legitimate business, like collecting for her museum, using it as a cover for what Fed did behind the scenes. And then the opportunity of a lifetime arose for Jasmin. That was the beginning of the end. Did she tell you she'd been invited to America to work at the Smithsonian?'

Flora shook her head. 'She wouldn't say why she was leaving. I just assumed she was tired of living in England.'

'She was tired, but mainly of hiding her relationship with Fed and keeping up the pretence that her little museum made any money at all,' John said wryly. 'Fed agreed they could make a fresh start, and arranged with the British Museum to buy their entire collection. And that's where Lucy Akopian, wronged wife and betrayed friend, came back into their lives. She had never lost her love of history, and was in the museum's gift shop that day when she saw Fed. She recognised him instantly and confronted him.'

Flora listened wide-eyed. Even Marshall was focused on John's every word. Flora slipped her hand into Marshall's and said, 'And then what happened?'

'Well, Fed pretended to be overjoyed to see her, probably gave her some story about trying to find her, and they arranged to meet later.'

'How do you know all this?'

John tapped the side of his nose. 'It's my job to know, Flora. Actually, it wasn't hard to put it all together. Once I'd found Lucy's home address and talked to her friends, had a look at her messages and emails ... Well, you know the kind of thing. You're a private investigator too.'

Flora laughed incredulously. 'Yeah, but it sounds a damn sight easier when you have access to all the stuff the police know. I have to get by on a bit of internet research and my intuition.'

'And you do very well with it, sweetheart,' Marshall put in kindly.

'So,' John continued, 'what we think happened is this. Jasmin panicked when Fed told her about Lucy. It could have ruined everything for her. The new job, the new life, everything she'd worked for. I think she made Fed promise to pay Lucy off, but of course, that's not what happened at all.'

'Instead,' Flora said, picking up the story as she saw it, 'Fed strangles Lucy and packs her in a crate on top of some old artefacts, including the priceless Lamassu, then drives up to Shrewsbury. He slips into the museum and swaps one of the recently packed crates for the one with Lucy's body in it, leaving the crate to look as though it's been forced open. Enough to spread confusion, and probably hoping the police would assume a burglary gone wrong. Jasmin comes in, sees her old friend dead as a dodo, and goes crazy.'

'Pretty much,' John agreed. 'From what I've overheard of their conversations, Fed took the Lamassu without Jasmin's knowledge, intending it as a lure for Lucy. Jasmin was furious when she found out later. And then when he told her he'd put it in the crate with Lucy's body, she knew she wouldn't see it again until the collection was unpacked.'

'So she really did think it had been stolen?' Flora said. 'At first, anyway. Well, she's seen it one last time now – when we went to the museum this morning the whole collection was set up with the Seventh Tablet front and centre.'

'Jasmin's doing,' John confirmed. 'She was there most of the night.'

The idea Flora had been incubating returned again, and this time she thought about one of the receipts she'd seen in Jasmin's filing cabinet. What would a museum owner need with a stonemason?

'When she came to our warehouse on the sixth night,' she said, 'I suppose that was when she planted the speaker in the armour? I thought it was odd at the time, how she shut herself inside the lorry. She *really* wanted me to believe in that curse.'

'You never told me about that,' Marshall remonstrated.

'You weren't talking to me, remember?'

'They must have been worried last night when they realised it was gone,' John said. 'And once Fed knew that you had it, Flora–'

'They got even more desperate to get rid of me,' she said. 'Speaking of Jasmin, did anyone see where she went? Ugh,' she groaned. 'I can't believe she got away. After everything that bloody woman has put me through!'

'I'm pretty sure she's sitting over there in the back of a squad car right now,' John said, patting Marshall on the back. 'This young chap's doing as well, I think.'

Marshall beamed with pride. 'I couldn't have grabbed her if you hadn't told me exactly where to stand, and pretty much predicted everything Fed would do.'

Flora rolled her eyes exasperatedly. 'Ugh, you two. I think I preferred it when you were fighting.' But secretly she was overjoyed. If Jasmin had been on the loose, Flora would likely have been hearing those midnight screams for the rest of her life.

'You got yourself a good one here,' John said, standing. 'Although watch out – I might poach him to come and work for us.'

'Don't get any ideas,' Flora told Marshall when his face lit up eagerly. 'I've had enough excitement tonight to last me a lifetime.'

'She says that now,' Marshall said to John as they began to walk towards the waiting police cars. 'But give it a couple of months and she'll be up to her neck in another mystery. You'll see.'

'It's true,' Flora agreed with a smile. 'I probably will.'

'And you'll have me around to help,' John Hopper said. 'If you'll have me.'

Flora said she would, she absolutely would.

The attractive police officer called John over to debrief him, and Flora and Marshall settled on a low wall nearby. Flora gazed out at the cars and the flashing lights, the police talking to potential witnesses, taking statements, speaking into their radios. She glanced across at Marshall, who appeared to be taking it all in his stride.

'Are you okay?' she asked. Marshall shook his head.

'No, Lively. I am not okay.' He scooted along the wall to be closer to her and kissed her gently on the lips. 'But I will be. So long as I've got you.'

'You've got me,' she whispered.

She noticed a pale face peering out of the back seat of one of the police cars. Jasmin. They regarded each other for a moment. Flora knew now that Jasmin had never intended for the tablet to go to the British Museum; she'd probably been planning the switch for months. If Fed hadn't killed Lucy, Jasmin's fake would have somehow found its way into the collection, with neither Flora nor Marshall any the wiser. Just another lump of old stone to be unpacked, and if they'd missed logging it, so what? Everyone makes mistakes.

The special tape was so Jasmin could easily reseal the crates without anyone knowing. And the specific type of crate so Fed could bring in yet more artefacts, keeping them under everyone's radar.

Clever, Flora acknowledged. But her past had caught up with her – Lucy's reappearance and Fed's penchant for violence scuppering her carefully laid plans.

'You found another way though, didn't you?' Flora said, so softly Marshall didn't hear her.

She opened her mouth to call to John Hopper. She had to tell him to check Jasmin's luggage; she was certain that her instinct was right. The stonemason, the secrecy, the desperate and deliberate attempts to sew confusion and conflict. And, the most compelling reason of all: there was no way Jasmin White would part with the Seventh Tablet of Lamassu. Therefore, the one in the museum was a cleverly constructed fake. Flora would stake her reputation on it.

But then she saw the reflection of the fourth plinth Lamassu in the car window. She looked behind her and there it was, shining in the bright blue lights, constructed by hand out of the rubbish that other people threw away, a reminder of what had been destroyed. She looked back at Jasmin, and realised that it wasn't Flora she was staring at. She was gazing into the past, at the invisible enemy. The invisible enemy who should not exist.

Flora took a deep breath and snuggled into Marshall's side. She was very cold, and also ridiculously hungry. After tonight, they would be on the road again, heading back to her gorgeous little apartment, her beloved Shrewsbury, her ramshackle removals firm. She had Marshall, and now she had a father too.

And what did Jasmin have? Even the love of her life had betrayed her in the end.

Hopefully she'd hidden that Lamassu well, somewhere no one would ever find it.

And once she was released, once her punishment for being Fed's accessory was over with, she and the carved winged bull could be reunited forever.

In the meantime, Flora wasn't going to say a word about it.

THE END

Acknowledgements

This book was a long time in the writing for a number of reasons, but we got there in the end! I'd like to thank Chris Howard for the awesome cover; he really knows how to bring Flora's mysteries to life. Special thanks to my daughter Lulu who has to put up with me disappearing into my office for hours on end and my constant cries of 'Just let me finish this sentence!' As always the support of my family and friends is indispensible. And finally, the biggest thanks of all to my readers and everyone who comments on my social posts or reads my emails - whenever writing becomes hard work, I think about those messages and it gives me the encouragement to carry on.

To find out more about my books and my writing life, visit me at **www.joannephillips.co.uk** where you can sign up to my mailing list and hear about new releases, giveaways and special promotions.

Printed in Great Britain
by Amazon